the lab test

BOOK SIX OF THE SYDNEY HARBOUR HOSPITAL SERIES

CHRIS TAYLOR

BOOKS BY CHRIS TAYLOR

THE SYDNEY HARBOUR HOSPITAL SERIES
(in order)

The Perfect Husband
The Body Thief
The Baby Snatchers
The Final Bullet
The Debt Collector
The Lab Test
The Stolen Identity
The Cliff Top Killer
The Likeable Fraudster

THE MUNRO FAMILY SERIES
(In order)

The Profiler
The Investigator
The Predator
The Betrayal
The Deception
The Negotiator
The Christmas Vigil
The Ransom
The Defendant
The Shooting
The Maker

Find out more about all of Chris Taylor's books, including the hugely popular Munro Family series by visiting her website at:
www.christaylorauthor.com.au/about/books

DEDICATION

This book is dedicated to my sisters, Nicole, Julie, Catherine, Marina and Donna.

And as always, to my wonderful husband, Linden. I love you.

Acknowledgments

As usual, no book comes into being without a lot of help and support by my friends and family. A world of thanks must go to my wonderful editor, Pat Thomas. Thank you for everything that you do to make my stories even more amazing than I could ever dare to dream. To Detective Superintendent Michael Kilfoyle, thank you for lending my story credibility. Any mistakes are wholly my own.

To Alisha and all of the staff at damonza.com, thank you for yet another fantastic cover. To my sister, Nicole Guihot and to my friend, Ally Thomson, thank you for your excellent editorial comments, proof reading skills and suggestions. I hope you like the final result.

To Amy Atwell and her dedicated staff at Author E.M.S. who are so much more than book formatters. Amy, once again, thank you for your magic.

To the fantastic writer organizations such as Romance Writers of Australia, Romance Writers of

America and Romance Writers of New Zealand for all the help, support and encouragement they offer new and aspiring writers, including me.

To my readers, thank you for your support and love for my stories. Your encouragement and enjoyment make this journey all worthwhile.

And lastly, to my friends and family, especially my husband and children. Thank you for putting up with late dinners and even later conversations as I've emerged day after day from the sometimes scary but always enthralling world I've created on my computer.

PROLOGUE

Dear Diary,

Why do I do this to myself? Why do I treat myself with such disdain? Where's my self-respect?

I could say it's just the way I am—a product of my dysfunctional childhood—but that would be a cop-out. After all, my little sister managed to rise above the filth and squalor of our home life.

Sabrina, the beautiful one, the perfect angel, the girl with the softest heart. I should hate her—the girl who has everything—and yet, I don't. Does that make any sense?

One thing is for certain. I'm on a fast road to nowhere.

———————

Danielle Porter braced herself against the hood of the pickup, her arms stretched as wide as her legs. Her black lace panties had been discarded, her short skirt was hitched up high. The man behind her continued to thrust into her, hard and fast and uncaring. His large hands were tight around her hips, digging into her flesh. She gritted her teeth and waited for it to be over.

"Give us a feel of your big titties," the man mumbled, still thrusting hard.

Releasing her hips, his hands came around her ribcage and found their way under her cheap cotton bra. He squeezed her generous breasts and then pinched her nipples. She bit down on a familiar surge of pain.

In high school, she was known as Dolly, after the country music star. She hadn't been with a man yet who wasn't fascinated by her breasts. It hadn't taken her long to realize her breasts garnered plenty of attention. She'd started wearing tight-fitting singlet tops to display them to their full advantage. After all, any attention was better than no attention at all.

The sound of a country music song playing from the jukebox could be heard over the grunts of the man who stood between her legs. He kept up his steady rhythm, almost in time with the music. His fingers squeezed and his hips thrust. His cock slid in and out. She half-lay, spread eagled across his hood and moaned every now and then for good measure.

She'd met him a couple of hours earlier, in a bar on the edge of town. All he'd had to do was buy her a drink or two and she was his. A frantic, meaningless coupling between strangers that meant for a few moments, she got to block everything out—her redneck family, her failing grades, her innocent little sister.

At the thought of Sabrina, Dani tensed. Shame warred with anger. She clenched her hands into fists. *Why couldn't she be more like her sister, accepting their unsatisfactory beginnings, but determined to strive for great things?* Instead, she was letting history repeat itself, as bad as her drunken, uneducated parents.

Tears burned behind her eyes and she hurriedly dashed them away. The man behind her grunted once, twice and then collapsed against her, spent. Filled with disgust and self-loathing, she didn't even look at him while he pulled up his jeans and buckled his belt and then offered to drive her home.

She shook her head rapidly back and forth, wanting nothing more than to be left alone. Tugging up her panties, she adjusted her skirt and took off toward the shadows.

"Hey! Miss! Come back! It's nearly midnight. It's not safe to head off down there in the dark. Come back. I'll take you home."

The concern in the stranger's voice was enough to fill Dani's eyes with hot tears. She couldn't remember the last time an adult had shown her kindness. His attitude probably had more to do with the fact she'd just had sex with him, but she appreciated the sentiment just the same. Still, his thoughtfulness didn't give her pause for long. She had no desire to prolong their brief association.

"Thanks," she called out over her shoulder, "but I'll be fine. I only live a little ways down the road. See ya 'round."

With the tears coming faster now, she hurried as quickly as her cheap plastic sandals would allow. Loose stones bit into the soles of her feet. A cool breeze blew in from the south and she shivered. The shots of tequila she'd tossed back earlier were now pounding in her head. She bit her lip against the pain of it and sniffled.

She didn't have to ask herself why she was crying. She knew darn well what was wrong. She was on a path of self-destruction and she didn't have a clue how she'd gotten there, or how she was ever going to get off. All she knew was if she didn't make some changes, her life would go completely off the rails and she might never get back on track.

Her parents wouldn't care. They'd hardly realize anything was amiss, but her little sister would be devastated...

The thought drew Dani up short. Sabrina's image swam before her. Her sister was sweet inside and out, with long blond hair and large blue eyes and the kindest heart Dani had ever known. Even now, she could hear Sabrina pleading for her to halt her self-destructive behavior, to look for the beautiful girl within. She was in there somewhere. Sabrina was sure of it.

It was Dani who was uncertain; who refused to believe her little sister might be right. The sad truth was, there was no good in Danielle Porter and everybody but Sabrina knew it.

Chapter 1

Twelve years later

Danielle Porter glanced at the cheap plastic clock that hung on the wall of the Sydney Harbour Hospital pathology lab and her heart skipped a beat. In just under an hour, her day would be over and with it, the end of the working week.

"Got any plans for the weekend, Dani?"

She held the test tube up to eye level and checked its contents before turning to respond to her colleague.

"Yes, Nigel," she replied to the lab tech she'd worked with for more than four years. "As a matter of fact, I'm going over to my sister's place this evening. We're having a little celebration."

Nigel's eyebrows rose and his expression filled with curiosity and hope. "What are you celebrating?"

Dani bit her lip in consternation and thought fast. She shouldn't have said anything. She could hardly tell a coworker she was celebrating her tenth year of sobriety and certainly not Nigel who had a crush on her and was hoping to be invited along. Nobody at the Sydney Harbour Hospital knew of her undesirable past and that was the way it was going to stay.

"Um, you know… It's kind of a family celebration," she replied. "Something personal to the two of us. Nothing special."

Nigel's face fell. "Oh. Are you sure I couldn't tag along? I don't have any plans and I'd love to meet your sister. You talk about her all the time. I feel I almost know her." He laughed a little nervously and scratched his head.

Dani looked away and wished she could find it in her heart to offer him even a scrap of encouragement. She'd known he liked her the first time they'd met, at an orientation day for new staff members of the hospital. When they realized they were both working in the pathology lab, he'd followed her around all day.

He was about her age and with his shaggy brown hair and friendly eyes, he'd reminded her of an overeager puppy and while she'd been happy for the companionship, she'd made it clear all those years ago that she wasn't looking for a boyfriend. Still, Nigel was nothing if not persistent and she had to admire that. It was persistence and sheer willpower that got her where she was— so far from the place where she'd begun. Though there wasn't much else, they had that in common.

"It's very sweet of you to ask, Nigel," she said now, aware that he was waiting for her reply. "But this is kind of a family thing. Maybe another time…"

She left the offer hanging in an effort to let him down gently. She hated to see the disappointment in his eyes.

"Yeah, okay. Maybe some other time," he muttered and then wandered away.

Dani sighed quietly and turned back to her desk. Sometimes she wished for the old Dani who would never turn down an offer from a man. The old Dani had been so much fun—at least, for some of the time. And then she remembered the pain and self-loathing that inevitably followed the fun and she was glad she was no longer that girl.

It had taken a long time, and a lot of hard work and determination, but she'd risen above her lowly beginnings and found the beautiful woman inside, just like Sabrina had promised would happen if she'd only give herself the chance. Having her sister meet and marry the man of her dreams had given Dani further impetus to stick to the plan.

She'd been free from men and alcohol for a decade. The two-year battle had been hard fought, but she was proud of the woman she'd become. A college graduate, a supportive sister, a loyal work colleague and friend. And the week before, she'd made the first mortgage payment on her very own unit. The tiny bedsit in North Sydney was hardly bigger than a shoe box, but it was hers and represented just how far she'd come.

Satisfaction surged through her and she squared her shoulders. She'd gotten to where she was all on her own and she had a right to feel proud, just like Sabrina said. Dani didn't need a man beside her to make her feel worthwhile. She didn't even need a date on a Friday night. An evening spent with her beloved sister and her sister's husband and the most recent addition to their family, their beautiful little girl, was all she wanted—and if her heart occasionally yearned for things to be different, she steadfastly ignored it. After all, she was only twenty-eight. Not exactly ancient. There was still plenty of time to find the man she wanted to spend the rest of her life with. *Wasn't there?*

Refusing to waste another minute thinking about a non-existent boyfriend and the future they might or might not have, she put away the tissue samples she'd been testing, tugged off her gloves and tossed them into the trash. Rinsing her hands in the sink fixed to the wall behind her work station, she returned to her desk and entered the results. She glanced again at the clock on the wall and sighed with satisfaction. Finally, the day was done. Logging off, she gathered her things. It was time for the weekend to begin.

Dani took a sip from her glass of iced tea and relaxed in her favorite recliner. Her sister smiled and raised her wine glass from where she sat on the leather sofa opposite.

"Here's to a decade of sobriety, Dani. I'm so proud of you," Sabrina said.

Dani was filled with warmth at the love and sincerity in her sister's gaze. "Thank you. It hasn't been easy."

"I'm sure. You deserve every happiness."

Dani acknowledged Sabrina's comment with a smile. Taking care not to spill her drink, she stretched her arms above her head and then flicked the lever to activate the chair. A moment later, she reclined in a prone position.

"Make yourself comfortable," Sabrina teased, a grin lifting the corners of her mouth.

Dani shot her a smug look. "Thank you. I intend to. As usual."

Sabrina pulled a face at her and tossed a cushion in her direction. It landed short, as her sister intended.

Dani laughed. "Ha! You missed! By the way, what are we having for my celebratory dinner?"

"You'll be lucky to get anything after that snide remark," Sabrina joked. She took another sip from her wine glass. "Actually, I had plans to prepare a feast tonight—succulent pork loin chops, new baby potatoes, roast peppers, heritage carrots and steamed beans, but Marnie's been out of sorts all day and I spent most of the time pacifying her. I'm afraid Chinese take-out is the best I can do."

"Hey, I'm all for Chinese take-out, as long as we can get deep-fried duck in plum sauce. So, what's with Marnie? Is she teething?" Dani asked, taking another sip from her glass.

"Maybe. But according to all the baby books, I think she's meant to have all her teeth by now. She'll be three next month."

Dani shook her head slowly in disbelief. "Three! It feels like yesterday."

Sabrina rolled her eyes. "Says Aunty Dani who hasn't spent a single night pacing with a sick child in her arms or had a long, long day where nothing she does can pacify the little mite." Sabrina softened her words with another smile and Dani took the gibe in the spirit it was intended and took another sip of iced tea.

All of a sudden, she was bombarded with memories. The panicked phone call from Franklin to tell her the baby was on its way; the race to the hospital with her heart in her throat; arriving just in time to see little Marnie enter the world, a squalling, red mass of humanity. It was a wondrous, amazing, magical time she'd never forget. In an instant, she'd fallen in love with her tiny, red-faced niece. The feeling hadn't dissipated over the years since her birth.

"How are things going on the boyfriend front?" Sabrina asked.

The question wrenched Dani back to the present. She choked on a mouthful of her drink, not at all fooled by her sister's casual tone. Sabrina had a keen look in her eye and Dani knew from experience that her sister had the tenacity of a bulldog when it came to seeking information. A simple, vague answer wouldn't be nearly enough. She swallowed a sigh of resignation and answered.

"I thought we were done with this conversation, Sabrina. Let's not go there again. We've only just apologized for the last time we argued over this." She looked her sister squarely in the eye and continued.

"I *don't* want a boyfriend and I'm not on the lookout for one, so stop setting me up with Franklin's friends. I'm perfectly happy on my own." Dani thought fleetingly of her recent yearning to have someone special in her life and then firmly set the thought aside. There was a reason she'd sworn off men more than a decade ago. Men came with complications and she'd worked darn hard over the past ten years to simplify her life.

Sabrina leaned forward, her beautiful blond hair falling across her face in a curtain of silken gold. Dani braced herself against what was coming. Her sister didn't disappoint.

"Bullshit."

Coming from that luscious, perfectly formed mouth, the expletive sounded shocking, but Dani knew her sister better than anyone. Sabrina looked like a golden angel and though she had the kindest heart, she also had a will of steel. She couldn't have grown up in the kind of household they had without acquiring a backbone. She knew from past experience it wouldn't be easy to convince her sister to leave the whole subject of Dani and her lack of a boyfriend alone.

"Sabrina, how many times do I have to *tell* you? I don't need a man in my life to feel fulfilled. I have a fantastic job, great friends, a sister who's mostly on my side and last month, I settled on a house. I'm finally in control of my life and I've done it all without a man in tow."

Sabrina's expression turned earnest. "Yes, you have, Dani, and I'm super proud of you! What you've managed to achieve is nothing short of amazing and you've done it all on your own. But that doesn't mean you have to go forth without the support of someone special. We're companion creatures. We're not meant to go through life alone."

Dani saw the care and concern that shone in her sister's eyes and a lump rose in her throat. Despite the horridness of her childhood, she'd never once blamed her sister, nor looked upon her with anything but love. Only two years separated them, but it could have been five times that amount. Her little sister had remained untouched, innocent—loved and adored by all. Even Sabrina's husband, Franklin, was convinced she'd hung the stars. It was the way it should be.

Dani wasn't the slightest bit jealous. Well, maybe just the tiniest bit. No matter how much she denied it to her sister and even to herself, more and more she wanted what Sabrina had—a man who adored her, a gorgeous baby—a perfect family all of her own. The problem lay in convincing herself she deserved it, too.

She'd paid for countless hours of therapy, but the truth was, she still had plenty of self-doubt. Her parents had done a real number on her. So many years of abuse and neglect were hard to erase. But she was getting there. Every day, was another step closer to the time when she'd finally be free of the pain and humiliation and the shame.

"Where's Franklin?" she asked instead, deliberately changing the subject.

Instead of the soft smile and twinkling eyes Dani expected, Sabrina's expression went blank. She averted her gaze and picked at a piece of lint that clung to her white linen shorts. Concern and confusion immediately flooded through Dani.

"Sabrina? What is it? What's happened to Franklin? Is he okay?"

"Yes, yes of course," Sabrina answered hurriedly, still not looking in Dani's direction.

Dani narrowed her eyes, far from convinced. "Sabrina Porter," she said, making deliberate use of her sister's maiden name. "What's going on?"

Sabrina bit her lip, her gaze still focused on the couch. "It's nothing. We... We're just going through a rough patch, okay? It happens to everyone."

Dani's heart clenched. If there were ever two people more in love than her sister and Franklin Cook, she hadn't met them. They'd been married nearly two years and had been together more than three years before Marnie's birth. Dani had yet to see them have even the tiniest disagreement. It was a little nauseating how much they doted upon one another. It concerned her greatly to hear they weren't getting along.

"What happened?" she asked quietly. "Is it anything in particular?"

Sabrina sighed. Lying back against the couch, she closed her eyes. "Franklin found some old love letters I'd received from Scott Wells. Do you remember him? We dated for a while in high school. I haven't seen him for years, but he wrote me for a long time after we broke up. Some of the letters Franklin found were dated after he and I got together. He went berserk and accused me of being unfaithful."

Dani stared at her sister in shock and shook her head in disbelief. Sabrina was the epitome of purity and innocence. It was ludicrous to suggest she could have been capable of such deceit.

"How on earth could he say such a thing? He was your first lover. He knows there was no one else."

Sabrina shook her head sadly. "Yes. The problem is, some of Scott's later letters got rather personal. He told me how much he loved me, how much he wanted me back. He urged me to break things off with Franklin, that I belonged to him and even though, when we were together, we'd done nothing more than some heavy petting, Scott wrote about it like it had been so much more."

"Surely Franklin believed you when you told him it wasn't true?" Dani exclaimed. "He's your husband! He knows you better than that!"

"I don't know why I kept them, why I didn't throw them away..."

Tears glinted in Sabrina's eyes. The sight of them filled Dani with sadness and pain. *How dare Franklin treat her sister like this!* She couldn't wait to give him a piece of her mind. Sabrina had been upset over her break up with Scott, but it was knowing he was hurting that truly caused her pain.

The truth was, Sabrina had moved on from her high school boyfriend and that was nobody's fault. It was just the way things went sometimes. Dani was sure Scott's heart must have mended. He was probably happily married now, with Sabrina a fond, distant memory. The thought that her sister's teenage relationship was causing problems for Sabrina and her husband made Dani sad.

"I had no idea Franklin was so insecure," she said.

Sabrina sighed. "I don't think it's that. He's been so stressed lately. He's not thinking straight. He's in the middle of a high profile case. I'm sure you heard about it on TV—the fifteen-year-old who's been accused of plotting a terrorist act. Franklin's law firm is representing the boy and Franklin's heading the defense team.

"He's been coming home so late, tired and overworked and then poor little Marnie's been miserable—waking several times during the night. Her daddy's usually such an understanding man, with endless patience when it comes to his little girl, but I guess the stress of work's been getting to him. He's even been short with her."

It was Dani's turn to sigh. Franklin was a junior partner in one of Sydney's most prestigious law firms. The firm was renowned for taking on high-profile cases and this one wasn't any different. She could understand how stress and fatigue might make him impatient and say things he didn't necessarily mean.

"You might need to give him a little space for a while," she suggested, eyeing her sister solemnly. "He's obviously not himself. I've never heard him say anything even halfway mean to you, let alone accuse you of infidelity."

Sabrina compressed her lips and nodded. Fat tears rolled slowly down her cheeks. "You're right," she whispered. "And I'm doing my best, but it's so hard to ignore it. The other week, he...he demanded a paternity test."

Dani gasped and her jaw dropped open in shock. The feeling was quickly followed by a surge of outrage. She leaped out of her chair.

"He *what?* How *dare* he? Has he gone completely *insane!* It's one thing to feel jealous over a few old love letters, but to accuse you not only of sleeping with Scott while you were with Franklin, but getting pregnant and then passing the child off as his! It's unbelievable! How could he *think* such a thing? Does he even know you at *all?* And how could you have kept this to yourself for a few weeks?"

Dani burned with indignation. Her breath came fast and her face was hot. *The bastard! How could he think so little of her perfect sister?* Sabrina wouldn't hurt a fly and she didn't have an ounce of deceitfulness flowing in her veins. Dani made a sound at the back of her throat and shook her head, still outraged at the thought.

"It's okay, Dani. Don't be mad." Sabrina's gentle words penetrated the fog of Dani's anger. Gradually, she slowed her steps and got her breathing back under control. Unclenching her fists, she forced herself to calm down. She moved to the couch and perched beside her sister.

"How can you be so calm, Sabrina? It's an awful thing for him to say. He's lucky he's not here right now, or I'd... I'd punch him in the nose! Nobody treats my sister like that and gets away with it!"

A tiny smile tilted up the corners of Sabrina's perfect rosebud lips. Dani's heart tightened at the sight of it. Despite everything, her sister could still summon a smile. Dani wished she had even an ounce of her little sister's goodness and strength.

"You always were my champion," Sabrina murmured and leaned closer to give Dani a hug. "Thanks for caring, big sis. It means a lot."

Dani's chest tightened with emotion and she had to blink back sudden tears. She loved her sister more than anything and hated to see her hurt. But this was Sabrina's battle. She was married now. Her loyalty was to her husband. Only the two of them could sort out this disagreement. Franklin had stuffed-up big time, but he was lucky in his choice of wife. Sabrina had the most forgiving heart imaginable. Dani was sure they'd work things out.

"What did you tell him?" she mumbled against Sabrina's shoulder.

"What do you mean?"

"Franklin. What did you tell him when he demanded a paternity test? I hope you told him to go to hell."

Sabrina pulled away and smiled sadly. "I wanted to, but it would have only made things worse. So, I... I agreed to it."

Dani stared at her, shocked for the second time. "You *agreed* to it? Why the hell would you do that? He had no right to even ask it of you! How could you—?"

Sabrina reached out and silenced her with a finger pressed against her lips. "*Shh,* Dani. Please, don't say anything more. I did what I thought was best. Franklin was spoiling for a fight. He wasn't in the mood to be reasonable. By agreeing to the test, it brought the matter to an end.

"The test will prove positive in Franklin's favor and that will be the end of it. Besides, he didn't need my permission. You know how these things work. The lab only requires a blood sample from him and Marnie. When he has time to properly reflect on his behavior, I'm sure he'll be appalled. He'll beg for my forgiveness and I'll give it, because none of us are perfect. We've all made mistakes."

Dani stared at her, once again amazed at her sister's capacity to love her fellow man. If Dani didn't know her as well as she did, she'd wonder if it were all an act. But from the moment Sabrina could talk, she'd always been kind and generous to everyone around her. Dani should have hated her perfect little sister, but instead, she was humbled and honored to be related to such a sweet girl.

"You're a better woman than I, Sabrina Cook," she murmured, slowly shaking her head.

"Nonsense," Sabrina replied. "You're a good person, too, Dani, if you'd only accept it were true. You protected me and loved me like no other throughout childhood and I haven't forgotten it. Mom and Dad could be so mean and nasty when they were drunk and that happened more often than not."

Sabrina's eyes flashed in a sudden show of spirit. "You don't think I know about all those times you shielded me from the worst they had to offer, but I *do* and I've never forgotten. If anyone's responsible for my soft and forgiving heart, it's *you*. *You* showed me what real love looked like, felt like, *was* like. If it were left up to our parents, I would have remained completely ignorant."

Fresh tears ran down Sabrina's cheeks and she lifted a hand to swipe them away. Dani stared at her, swallowing hard.

"I'm so proud of all that you've done with your life, Dani," Sabrina whispered. "I used to look at you as a wild teenager, and my heart would fill with despair. You were so much better than that. I ached for you and longed to help you, but I didn't know how, and then, somehow, you found the strength to bring an end to your reckless ways. You went to college and graduated. You found a job that you love. You've come so far and you have yourself to thank for it and I couldn't be happier."

Dani sniffed and Sabrina made another attempt to wipe the tears from her eyes. "Don't worry about me, Dani," Sabrina whispered. "I'll be all right. Franklin and I love each other. We'll get through this and be stronger for the experience."

Dani clamped her lips together in an effort to contain her emotions. She nodded in acceptance. "When do you get the results?"

"Franklin and Marnie had the blood test a week ago. We were told the results would take three to five days. They should be arriving in the mail any day now."

Easing her breath out, Dani reached for her sister's hand and squeezed it. "Well, at least it will be sorted out quickly. Let's hope Franklin doesn't take too long to come around."

"He won't. He loves me. In fact, I'm sure he's upset about the whole sorry argument. He came home with a dozen red roses yesterday. Anyway, it will be over soon. The results will prove he's Marnie's father and that will be the end of it."

Dani nodded, relieved by her sister's calm demeanor. She wished she could remain so unaffected in a time of crisis.

"I'm going to suggest to Franklin that we take a holiday—even just a few days," Sabrina continued. "He needs to get away from the office and remember what it's like to relax. This case has him twisted into knots. He barely sleeps half the night. It's not good for either of us, or for Marnie."

"A holiday sounds like a good idea," Dani agreed. "It will give you both time to regroup and reconnect. Put work and life and everything else in perspective. We all need time-out once in a while."

Dani looked around the lavish condominium with its costly furnishings and spectacular view of Sydney Harbour. Sabrina was surrounded by beautiful things, but what good were they if the owners weren't in the right frame of mind to appreciate them? She'd take her modest bedsit over Sabrina's north shore mansion any day. *Well, most days.*

"Thanks for coming over," Sabrina said and turned and hugged Dani again. "And thanks for listening. You've always been good at that."

Dani smiled at her sister and her heart filled with love. "Anytime, Sabrina. What are big sisters for?"

CHAPTER 2

Detective Constable Jett Craigdon picked up the pile of closed police files off his desk and dumped them in a box. They'd be taken down to the secure storage facility by a couple of the administration staff at a later date. He always enjoyed the moment when an investigation came to a successful conclusion and the case was closed. It was what his job was all about: finding the bad guys and locking them up.

Jett headed toward the tea room, intent on making himself a cup of coffee. He was already halfway through his morning shift, but Mondays tended to be slow. It was almost like the people with evil on their minds had worn themselves out over the weekend and needed time to regroup. Jett didn't mind. The slower pace gave him a chance to catch up on his paperwork and there was always plenty of that.

He passed by one of his colleagues who was sipping coffee at his desk. "Hey, Lane, what are you up to?"

"This and that," Detective Sergeant Lane Black replied. "You know how it is. Days like this can be a bitch. Let's hope we don't die of boredom."

Jett chuckled. He'd worked many a shift at the State Crime Command in Chatswood with Lane. The man was an excellent cop and he was also a terrific dad. His twin sons were eighteen months old and Lane doted on them. He reminded Jett of his own father and the special bond they had. He couldn't wait to have kids of his own.

Still, he had to find a girlfriend first, and not just any girl. She had to be the woman of his dreams, the woman he wanted to spend the rest of his life with, before he'd let things get serious.

He didn't believe in casual dating and casual sex was beyond what he could comprehend. He'd been raised in a strong Catholic household where love and marriage were sacred and women were treated with respect.

No doubt his colleagues would be surprised and amused to discover he was a virgin. At twenty-eight, it was assumed he'd had plenty of experience with women, including going all the way. The truth was, he was saving himself for his wedding night.

It was old fashioned and almost unheard of in this modern day and age where sex was a casual commodity and marriage was treated with disdain. Complete strangers vowed to love each other until death did they part and all the time the TV cameras were rolling and the ratings shot through the roof.

Fewer and fewer people were marrying, making

that commitment for life. It saddened Jett that society had let something as special and sacred as love and marriage become such a quick and cheap thrill. He didn't know how to halt the movement toward frivolous relationships, but it certainly wasn't for him. If that made him odd, then so be it. He was sure he'd find the girl of his dreams who appreciated his outlook and felt the same way and he was prepared to wait for her.

"What did you do on the weekend?" Lane asked, idly scrolling through a training manual on the latest police issue handgun.

Jett shrugged. "Cleaned my apartment. Hung out at the beach. Finished reading the latest James Patterson book."

Lane stared up at him, a smile lifting one corner of his lips. "Are you for real? You're twenty-something, reasonably good looking, footloose and fancy free. Why aren't you out hitting the nightclubs? Picking up women? Doing what other young blokes do?"

Jett chuckled, not taking offense. "Is that what you used to do?"

Lane grinned. "Too right! I could party all night, go home with a girl. Sleep in until noon. Those were the days." He shook his head, reminiscing.

Jett laughed. "You might not want to let your wife hear you say that."

"Zara and I have no secrets," Lane replied with another grin. "She knows all my faults and failings. Besides, she was only complaining the other morning how nice it would be to stay out late and sleep the whole day away. The twins make sleeping in impossible and we've learned to be in bed by nine." He sighed dramatically. "Late nights out are just not worth the headache. Literally."

Jett chuckled again. "You're all talk, Lane. You wouldn't have it any other way."

Lane's grin faded and he nodded. "Yeah, you're right. I wouldn't. Still," he added, holding Jett's gaze, "I sure had fun back in the day. You ought to try it sometime."

Jett offered a noncommittal shrug of agreement. He didn't need to be told how to have fun. It was just that his idea of fun wasn't exactly the same as every other single, twenty-eight-year-old. There was nothing wrong with that.

Detective Superintendent Michael Collins strode toward them, a grim expression on his face.

"Lane, Jett, a call's just come in from the dispatcher. They've received an emergency call from a man claiming that someone's murdered his family."

Adrenaline surged through Jett at his boss' announcement. Lane immediately became alert.

"Where did the call come from?" Jett asked.

"An address in Hunters Hill," Collins answered.

Lane frowned. "Why did it come through to us? It's not like the boys in Hunters Hill can't deal with a suspected homicide and they're much closer."

Collins' lips compressed into a grim line. "The caller identified himself as Franklin Cook."

It was Jett's turn to frown. "Franklin Cook? Why does that name sound familiar?"

"He's a partner at Harris & Birmingham and the lawyer heading Bilal Al-Jabiri's criminal defense team."

"The boy accused of plotting a terrorist act against the state," Jett finished.

Collins' expression hardened and he narrowed his flint-eyed gaze. "Yeah. Now you can see why it's come to us."

By the time Jett and Lane arrived at the modern, ten-storey cement-rendered condominium block, the place was teeming with police. An ambulance was parked off to one side, it's red and white strobe emergency lights still flashing, bouncing off the adjoining buildings. Splashes of blue and red and white light from several police vehicles added to the colorful display. A crowd of curious onlookers, mostly women and children, gathered on the well-manicured lawn. The mid-afternoon sun sparkled off the crystal blue water of nearby Sydney Harbour.

Jett and Lane strode up the slight incline that led to the paved front entryway. Double glass doors, sporting a fancy engraved insignia, blocked their way. A general duties officer guarded the entrance. Jett flashed his ID and Lane did the same.

"Which floor?" Jett asked the younger officer.

"The penthouse suite."

Jett nodded. Only the best for a partner of the prestigious Harris & Birmingham Law Firm.

"Who's inside?" Lane asked.

"Detectives Bennett and Jackson from Hunters Hill were among the first responders... They're up there, along with a guy from forensics. We're still waiting on the morgue."

"Has anyone left the building?" Jett asked.

"Not since I got here and I was among the first on the scene."

"Good," Jett answered. "Don't let anyone leave without taking their details. I don't care if they live here or not. I want to know who's in the vicinity."

"Sure thing, Detective," the constable replied. "I'll see to it myself."

Jett nodded his thanks and pushed through the double glass doors, Lane on his heels. Together, they rode the elevator up to the tenth floor. The doors slid open silently and they were met with another set of double doors. These ones were made from thick panels of oak and looked solid enough to withstand an earthquake. One of the doors stood slightly ajar and they pushed their way through. Jett came to a halt at the breathtaking scene laid out before him.

The building clung to the foreshore and through the floor-to-ceiling plate glass windows that took up one entire wall, the glory of Sydney Harbour lay spread out before them. The water was dotted with yachts and sail boats, moored or tied to jetties and wharves and buoys. The sun reflected off the glass of the tall city skyscrapers across the other side. It was a scene from a postcard, an invitation to enjoy the prettiest, cleanest city in the world.

The room was designed to take advantage of the view, with a large, wide open-concept style. A kitchen with black marble countertops and shiny stainless steel appliances stood off to the left and beside it, a heavy, dark wood dining suite. Twelve carved wooden chairs, upholstered in an expensive-looking blue fabric, stood around it. On the opposite side of the room, centered in front of the view, was a large modular sofa made from the softest leather.

"She's in here."

The somber words of the man who introduced himself as Detective Sergeant Christian Bennett broke into Jett's thoughts. About Jett's age, the man had an air of confidence and authority about him that bespoke experience and Jett was glad it hadn't been a rookie who'd been among the first to attend the scene. If Cook's family had been murdered, this case had all the hallmarks of a publicist's nightmare.

After shaking Bennett's proffered hand, Jett followed him down a long corridor. Bedrooms stood on his left and his right, both of them silent and still.

Walking forward, Jett came to a bathroom and stepped onto glossy black Italian tiles. A man in blue overalls and holding a camera squatted over the large, freestanding bathtub that was aligned next to another oversized window. Jett recognized the man from the specialist forensics team and nodded a somber greeting.

Dark red blood spattered the walls in almost every direction. It looked like something out of a horror movie. Familiar dread settled in Jett's gut. Moving closer, he forced himself to look in the tub.

The naked body of a woman lay still and silent in the red-tinged water. Numerous stab wounds decorated her abdomen and chest. As if that wasn't enough, her throat had been slit, almost from ear to ear. With her head thrown back against the bathtub, she was left with a garish imitation of a smile.

Bile rose in Jett's gut and he put a hand up to his mouth to force it down. He'd attended his fair share of bloody crime scenes, but this one topped them all. The woman looked to be in her mid-twenties with fine, golden hair piled up on top of her head. More blood congealed in the mass.

"It's not hard to determine cause of death," the forensics officer said, indicating the spray of arterial blood that painted a good portion of the wall. "Someone did a number on her, that's for sure," the man added. "Apparently there's a knife missing from the knife block in the kitchen. The poor woman didn't stand a chance. And the baby..." He shuddered. "That's just not right at all."

"The baby?' Jett repeated, dreading the answer.

"Yeah. There's a baby dead in her cot next door. Still wrapped in a pink blanket. I already checked for signs of life."

The dread in Jett's gut weighed even heavier. If there was one thing difficult for him to take, it was the needless death of a child. Backing out of the bathroom, he entered the room adjoining it. Lane stood at the cot, shaking his head.

"What kind of sick fuck does something like this?" he muttered to no one in particular.

Jett forced his feet forward and looked down at the baby. Like the forensics guy had told him, she was securely wrapped in a pink, satin-edged blanket. In fact, apart from the existence of blood smears on the sheets and the gray-blue color of the baby's skin, the infant could almost be mistaken for being asleep.

"Stabbed?" Jett asked quietly.

"Yep. Three times in the chest. Neat as you like. And then the prick had the audacity to re-wrap her, like nothing had ever happened."

The anger in Lane's voice reverberated through Jett. He was also having a hard time keeping his temper in check. The senseless violence was mind blowing and sent white hot fury gushing through his veins.

"What do we know about the intruder?" he rasped, barely able to speak through his anger.

"Not much. I understand the husband came home at lunchtime and found them like this. He's in the master bedroom, talking to Detective Jackson."

Jett compressed his lips and nodded, bracing himself for what was to come. The husband was always the first suspect, even if he'd done nothing wrong. The initial interview was never easy. The husband was not only grieving, he was usually on the defensive. If he were smart—and this guy was a top notch lawyer—he'd understand and do what he could to cooperate, but it didn't always go down that way.

"Do you want to do this, or will I?" Lane asked, his voice rough with emotion.

Jett turned his head away from the child in the cot and stared at his colleague. "Leave it to me."

———

Franklin Cook sat on the edge of the bed he shared with his wife and hung his head in his hands. Shocked and bewildered, he did his best to keep himself in check. His wife and baby had been savagely murdered and nobody seemed to know why. He stared down at his hands, at the blood that stained them and realized it was Sabrina's. His clothes were also covered in it because he'd tried to haul her from the tub. He still couldn't believe his wife and beautiful baby girl were dead.

A sob of anguish escaped him and then another. He pressed a fist against his mouth in an effort to hold them in.

"Franklin Cook?"

The firm voice snagged his attention. He looked up into the face of a man about his age who had the bearing of someone in authority. His dark suit was expensive, although not nearly as costly as the tailored charcoal-gray suit Franklin wore, with its matching, designer shirt made from the finest of cottons and in his favorite pale blue. In a distant part of his mind, he mourned the fact his clothing was ruined, stained with his wife's blood.

"I'm Detective Constable Jett Craigdon," the man said, pushing back a hank of black hair. Worn longer than was currently in fashion, it had fallen across his eyes. He pointed to the other man beside him. "And this is Detective Sergeant Lane Black. We're here from the State Crime Command. I work in the Homicide Squad and Detective Black is part of our Middle Eastern Crime Squad."

The words slowly penetrated the fog that had enveloped Franklin's brain ever since he'd arrived home. Comprehension dawned and he gasped in surprise. The State Crime Command had jurisdiction over more serious criminal matters. Their presence only reinforced the fact these were no ordinary murders.

"You think this might have something to do with the court case? With Bilal Al-Jabiri? Is that what you're saying? That... That *I* brought this violence to our door... That *I'm* responsible?" His voice broke. He gasped again and blinked back a rush of tears.

"At this stage, we don't know anything," Detective Craigdon replied. "We have officers reviewing the CCTV footage from the cameras situated outside the entrance to your building. We're not sure if you and your work are connected in any way to what's happened, but we're covering all bases. You've managed to annoy some people lately."

Franklin shook his head, aghast at the thought. "Oh, my God! This is all my fault! If I hadn't taken on the case—"

"We don't know anything yet," the older detective interrupted. "We're hoping you can give us some answers."

Franklin spread his hands wide and implored

the officers. "Ask me anything you want. I don't have anything to hide. All I want to do is find the bastard responsible and see him locked up for life. My beautiful wife, my sweet, little girl..." He was suddenly overwhelmed with emotion and sobbed uncontrollably in his hands. At any other time, he might have been embarrassed, but right now, he was beyond caring. All he could think about was his beautiful Sabrina and sweet baby Marnie, lying in a pool of blood.

"Have you received any death threats since you took on the Al-Jabiri case?" Detective Craigdon asked, staring down at him.

"It's only been three weeks, Detective. We haven't even set a trial date." Franklin cleared his throat and tried to stop the shaking in his voice. "I've taken on high-profile cases before. I've never feared for my safety, or the safety of my family." He stared down at his hands and once again, noticed the blood stains on them.

"Have you and your wife been having any problems, Mr Cook?"

The question came from the other detective, the one who'd been introduced as Lane Black. Franklin shook his head.

"No, of course not. We're very much in love. We have the occasional squabble, but who doesn't? Are you married, Detective?"

Lane Black nodded. "Yes, Mr Cook, I am."

"Then you understand."

"Who had access to your condo?" Detective Craigdon asked. "The forensics guy says there are no signs of forced entry."

Franklin stared at him and shook his head, his mind awhirl with emotion and the images of his dead wife and child.

"I don't know, Detective. No one, apart from the building manager. He's responsible for maintenance and that sort of thing. We pay high monthly rates for the upkeep."

The detective pulled out a notebook and jotted down some points. Another thought struck Franklin. "Oh, I almost forgot. My wife's sister has a key. She's often here in her spare time and occasionally stays overnight."

"What's her name?" Craigdon asked.

"Danielle Porter. She's a pathologist at the Sydney Harbour Hospital."

"Have you any reason to suspect that your sister-in-law might do your wife and daughter harm?" Again, the question came from Craigdon.

Franklin shook his head. "No, I can't imagine Dani doing anything like this. She loves Sabrina and she loves Marnie like she's her own. The sisters have had their odd arguments, of course. No one's perfect. In fact, now that I think about it, the last time I saw them together, they were arguing."

Both detectives came alert. Craigdon scribbled again in his notepad. "What were they arguing about?" the older detective asked.

"I'm not sure. I try to keep out of it, but Sabrina was upset for quite some time afterwards. Come to think of it, I haven't seen Dani around here recently."

"Is that unusual?" Craigdon asked.

"Yeah, it is," Franklin replied slowly. "I've been

so busy, I didn't give it any thought, but Dani's almost part of the furniture around here. She spends a lot of her free time with my wife. But lately, they didn't seem to be getting on so well. At least, from what I could tell. I haven't been here much myself and when I have been around, I haven't exactly been paying attention. The Al-Jabiri case has been consuming almost every second of my day."

"Mr Cook, do you own a life insurance policy on your wife?" The question came from Black.

Franklin tensed and then forced himself to relax. He knew what the cop was doing. The spouse of a murder victim was always suspect number one. It was a routine question and needed to be treated as such.

"Yes, of course. We have one on each other. Mine's worth a whole lot more than hers." He shrugged. "I support the family."

"What's the value of the policy you own on your wife?" Craigdon asked.

Franklin held his gaze and replied without flinching. "One hundred thousand dollars."

Craigdon recorded his answer and the details of his insurance company, but Franklin could tell the amount didn't raise any alarm bells. And neither should it. One hundred thousand was a pittance. Certainly not worth murdering for. He eased out his breath.

"What happened to your hand?"

Once again, it was Craigdon who posed the question. Franklin's breath snagged and his heart skipped a beat. His wife and child had just been murdered and he had a fresh cut on his hand. Of course the police would be suspicious. He tightened his hands into fists and ignored the surge of pain.

"It's nothing," he replied. "A scratch. I cut it with a knife while I was preparing dinner on the weekend."

The detective nodded in acknowledgement. Franklin eased out his breath. And then the detective spoke again.

"We're going to need to photograph it—standard procedure. I'm sure you understand."

Franklin held the man's gaze. "Of course."

Detective Craigdon murmured to one of the other detectives, who quickly left the room. A moment later, a man wearing overalls emblazoned with the word "Forensics" came into the room, a camera at the ready. Craigdon and Black stood back while the other officer took photos of Franklin's hand.

"That cut looks quite deep," Craigdon commented as soon as the forensics guy was finished. "You ought to drop by the emergency department. It might require treatment."

"It will be fine, I'm sure," Franklin replied quickly. Attending to his injury was the last thing on his mind. His wife and baby were lying dead in the condominium, brutally murdered, and so far, the police hadn't figured out why. A slight discomfort from the pain in his hand was the least he was forced to endure.

"What's going to happen now?" he asked quietly.

"We'll have a look around, take some more photos. We'll talk to the neighbors. Review the CCTV footage, like I mentioned," Craigdon replied.

"What about...my wife? And my baby?"

Compassion filled Craigdon's face and his tone softened. "They'll be taken to the morgue for autopsies. Once the forensic pathologist is finished, the bodies will be released to whichever funeral home you nominate."

A fresh wave of shock rolled over him. He gasped on another sob. He still couldn't believe it. They were dead. They were *dead.*

What the hell was he going to do without them?

———————

Jett motioned to Lane and together they moved away from the broken man who remained on the bed, his head hanging between his legs.

"What do you think?" Lane murmured.

Jett shrugged. "His grief seems genuine, but he does have a knife wound on his hand. Franklin Cook wouldn't be the first husband to put on a good show of grief after murdering his wife and child."

Lane's lips twisted into a grimace. "Yeah, ain't that the truth. And there's also the insurance policy."

Jett shook his head. "I don't think money's a motive. Assuming it checks out. And why would

Cook lie about something that can be so easily verified? It's a pittance compared to the obvious wealth enjoyed by this family. The man's wearing a suit that costs more than my monthly salary and as garish as that yellow tie is, it's worth more than most people make in a week. And take a look at this place. I'm betting the annual condo fees on this penthouse would cost more than that."

"So, if money wasn't a motive, what was?"

Jett blew out his breath on a heavy sigh. Sabrina Cook had died from at least twenty to thirty stab wounds. Jett hadn't counted them, but there were a lot of them. It was obviously overkill. The slit across the woman's throat alone would have done the trick. There was no need for the other wounds. Jett had seen his fair share of murder scenes and this one displayed all the signs of being personal. This was a crime of passion, of anger, of devastation, of a total loss of control. Coupled with the fact there was no forced entry, Jett couldn't help but conclude the Cooks had known their killer.

"I guess that's up to us to find out. That's why they pay us the big bucks, right?"

Lane's wry smile was cut short by the reappearance of Detective Bennett in the open doorway of the master bedroom. He headed toward them.

"Excuse me, Detectives," the man murmured, his voice low.

"What is it?" Jett asked.

"I have Marcia Willis in the living room. She's a resident of the building. She told one of the constables downstairs that she saw someone outside the Cooks' condominium earlier today. Do you have time to speak with her?"

Jett nodded. "Of course. We'll be right out."

Bennett left. Jett and Lane walked toward the door. On his way out, Jett spared Franklin Cook a glance. The man was still hunched over the bed, staring into space. Tears streamed down his cheeks.

Jett felt a wave of sympathy. *Poor bastard*. With a determined effort, he blinked to clear his head and followed Lane out of the room.

Marcia Willis was a woman in her fifties, but time had treated her well. She was dressed in a pale pink linen pantsuit that skimmed the lines of her trim body. Her hair was cut into a stylish bob and dyed a tasteful honey-blond and her makeup was impeccable. A bright pink-and-blue-and-yellow scarf was tied with expert precision around her neck.

"Tell us what you saw, Mrs Willis," Jett said, after making the introductions.

"I'm a friend of the Cooks. I live on the floor below with Trevor and Kiki."

Jett raised an eyebrow and the woman hurriedly explained.

"My husband and dog."

Lane nodded. "What brought you to the penthouse?"

"I hadn't caught up with Sabrina and Marnie for a while. Trevor and I have been traveling overseas. We only got back a few days ago. With jet lag and everything else interfering, I hadn't been up to see her."

"Okay," Jett said, making notes. "So, you came up to the penthouse."

"Yes, but first I spoke to Sabrina on the phone."

"What time was that?" Lane asked.

"About eleven-thirty, I guess. I asked her if it was convenient for me to come up and see them both before Sabrina put Marnie down for a nap."

"When did you come up to the penthouse?" Jett asked.

The woman frowned, in thought. "It was about half an hour later. I received another telephone call right after I'd hung up from Sabrina and I got caught up for a while."

"Did you see Mrs Cook?" Jett asked.

"No, but I saw Kevin Thompson outside her door. He's the maintenance man. He had a toolbox with him. I assumed he was there to do some repairs. I decided to come back later." She leaned in closer and whispered behind her hand. "He's black, you know."

Jett stared at her and frowned. Her attitude should have surprised him, but sadly, it didn't. In his line of work, he came across racism and prejudice all too often. Instead, he gave her a curt nod of acknowledgement and jotted her information down. "Thank you Mrs Willis. We appreciate you coming forward."

The woman shuddered. "I just hope you find the man who did this. It's just terrible what happened to Sabrina and that poor little baby girl. I still can't believe it."

"Yes and we're going to do everything we can to see that whoever did this is punished. Do you mind giving us your contact details, in case we need to speak with you further?" Jett asked.

"No, of course not," the woman replied and hastily supplied them.

Jett fished out a card and handed it to her. "Here's my number. If you remember anything else, please give me a call."

"Thank you, Detective. I will."

"I'll get someone to show you out, Mrs Willis," Lane offered. "And thank you for speaking with us."

After the woman left, Jett turned to Lane. "It sounds like we need to talk to the maintenance man."

"Yeah. The morgue staff just arrived. We'll be able to confirm a time of death."

"What time did the husband find them?"

"The emergency call came in at one thirty-six. According to Bennett, Cook told him he arrived home for lunch about one-thirty. He left for work at seven this morning. Said good-bye to his wife and kid."

"We know Marcia Willis spoke to Sabrina about eleven-thirty. Let's hope the maintenance man can shed a little more light on the matter. If he spoke to her at twelve, that narrows the possible timeframe for her death to an hour and a half. Even if he didn't, we're still talking a very small window of opportunity."

"Indeed," Lane agreed, his expression grim.

"We need to move as quickly as we can," Jett said. "I'll leave you to track down Kevin Thompson. I'll try and find the sister. If she's not involved, I don't want her hearing about the brutal deaths of her relatives on social media."

Lane nodded grimly and Jett knew what he was thinking. At this early stage of the investigation, they couldn't rule anyone out.

"I'll meet you back at the station. We'll compare notes," Jett said.

On his way out of the penthouse, his gaze scanned the opulent furnishings, the amazing view and he couldn't help but think where their wealth had gotten them. The Cook family had been torn apart at the seams and couldn't be put back together again, no matter how much money was put on the table.

Sometimes, life just sucked.

CHAPTER 3

"Dani, there's someone outside waiting to see you."

Dani looked up from her microscope and blinked at the receptionist.

"For me, did you say?" she asked, surprised because in the four years she'd worked in the pathology lab of the Sydney Harbour Hospital she'd never had a visitor. Not even her sister called upon her there. Sabrina understood Dani was often knee-deep in body tissues and fluids and couldn't just drop everything at short notice.

Tugging off her latex gloves, she tossed them in the trash can and then rinsed her hands in the sink. Patting them dry with some paper towel, she headed out of the lab. A tall, broad-shouldered man who looked about her age stood in the waiting room. His longish black hair fell across a wide forehead and concealed part of one eye. He wore a dark-colored suit and tie and a pristine white shirt. She walked toward him, wondering who he was.

"Excuse me? I'm Danielle Porter. I understand you're looking for me."

The man came to attention. He was tall, at least a head taller than her. Dark stubble that matched the color of his hair shadowed his cheeks, as if he was overdue for a shave. He brushed the hair from his eyes, revealing eyes so blue they reminded her of the ocean in the middle of the morning. Inexplicably, her heart picked up its pace.

"I'm Detective Constable Jett Craigdon. Is there somewhere else we might go to chat?"

Surprise held Dani momentarily immobile. Did he say he was a *detective?* Why would a detective be needing to see her? It had been more than twelve years since her last brush with the law. A sense of foreboding trickled through her veins.

"Um, sure. Follow me," she managed and led him into a small room just off the waiting area.

Turning to face him, she jammed her hands into the pockets of her white lab coat. "What can I do for you?"

"Are you the sister of Sabrina Cook?"

Her anxiety ratcheted up another notch. "Yes," she replied cautiously.

His expression remained grave. "I'm afraid I have some bad news."

Dani stared at him. She saw his lips form the words and heard them echo in her ears, but she refused to grasp their meaning.

She blinked rapidly in an effort to clear her mind. "I'm...I'm sorry?"

"There's no easy way to tell you this, Ms Porter,

but your sister and her daughter were found murdered in their home this afternoon."

Dani gaped in disbelief. Blood pounded in her ears, blocking out the rest of his words. Nausea swirled in her belly and she gasped for breath. She must have misheard. It couldn't be right. Sabrina and Marnie...*dead*? No, it couldn't be true. She refused to believe it. There'd been some mistake. It was some other Sabrina Cook he was talking about, not *her* Sabrina. Her Sabrina was at home, enjoying life with her husband and baby daughter. Dani had seen the two of them just the Friday before. They couldn't possibly be dead.

"I'm sure this has come as a shock," the detective was saying, looking grave. "I'm afraid I'm going to have to ask you a few more questions. Would you mind accompanying me to the station?"

Dani gaped again. *Why the hell would he need to speak to her at the station? Couldn't he speak to her here?* It wasn't as if she had any knowledge of what had happened.

"I'd rather answer any questions you have, right here," she said, amazed she was even able to form the words. Her head spun. Her heart pounded. She didn't want to accept it was real, even that *he* was real.

He shrugged. "Suit yourself."

He pulled a notebook out of the inside of his suit jacket. Feeling detached from the news he brought, she wondered vaguely how he was faring in the mid-afternoon heat. She'd gone outside at lunchtime and had been hit with a blast of summer sun. She'd been pleased she'd opted for a short-sleeved cotton blouse and light cotton pants. Not that it mattered what she wore most of the time. The majority of her day was spent at her desk or poring over a microscope in the climate-controlled comfort of the pathology lab.

"Ms Porter, where were you between the hours of eleven-thirty and one-thirty today?"

For a third time, the woman who stood before Jett with the startling green eyes and over-large breasts gaped at him in shock. Her face paled momentarily and then twin spots of anger colored her cheeks.

"You... You think *I* had something to do with this?" she sputtered.

He schooled his features to remain impassive. With her dark hair pulled back into a neat bun at the nape of her neck and the white lab coat giving her an implied authority, she looked more like a wise and kindly doctor than a killer, but he'd never been one to be taken in by the way a person looked. He'd more or less accused her of being involved in the awful crimes. It was important to note her reaction.

"The attack against your sister was personal," he continued, leveling his gaze on her. "As a close family member with a key to their condominium, questioning your whereabouts at the time of the murder is standard procedure."

The woman blinked and shook her head. She looked dazed and bewildered, exactly like he'd expect someone to look when they'd just discovered their sister and niece had been murdered. *But was it all an act?* He'd need to delve deeper to find out.

"I... I arrived at work at eight and was here until my lunch break," she finally replied.

"When did you leave for lunch?"

"Twelve-fifteen."

"What time did you get back?"

"My lunch break's usually only half an hour, but today I took a little extra time because I...had an appointment."

"Okay," Jett replied. "What time was your appointment?"

"Twelve-thirty."

"Where did you go?"

"I met a...friend on No.1 Oval at the Sydney University. It's right behind the hospital."

Jett's curiosity spiked. She was being evasive. "Does this *friend* have a name?"

Her eyes flared with impatience. "Is this really necessary, Detective? I can tell you right now, I had *nothing* to do with my sister's murder or the murder of my niece." Her voice broke on the last word and her hand came up to cover her mouth. Her eyes welled with tears, as if suddenly recalling the reason for his visit.

Her obvious distress made him want to soften his tone, but something inside him rebelled at the thought. The woman might look like she could grace the covers of a glossy magazine, but that didn't mean she wasn't capable of murder, no matter how upset she appeared. She could be an excellent actress. Until he had more evidence to the contrary, everyone he spoke to that had access to the deceased would be treated as a suspect.

He narrowed his gaze on her. "You seem to forget, Ms Porter, that I'm investigating a brutal double homicide. You don't get to decide which questions are important. Right now, we're trying to establish your alibi. I'd appreciate a little more cooperation. What was the name of your friend and what was the purpose of your...appointment?"

She looked away. Her bottom lip trembled and fresh tears slid down her cheeks, but eventually, she lifted her gaze to his and stared at him, almost defiantly.

"His name is Ben Fitzgerald and he's my... My sponsor."

Jett started in surprise. "Sponsor? As in AA?"

She lowered her gaze and nodded, her lips compressed. "Yes. I met him at a meeting ten years ago. I've been sober ever since."

Jett noted the information, still trying to get his head around the fact the confident, intelligent woman before him was a recovering alcoholic. *What other dark secrets did she hide?*

"How long did you meet with Fitzgerald?" Jett asked, forcing the thought away.

"We talked for about forty-five minutes. Usually it's longer, but I received a phone call from one of my colleagues. A tissue sample had gone missing.

I was the last person with it, so I agreed to come back to the lab and help locate it. It meant I had to cut our visit short."

"What time did you get back to the hospital?"

"The oval's not far from my building. It was probably about one-thirty when I got back."

"I'll need Fitzgerald's contact details to verify your story. Did you speak to anyone else while you were out?"

She shook her head and then paused. "Oh, yes. I bought a sandwich from one of those mobile vendors on my way back to the lab. He probably won't remember me. It was lunchtime. He was busy."

"Let's hope for your sake he does. Right now, your alibi's a little shaky." Jett held her gaze.

She frowned. The movement caused a tiny line to form across the bridge of her nose. "If I'd known I was going to be a suspect in the murder of my sister and her child, instead of enjoying the sunshine, I'd have made sure I spoke to as many people as I could. In fact, I wouldn't have gone outside at all. I would have stayed at my desk, like I often do, and ensured there were several work colleagues who could verify my presence. That is, if I were looking to cover the fact I'd dashed out over my lunch break to commit a double homicide."

Her voice dripped with sarcasm. It was reflected in the brilliant green of her eyes. Even her tense stance challenged him. He nodded grimly, a little embarrassed.

Okay, her alibi wasn't watertight, but as she

said, she wasn't expecting to need one. It made sense that her movements during the relevant time didn't exactly strengthen it. He changed tack.

"Tell me about your brother-in-law. What do you think of Franklin Cook?"

The defiance in her eyes slowly faded to be replaced with a look of sadness and concern. "Poor Franklin," she murmured. "He must be devastated."

Jett noted her reaction. There was no anger or resentment in her tone. In fact, just the opposite, but he needed to be sure.

"In cases such as these, the husband is always our prime suspect. Do you think he's capable of murdering his wife and child?"

She was shaking her head vehemently side to side even before he finished. "Oh, goodness, no! Franklin doted on the two of them. I've never seen a man so in love with his wife and he was besotted with little Marnie. It's inconceivable to think he could have done something like this!"

"Are you sure?" Jett persisted. If she was the murderer, this was her perfect opportunity to implicate her brother-in-law. The woman was close to the people involved. Her opinion counted.

"Of course I'm sure! Until recently, they'd never even had a major argument and they've been together for at least seven years."

Jett's attention snagged on her words. "They argued recently?"

The woman sighed and looked away. "Yes, but

Sabrina was certain they'd sort things out and come through it stronger for the experience."

"What did they argue about?"

Her gaze flicked up to his and then moved away. "Does it matter, Detective? They had an argument. Couples argue all the time. It doesn't mean anything."

Jett stared at her. "Yes, except you've just told me *this* couple didn't argue all the time. In fact, they *never* argued. I'd say any argument between them in that context could be important."

She bit her lip and Jett could tell she was debating what to tell him. "Have you spoken to Franklin about this? I... I assume he...knows?" she asked.

He nodded. "Yes, he knows. He was the one who found them."

"Oh, dear God!" She brought a hand up to her mouth. Her exclamation was laden with horror. "Poor Franklin."

Jett compressed his lips and nodded. "I can't imagine it was pleasant. Unfortunately, at this early stage of the investigation, everybody's a suspect, particularly those close to the deceased. I met your brother-in-law at the scene and spoke to him briefly, but until now, I wasn't aware of any specific argument between him and his wife. My colleague's still at the scene, taking statements. I came to speak with you, break the news, before you heard it from the media."

She stared at him and once again, her eyes filled with tears. "Thank you," she whispered. "It was very thoughtful of you."

Jett squirmed under the gratitude that shone from her eyes. He needed to stay impartial. Everyone was a suspect, although he'd already begun to doubt she was involved. He'd been a detective for years. He trusted his instincts and right now, his gut was telling him she'd had nothing to do with the terrible tragedy. He cleared his throat and asked her again about the argument.

She swiped at her eyes and took an unsteady breath. "You have to understand," she began hesitantly, as if unwilling to be disloyal. "Franklin's been under a lot of strain at work. He's representing that boy accused of plotting a terrorist act. It's been all over the news."

She glanced at him and he nodded. "Bilal Al-Jabiri. Yes, I know the case you mean. What does that have to do with the argument?"

She bit her lip. Her shoulders slumped on another sigh. "Franklin's been working so hard, preparing for the trial. He's been more stressed than usual and little Marnie's been out of sorts. Sabrina told me he... He found some old love letters written to her by an ex-boyfriend. They were from years ago, but Franklin overreacted."

Jett tensed, his senses alert. "In what way?"

"He accused her of being unfaithful."

"Okay," Jett replied, keeping his expression neutral. "What did your sister say?"

"She told him he was being ridiculous, of course. That she hadn't been with anyone but him."

"Did he believe her?"

"No. Not at the time, anyway, but Sabrina told me how tired and stressed he was."

"What did he do?" Jett asked.

"He didn't hurt her, if that's what you're thinking. Goodness, he'd never do anything like that! Franklin might have been angry, but he's not a violent man."

Jett made a note of her response. "So, what happened? I assume he didn't just forget about it?"

The woman compressed her lips and shook her head, her eyes full of sadness. "No, he didn't just forget. He... He demanded a paternity test."

Jett's eyes widened in shock and he took a step backwards. "He accused your sister of deceiving him about the paternity of their child?"

"No! Yes! I... I guess so, but you have to remember, he wasn't thinking straight. Even I thought it was completely out of character. I was wild as hell when Sabrina told me about it, but she begged me to understand. It was the pressure of this case, the lack of sleep—it wasn't the real Franklin saying these things."

"Did your sister agree to the test?"

Once again, the woman nodded, her expression one of resignation. "Yes. She told me it wasn't worth arguing over. It would only make Franklin worse. Besides, she knew Marnie was his and that the test results would prove it."

Jett stared at her. "Sabrina told you that? She told you she was certain the baby was his?"

Anger flared in the green depths. "Yes, Detective. She did. My sister was the most beautiful, kind, warm, innocent woman you'd ever meet. She wouldn't know *how* to tell a lie. There was no way she'd been unfaithful to her husband and *nobody* could ever make me believe otherwise."

"How long ago did this conversation take place?"

"Last Friday night." Her voice broke and once again, tears filled her eyes.

Jett's instinct was to offer her comfort, to reassure her things would be all right, but he needed the information she could give him and the sooner he got it, the better.

"Franklin told us you hadn't been over to his condo for a while."

She sniffed back a quiet sob and used a Kleenex to dab at her eyes. With a deep breath, she spoke again.

"That's not true. I... I went over to her place after work. We shared an early dinner and talked. Franklin wasn't there. He was working late at his office. He hasn't been there so much lately when I've visited. Like I said, he's been busy with his case."

Jett scribbled a few notes on the notepad and then addressed the woman once again. "Do you know if they had the DNA test?"

"Yes. She told me they'd done it about a week earlier. She was expecting the arrival of the results any day."

Jett frowned. Although it sounded like the results would hold no surprises, it was worth following up. "Do you know what lab conducted the testing?" he asked.

"No, I didn't ask. There are a heap of private clinics in the city. It could have been any of them."

Jett filed the information away. The paternity test was probably a dead end. Sabrina Cook had assured her sister the results would prove Franklin was the father and Danielle Porter was adamant that her sister had spoken the truth.

If that were the case, it was highly unlikely the results could have triggered the level of violence that had been exhibited in the penthouse, although it was worth checking the results with the husband. And there was still the maintenance man. It would be interesting to talk to Lane and see what he'd uncovered in that interview.

Tucking the notepad back into the inside pocket of his suit jacket, Jett held out his hand to Danielle.

"Thank you for your time, Ms Porter, and please accept my sincere condolences on your loss. This must be very difficult for you."

Once again, her lip wobbled with the effort of holding back more tears. "Thank you, Detective. Please stay in touch. I need to know that you've found whoever is responsible."

"Of course," Jett replied and took down her contact details. He noted with surprise she lived only a couple of blocks from him. His gut clenched. *What he wouldn't give to have met her under different circumstances and be given an opportunity to get to know her better...*

With an impatient sound in the back of his throat, he forced any such thoughts from his head.

She was involved in a murder investigation. Spending time with the woman out of work hours was out of the question at this time.

Swallowing a sigh of resignation, he handed her a card. "Call me if you have anything further to add."

Chapter 4

Dear Diary,

I thought I'd reached my lowest low, but it has nothing on the way I feel right now. My sister and her baby— dead. Not just dead, but murdered and in such a horrible, devastating way. I can't imagine what kind of person could do such a thing! My sister, a beautiful, kind, generous woman who wouldn't hurt a soul and her sweet little innocent child...

Dead. Killed so cruelly. The very thought of what the two of them endured in the moments before their deaths tears my heart in two.

And Franklin, poor Franklin. He's a broken man. He doesn't want to go on. He can't go on. They were his life. They were his everything...

I can only hope and pray the police find the person responsible and see that justice is done. It's the only thing that keeps me going...

I miss them so.

———

Dani leaned tensely against the black marble counter of her sister's gourmet kitchen and stared at Franklin. No expense had been spared in the top-of-the-line appliances—the stainless steel Bosch oven and hot plate, the matching fridge and freezer combination with its chilled water and ice cubes available at the touch of a button, the shiny metallic dishwasher. The dream kitchen her sister would never grace again. Fresh pain washed through Dani and she bit her lip at the surge of hot tears that burned behind her eyes.

Ever since the detective had attended upon her with the news, she hadn't been able to stop crying. Her eyes were hot and swollen. She looked a mess. But she couldn't care less. *What did it matter what she looked like?* Her beloved sister and niece were dead, never coming back.

Franklin made a sound of distress from where he sat on the couch and Dani's heart clenched with pain. Sabrina and Marnie had been his world. What would he do without them? No doubt he'd bury himself in his work. At least he had that to take his mind off the horror. Dani wished she were as lucky.

While she loved her job as a pathologist, it didn't consume her. Not in the way Franklin's work consumed him. It had been a running joke between the three of them: If Sabrina had been the least bit insecure, she could have been forgiven for thinking there was something else—or *someone* else—taking up so much of his time.

The very thought that Franklin might be

unfaithful to his wife was as ludicrous as Sabrina sleeping with her old high school flame. At the reminder of Scott Wells and Franklin's discovery of Scott's ill-fated love letters, Dani moved forward and sat next to him. She took his hand and squeezed it.

"I... I told the detective about the paternity test," she said quietly, wanting him to be prepared. She'd gone straight to his place after meeting with the tall officer. She was counting on the fact the detective wouldn't have spoken to her brother-in-law again.

Franklin lifted his head to stare at her. Surprise flared in the dark depths of his eyes. "You knew about that?"

She nodded. "Sabrina told me about it last week—on Friday night. I came over for a visit. You were at work."

A soft curse escaped him. His expression was so sad and remorseful, Dani caught her breath.

"I was so stupid!" he cried, his hands clenching into fists. "How could I have said such things to her? Accused her of such deceit? My beautiful, perfect Sabrina! I must have been mad! And now...she's gone. What am I going to do without her?"

His voice cracked with emotion. Desolation flooded his face. Dani swallowed the lump that formed in her throat and blinked away her tears. Slowly, she shook her head.

"It's not fair, is it?" she whispered hoarsely. "How could God be so cruel? Sabrina...and wee, innocent Marnie. I still can't believe it."

Franklin stared at her, his face ravaged with grief. "God had nothing to do with this, Dani!" he cried. "This is pure evil."

Dani lowered her gaze and stared at her hands where they lay clenched in her lap. Franklin was right. This wasn't God's fault. A surge of helplessness rushed through her. *Who could have done this, and why?* Sabrina hadn't had an enemy in the world.

"Do the police have any leads?" she croaked, swiping at her tears.

Franklin's lips compressed and he shook his head. "Not as far as I know. One of our neighbors saw the maintenance man outside our place earlier in the day. The police are looking for him. But I know Kevin Thompson. He's a good man. He's worked here for years."

Dani agreed with Franklin, immediately dismissing the idea that Kevin could be responsible. He'd been the maintenance man there for as long as she could remember. At a guess, she'd put the aboriginal man in his late forties and a nicer, friendlier guy you couldn't meet. He always greeted her with a wave and a smile when she dropped by. More often than not, he had a joke to share or a report on his three grandbabies who lived out west, in Penrith. No, Kevin Thompson was the last person she'd suspect.

"There's no way it was Kevin," she said adamantly.

"Yeah," Franklin slowly agreed.

Dani gazed blindly at the floor, filled with helplessness and anger. "Then who? *Who?*"

Franklin drew in a deep breath and blew it out on a heavy sigh. His face flooded with guilt. Dani stared at him, her heart pounding.

"What is it, Franklin? What do you know?"

"I don't know anything!" he cried and dragged a hand down his face. "But, I can't help wondering if it has something to do with a case I've been working on. The detectives even hinted at it."

"Bilal Al-Jabiri?" Dani murmured.

"Sabrina mentioned that too?" Franklin asked.

"Yes, of course, but I'd already seen you on the news. Do you really think this could be connected?"

Franklin's shoulders slumped. "I don't know, Dani, but it makes a mad kind of sense and the police seem to think it's a possibility. I've pissed off a lot of people by taking on this case. People with radical viewpoints and tempers to match. I can't believe I did this to my family. That I brought this to our door." Once again, his voice cracked and he bent over with his head in his hands. Harsh sobs shook his shoulders.

After a while, she spoke again. "We have to talk about the funerals. Did Sabrina make any requests?"

Franklin lifted his head and stared at her blankly. "What the hell are you talking about? What kind of requests?"

Dani blinked back tears. She was just as on edge as Franklin. Couldn't he see that? But someone had to sort out the arrangements, no matter how difficult it was to do.

"I... I don't know, Franklin. Were there any special hymns she liked?"

Franklin dropped his gaze to the floor and shook his head from side to side. "I can't talk about this, Dani. I can't do it. I just can't." He choked on another sob.

Dani clenched her teeth against a surge of emotion and moved closer to pat him awkwardly on the arm. There was nothing she could say to ease his desolation and she wouldn't even try. How could she console someone when *she* was inconsolable? At that moment, a mere handful of hours after the deaths of her niece and sister, the future looked dark and bleak.

Jett dropped into his office chair with a sigh. His shift had ended hours ago, but when a case like the Cook double homicide happened, nobody got to go home. He glanced across at Lane where he sat at the desk opposite.

"How did you go with the maintenance man? Did you manage to track him down?"

Lane shook his head and ran a hand tiredly through his hair, leaving it standing on end.

"No. There was no sign of him, but I spoke with the building supervisor. Matthew Phillip is Kevin Thompson's boss. He confirmed Kevin had been booked in to clear a drain in the Cook condominium earlier in the day, but he expressed shock at the possibility the man was responsible for the deaths. Thompson's worked there for ten years and has never caused him a moment's trouble."

"Did we get a contact number for the guy?"

"Yeah. Phillips called him while I was there. The call went straight to voicemail. I took down Thompson's details. We sent a car around to the same address his pay slips are sent. There was no one home."

Jett scratched at the stubble on his chin. "When did the super last see Thompson? Do we know if this guy entered the Cook condo?"

"That's unclear. Phillips hasn't seen Thompson since their tea break at eleven. At that time, Thompson confirmed the blocked drain in the penthouse was still on his list."

"How did he seem, to Phillips?" Jett asked.

"He seemed like his normal self. Phillips didn't notice anything out of the ordinary. Definitely no signs that the man was about to stab a woman and her child to death."

Jett's lips compressed at the memory of Sabrina and Marnie Cook and the state in which they'd been found. A wave of anger surged through him, quickly followed by cold determination. Nobody deserved to die that way. It was plain wrong, no matter how anyone looked at it. He would find the killer and bring him to justice, if it were the last thing he did.

Lane bent low and pulled something out of his briefcase and tossed it on Jett's desk. "I asked the husband for his wife's phone. I haven't had time to go through it, yet. I thought we might find some clues in her phone and text log. It might be a long shot, but you never know."

Jett nodded and reached over and picked up the phone. It was sealed in a clear plastic evidence bag. The iPhone was protected by a hot pink-and-silver Dolce & Gabbana phone cover. Given the overt display of wealth evidenced in the condominium, Jett assumed the designer accessory was genuine.

"How did it go with the sister?"

Lane's question startled Jett out of his thoughts. In the blink of an eye, his mind zeroed back to the dark-haired beauty he'd spoken with earlier in the day. He wondered where she was right now and whether she still felt as devastated by his news as she'd looked.

"She's a pathologist at the Sydney Harbour Hospital," he said. "I broke the news to her at work."

Lane held his gaze. "What was your take on her?"

Jett shrugged. "She seemed genuinely shocked and distraught. Then again, she might just be a good actress. Who knows? She's almost as tall as I am and looks strong enough to be able to carry out the deed, but so far, I'm struggling for a motive."

"Jealousy?" Lane suggested. "From the photos Franklin Cook supplied of his wife, Sabrina Cook was a stunner and everybody I interviewed emphasized how good and kind she was. She was married to a successful lawyer, with wealth far beyond what most of us ever hope for. To top it off, she had a sweet baby girl. She was living the dream."

"Yes," Jett replied. "It seems even more unbelievable that somebody purposely destroyed all of that. Sabrina's sister is every bit as good looking and furnished me with an alibi. Apparently she was meeting with her AA sponsor. I tracked him down at No. 1 Oval at Sydney University. He corroborated her version of events."

Lane nodded. "Samantha Coleridge called from the morgue with the initial autopsy results. Sabrina Cook was stabbed thirty-seven times before her throat was slit from ear to ear." He shook his head, his expression grave. "This was personal. It's why the Al-Jabiri angle doesn't seem to make any sense."

"Unless it was someone close to the legal action. Who had the most to lose?" Jett wondered aloud.

"There are a number of potential suspects," Lane replied. "I spoke to one of the senior partners of Franklin Cook's law firm. Mike Harris told me they'd received hate mail from members of the public the moment they announced they were taking the case. Franklin was often in the media, loudly defending his client's right to a fair trial. That kind of thing's bound to raise hackles and put certain people on edge."

Jett regarded him curiously. "Were there any standouts?"

"We have a couple of names. Fanatics who took to social media about the case to vent against Harris & Birmingham. Franklin Cook gathered his fair share of haters."

"Could the hate campaign have turned this personal? Personal enough to slaughter the man's wife and child?" Jett asked, shaking his head. "What the hell are we coming to?"

Lane sighed heavily. "You're asking me." Glancing at his watch, Lane pushed away from his desk. "I'll leave you to it, mate. I'm heading home. There isn't much more we can do tonight and I, for one, am beat."

Jett nodded. "Yeah, no worries. I won't be far behind you. I might take a quick look through Sabrina's cell phone before I call it a night."

Lane nodded and lifted a hand in farewell. Jett turned back to his desk. He pulled on a pair of latex gloves from the box he kept in the bottom drawer of his filing cabinet and emptied the phone onto his desk. Activating it, his heart skipped a beat at the screen saver.

It was a close-up shot of Sabrina and her sister. Jett whistled beneath his breath. Lane hadn't been exaggerating when he'd called Sabrina a stunner. The woman was breathtakingly beautiful. Golden blond hair fell in loose waves around a picture-perfect face. Clear blue eyes shone with happiness and warmth. A luscious mouth, perfectly formed, was opened in a wide smile.

She was cheek to cheek with her sister. The two of them grinned into the camera. Danielle Porter's dark coloring contrasted starkly with her sister's, but the impact of her emerald green eyes remained as dramatic as he'd found them earlier.

Today, her brown hair had been tied back in a neat bun at the nape of her neck, but the photo on the screen showed her hair loose, like her sister's. It curled around her shoulders and fell in long waves across her chest. The informal hairstyle made her look much younger than her stated twenty-eight years.

Jett swiped his thumb across the screen and the phone opened to the text messages. It was curious the phone wasn't protected with a password. Most people felt the need to secure their phone that way. Still, maybe there had been a password and Lane had asked Sabrina's husband to remove it. Not that it mattered, one way or the other. The lack of a password would hardly point them in the direction of the killer, but her text and phone logs might.

Going straight to the messages, Jett scrolled through the list of texts, starting at the most recent and working his way back. Between nine fifty-one and ten-thirteen on the day of the murder, Sabrina had received and replied to messages from "Sonia" and "Wendy" about a playdate the girls had organized for Tuesday of the following week. Apparently, it was Timothy's birthday and they were all meeting at the park.

Two days earlier, there was a brief message from Franklin, telling his wife he'd been caught up at work and would be home late. Sabrina had replied with a thumbs-up emoji and two red hearts.

Jett recalled Sabrina's sister telling him about the recent disagreement between Franklin and his wife. He'd accused Sabrina of infidelity. It wasn't the kind of accusation one made lightheartedly.

According to Danielle, the couple had been expecting the results any day. Jett made a note to follow the matter up with Franklin. From what Danielle had told him, it was unlikely the results had caused a stir, let alone a double homicide, but it was a loose end that needed tying up so that they could focus on other areas. Like the maintenance man and the middle-eastern angle.

Jett scrolled back through the texts a bit further and paused on the name "Dani." The most recent message was over a week before. He opened it and scanned the words and then started in surprise.

How many times do I have 2 tell u, Sabrina? Butt out.

The texts from Sabrina were less aggressive, but all the same, it was clear there was tension between the two girls.

Get off your high horse, Dani and just LISTEN to me for a change!

And: *You're so darn stubborn! I'm only trying to help you! Please let me help you!*

Dani's reply was more forthright.

I don't need your help, Sabrina. I can do this on my own.

Jett scrolled forward, but the argument ended abruptly with the first jab. It wasn't clear what they'd been fighting about. According to Franklin, the girls had been on less friendly terms more recently. Jett wondered if the anger he felt in Danielle's responses to her sister could have morphed into the kind of rage exhibited at the scene of the murders.

He shook his head and sighed. It was definitely a stretch. It wasn't unusual for siblings to argue. Hell, he argued with his brothers and sisters all the time. It didn't mean he wanted to kill them. He'd talk to the woman about it the next time he saw her, but as far as he was concerned, there were far more viable suspects than Danielle Porter.

CHAPTER 5

The day of the funeral dawned bright and sunny—a beautiful, clear summer's day. Dani rolled over in bed and squinted at the light that shone through the window. It had been late when she'd finally collapsed into bed and she'd forgotten to close the curtains. Sunshine now spilled into the room and across the pale carpet, like a ribbon of gold. Groaning aloud, Dani drew the sheet up over her face and tried hard to pretend this day wasn't happening.

It had been well after midnight when she'd finally left Franklin's condominium—yes, it was just Franklin's, now—and had made her way back to North Sydney. The familiar sound of late night traffic outside her window had calmed her, along with the camomile tea, but still, it had been a long time before she'd succumbed to sleep.

The bodies of her sister and niece had been removed by the time she'd reached their Hunters Hill condominium, but still, she hadn't been able to bring herself to enter the rooms where they'd been found. Franklin had told her, in halting sentences, that Sabrina had been murdered in the bath. It appeared poor baby Marnie had been sleeping in her crib.

Even now, with the morning sun urging her upright, Dani still couldn't accept the truth. *Someone had murdered her beautiful, sweet-natured sister and an innocent baby. Who could have done that?* The world had been turned on its axis. Nothing made sense.

Then again, Franklin was a well-known lawyer who'd recently taken on a very high-profile case. She'd seen the crowds of angry protesters outside the courthouse on the early morning news the day of the murders. They'd been shouting and holding placards. Some had been protesting against Jamal Al-Jabiri's charges, but most had been angry he hadn't already been found guilty and locked up for the rest of his life.

At the time, she'd shuddered at the implacable fury on the faces of the demonstrators in both camps and had wondered why the hell Franklin had found it necessary to take on such a case. Still, this was Australia. Though the demonstrators' anger had unsettled her, she never dreamed it might result in the murders of her little sister and baby niece.

She sighed heavily. No amount of time lingering beneath the covers would make the next few hours disappear. With reluctance, she pushed back the sheets and climbed out of bed. Padding into the bathroom, she stared at her reflection in the mirror and grimaced. Her long curly hair stood out in every direction, a tangle of snarls and knots. She'd been too tired to run a brush through it before bed the night before and now she was paying the price. There was nothing for it but to tame the wild mass with water.

Reaching into the shower, she turned the spray on full force. Stepping under the steaming water, she took the time to shampoo and condition her hair. It was the day of her sister's funeral, along with her little niece's. She was determined to look her best, if it killed her.

It had been five long days since the detective had attended upon her workplace and given her the terrible news. Sabrina and Marnie had required autopsies and that necessity had added to the delay. The whole sad ordeal had been drawn out.

She'd been numb with grief ever since she'd been told what happened, but burying her loved ones was another something that had to be done. It wasn't easy on any of them, but she'd been frustrated at Franklin's unwillingness to make the arrangements. It was almost as if the deaths of his wife and baby had placed him in a catatonic state. He hadn't left the condominium since it happened. It had been up to Dani to meet with the funeral director, choose the caskets, the flowers, and arrange the service, even the hymns.

She hadn't wanted to do it, but there was no one else. Franklin was an only child. His parents were both deceased. Dani was the sole surviving sibling and though she assumed her parents were still alive, she didn't know for certain and she sure as hell wasn't going to waste time finding out. They'd made their choices years ago, effectively abandoning their daughters to fate and the random kindness of strangers. They didn't deserve the honor of saying good-bye.

With a sigh, Dani turned off the faucets and wrung the water from her hair. Stepping out of the shower, she reached for a towel. She wrapped a fluffy one around her body and twisted another around her hair before returning to her bedroom.

She surveyed the contents of her meagre wardrobe. She'd never been one for fashionable clothes. Sabrina had owned a stylish outfit for every occasion, but Dani spent most of her time in a lab coat and her weekends at her sister's. There just didn't seem the need for an extensive wardrobe.

Her chest tightened with emotion at the thought she'd never spend an evening or a weekend with Sabrina again. Tears sprang to her eyes and trickled down her cheeks. She swiped at them a little impatiently, wondering when they were ever going to stop. And then she was tired of being strong and she bent over with a wrenching sob.

Making her way unsteadily to her bed, she sank down onto it and leaned over with her head in her hands. There were hours and days ahead where she'd have to be strong. Right now, she needed to cry.

The sobs rose up from deep inside her and poured out through her mouth. She gasped and heaved and mourned the loss of her beautiful sister and her innocent baby niece. The anger and frustration at not knowing who was behind this only made the whole thing worse. She didn't even have a name or face to lay the blame.

She hadn't heard anything from the police and she didn't think Franklin had either. Not that he was in any position to carry on a conversation, but he hadn't mentioned progress on that front.

Another surge of anger at the injustice of it all rushed through her and she clung to the strength it gave her. Anger was good. Anger was productive. Anger would see her through.

Jett hung back from the crowd of funeral-goers, content to listen and observe. A gaggle of reporters with television cameras stood off to one side. He guessed it was Franklin Cook's high profile that had drawn them and the fact his wife and daughter had been brutally slain. It wasn't surprising that the story had already made headlines and had been the lead story on the six o'clock news.

Jett was there as an observer, keen to know who was interested enough to attend the funeral of Sabrina Cook and her daughter. Beside him, Lane also scanned the crowd. His experience with the middle-eastern activists would hold them in good stead.

"Look over to your left," Lane murmured, his lips barely moving. "The man with the black beard standing near the gum tree. That's Mohammed Abdul Sharif."

Jett looked in the direction Lane mentioned and spied a middle-aged man wearing black-rimmed glasses dressed in loose white pants and a matching, long-sleeved tunic that fell below his knees. Around his head, he wore a black Keffiyeh wrapped in the traditional Islamic style. He stood with three other men, similarly attired.

"Who's Mohammed Abdul Sharif?" Jett asked.

"He's the self-proclaimed leader of one of Australia's largest Islamic communities. He has a lot of influence among his followers."

"Is he an extremist?" Jett asked, pitching his voice low in deference to the other funeral-goers standing nearby.

"No, in fact, just the opposite. He does all that he can to talk in terms of peace and respect for religious and cultural differences, love and getting along with each other."

"What's he doing here?"

Lane shrugged. "Paying his respects? Perhaps he's keeping an eye on things. There are some people within his community who are getting a little fed up with all the talk about peace, especially with one of their own, a teenager, no less, currently warming his butt in jail."

Jett acknowledged Lane's comment with a nod and continued to scan the crowd. A shiny black limousine pulled up at the curb and the reporters and photographers swarmed forward. The car door opened and Franklin Cook stepped out, followed by his sister-in-law.

The air was filled with the sound of clicking cameras. One or two photographers even had the audacity to call out, hoping to get a better shot. Danielle was dressed in a simple black sheath that skimmed the curves of her body. Her long, slim legs appeared even longer because she wore a pair of five-inch heels. Dark sunglasses hid her gaze from his view, but her mouth was compressed into a tight line. Despite his training and the importance of remaining impartial, Jett's heart went out to her.

Her brother-in-law offered his arm and Jett noted she took it without hesitation.

"It doesn't look like she's harboring any blame," Lane murmured.

Jett watched as the two of them walked slowly into the church, heads bowed low in grief. They looked neither left, nor right.

"Yeah," he replied quietly, "though it's interesting. Danielle Porter told me Sabrina and Franklin never argued and yet a couple of weeks before her death, he accused her of being unfaithful."

Lane's eyebrows rose and his forehead lined with creases. "Wow, that's one helluva way to trigger an argument. What happened?"

"Franklin demanded a paternity test. The results were due about the same time she and her daughter were murdered."

Lane frowned and his voice sharpened. "And why are you only just now sharing this information?"

Jett held his gaze. "Danielle also said the

accusation was groundless. Sabrina had assured her the results would prove Franklin was Marnie's dad. I'll follow it up with him after the service. It should be easy enough for him to clear the matter up, one way or the other."

"Given that all other lines of enquiry so far have drawn a blank, we need to investigate every possible clue," Lane replied.

"Yeah," Jett agreed. "But I'm not sure it's going to lead anywhere."

Lane let out a sigh filled with frustration. "It doesn't seem to matter where we look, we keep running into brick walls. I interviewed some members of the Islamic community. They'd heard of the murders, but they had nothing to impart that would implicate anyone. That poor woman and her child have been dead almost a week and we're not even close to finding the killer."

"Yeah, I went by Kevin Thompson's apartment Tuesday afternoon and again, yesterday morning. Same story. His sister hasn't seen him since the morning of the murders."

Lane nodded, his expression grim. "At this stage, the maintenance man's our best bet and he's not doing himself any favors. What's he hiding from?"

"I'll run his name through the system when I get back to the office and see what I can find," Jett offered. "I'll also check if he has a vehicle registered in his name."

"Good. In the meantime, I look forward to hearing about the paternity results."

"Yep. I'll let you know as soon as I talk to Cook.

I'm not holding out much hope it's going to move things forward, but it's worth following up."

Lane acknowledged Jett's comment with a brief nod. "I guess that's it. There's no point in both of us hanging around. I'll see you back there." With a wave, he disappeared into the crowd.

Forty-five minutes later, Jett followed the funeral procession as it snaked its way to the Macquarie Park Cemetery and Crematorium. Unlike the swarm of media, he kept a respectful distance as the final hymns were played from an iPod and a Bluetooth speaker and the caskets were lowered into the ground. One was made of dark cedar and was liberally embellished with shiny brass fittings. The second coffin was small and white and lacy. Jett's gut tightened at the sight. It was decorated with bright, yellow-button daisies and soft green ferns. A pink teddy bear sat on top of the flowers.

Finally the crowd thinned until only Franklin and Danielle remained. Sabrina's husband sat in the cheap plastic chairs provided for the family by the funeral home. Danielle kneeled by the gravesite and stared at the hole in the ground.

Jett moved closer and could see her lips moving silently. He wasn't sure if she was praying or bidding the occupants a final farewell. He felt uncomfortable interrupting either scenario, but he still sought some answers and in a homicide investigation, there was never a good time to ask.

"Mr Cook, Ms Porter. Please accept my condolences," he said quietly, gazing from one to the other.

Danielle stood a little awkwardly and inclined her head, but didn't speak. Her hair was pulled back into an uncompromising bun. Her face was drawn and wan. Without the protection of her sunglasses, he could see her eyes were red and swollen and glazed with pain. In contrast, Franklin Cook looked stoic. He regarded Jett with a frown.

"Detective Craigdon," he said, his voice toneless. "Thank you for coming."

Jett inclined his head. "I... I'd like to ask you both a couple of more questions."

Franklin's frown deepened. "*Now?*"

"Yes. I understand this is a difficult time, but we're working around the clock on this and so far, we have very few leads." He flashed another look at Danielle and then returned his attention to Cook. "I wanted to ask you about the DNA test. The one you requested not long before this happened."

From the corner of Jett's eye, he saw Danielle stand and fold her arms across her chest, but he kept his gaze on Franklin, watching closely to gauge his reaction. The man's expression didn't alter. He certainly didn't appear surprised by the question.

"What is it you want to know, Detective?" he asked in the same toneless voice, as if nothing and nobody mattered anymore. *And perhaps that was true...*

"Have you received the results?" he asked.

Franklin nodded wearily. "They came in the mail the day...the day this happened. I received them at work. I have all of our mail delivered to my office. It's more secure that way."

"And what did they say?" Jett persisted, feeling churlish that he had to ask, but wanting to put this line of questioning to rest.

Danielle Porter's eyes blazed with fury. She pushed herself into Jett's space. "What the hell do you think they said? My sister was good and kind and honorable. She didn't have a deceitful bone in her body. Of course Marnie belonged to Franklin!"

Jett studied her closely and tried not to be moved by her fierce beauty. Her breath came fast and her chest rose and fell, drawing her generous proportions to his attention. With a sound of self-disgust coming from the back of his throat, Jett forced his attention elsewhere. Once again, Franklin bent forward and held his head in his hands.

"The truth is, Detective," Franklin said, his words muffled behind his hands, "I haven't even opened the results. I should never have requested proof in the first place. I knew when I demanded it, that it wasn't right. My wife would never be unfaithful. But it was like, once it was out there, I couldn't take it back. It seemed easier to go ahead with it than call it off."

He lifted his head and gazed at Jett, his eyes now filled with pain. "I never got to tell her I was sorry. She died before I got the chance. How will I forgive myself? She died thinking I believed she'd been unfaithful. She died uncertain of my love. It's wrong! So wrong! I don't know what to do. There's nothing I can do and it's killing me!"

His words were drowned out by noisy sobs as,

once again, he held his head in his hands. Danielle looked stricken. Seating herself beside him, she put an arm around his shoulders and offered him murmured words of comfort.

"*Shh,* Franklin, it's all right. And don't be upset. Sabrina knew how much you loved her. She *knew.* She told me about the roses. She knew you hadn't meant what you'd said. She understood you were tired and stressed and those words had come out without thought or premeditation."

Franklin lifted his head and stared at his sister-in-law, his eyes wide with surprise. "She... She told you about the roses?"

Danielle held his gaze. It was like Jett was no longer there. "Yes, she told me and she knew exactly what they meant. She told me it was your way of apologizing for your behavior. So please, stop crying. Let's remember her and Marnie, the way they were, full of sunshine and love. They deserve nothing less."

Jett stared at Danielle with admiration. She'd just lost her niece and sister in the most horrific way. She was standing mere feet from their grave and yet, despite her obvious pain and loss, she cared enough about her brother-in-law to comfort him and ease him through his grief. Jett's certainty that she wasn't involved in the deaths was strengthened, but he still had one more question. He cleared his throat to get her attention.

"Ms Porter, I read through some of the text messages on your sister's phone. I noticed you two seemed to be arguing over something a week before her death. Can you tell me about that?"

She turned her head and glared at him. "I don't know what you're talking about."

He dug into his pocket and pulled out his phone. He'd taken a screenshot of the messages.

"This might refresh your memory," he said and handed her his cell.

She looked down at the screen and scanned its contents. A frown creased the smooth skin of her forehead. A moment later, it cleared and a hint of embarrassment colored her cheeks.

"Okay, I guess you could call this an argument, but it was nothing. A disagreement, that's all."

Jett eyed her curiously. "What were you disagreeing about?"

The color in her cheeks deepened and she kept her gaze fixed to the ground. "It's not what you're thinking, Detective. It was nothing."

He regarded her steadily. "I think I need to be the judge of that."

She drew in a deep breath and then let it out on a sigh. "Sabrina was trying to find me a boyfriend. A few times she'd tried to set me up with men from Franklin's work. She wouldn't believe me when I told her I wasn't interested." She threw her head back and stared at him, a look of challenge in her eyes.

He stared back at her, refusing to acknowledge the leap in his pulse when she revealed she was single.

"All right," he finally replied, giving her a nod.

"Will that be all, Detective?" she asked pointedly.

"For now." He looked at Franklin. "I'd like a

copy of those paternity tests, if you don't mind."

Franklin barely acknowledged his request. His gaze remained fixed on the grave. Jett felt a wave of sympathy.

"Thank you for your time, Mr Cook, Ms Porter," he said quietly. "And once again, I'm so sorry for your loss."

"Just find the bastard who did this to my family," Franklin urged, his voice rough and unsteady.

Jett compressed his lips and nodded, feeling the full weight of their joint stares. He was responsible for finding the killer. In silence, he vowed not to rest until that was done.

CHAPTER 6

J ett closed the door to his squad car and approached the four-storey red brick apartment block that was surrounded by similarly ugly buildings. Built in the 1950s and subsidized by the government in an effort to provide cheaper housing options, they dotted the Sydney skyline. Though many of them had been demolished and replaced with sleeker, more modern versions, a few of them still remained, including the one where Kevin Thompson lived with his sister.

Fuelled with renewed determination after his conversation with Franklin and Danielle, Jett had run Thompson's name through their system and discovered the man had a record. Given Thompson's employment, the discovery had taken Jett by surprise. For some time, almost every employer demanded a criminal history check prior to commencement of work. He wondered how Thompson had managed to avoid it.

Though the most recent entry on Thompson's

record was added more than a decade ago, previously, there were a number of convictions for break and enters and assaults. Fifteen years earlier, Thompson had done jail time for assault with a weapon, namely a knife. Jett didn't know if Thompson had finally cleaned up his act, or if he'd just gotten better at evading the law, but this time, he was determined to find out.

His sharp knock on Thompson's front door was answered quickly, as if someone had been watching his approach. Margaret Thompson opened the door the length of the security chain and peered at him, with a narrowed gaze, through the crack.

"Go away. He's not here. I already told you I'd call you if he showed up."

Jett held her gaze. "I need to talk to him, Margaret. He's not doing himself any favors hiding himself away. It makes me think he's guilty of something and I don't want to jump to any conclusions. You're his sister. Talk to him. Try and make him see sense."

Her mouth set in a mutinous line. The flicker of a curtain in the window beside the front door snagged Jett's attention. Someone else was inside. He turned back to Margaret and gave her a hard stare.

"He's in there, isn't he? Let me come in. I need to talk to him."

She shook her head. "No, he's not home. I already told you. Now, go away before—"

A dark hand flashed in the narrow space of the open doorway and a moment later, the security chain was released. Kevin Thompson pulled the door all the way open and stared down at Jett with his arms crossed over his chest.

"What do you want?" he growled.

"Kevin, don't say anything. I'm going to call—"

Kevin shot his sister a look and the rest of her protest died in her mouth. "Don't go callin' nobody, Margaret. I ain't got nothin' to hide." He turned back to Jett. "Ask your questions and then leave us alone. We ain't done nothin' wrong."

Jett nodded and pulled out his notebook. "Why did you stop going to work, Kevin? Your boss tells me he hasn't seen you since the morning Sabrina and Marnie Cook were murdered. You were seen by one of the residents outside the Cooks' condo not long before her husband found them dead. Is that why you stayed away? Did you have something to do with their deaths?"

Kevin's hard gaze remained on Jett's. "It's like I already told you, I had nothin' to do with what happened."

"Then why did you run, Kevin?"

The man shrugged and looked away. He scuffed the toe of his shoe on the doorstep.

"I ran your name through our system," Jett continued, retaining his conversational tone.

Kevin's dark skin lost a little of its color and his gaze stayed fixed to the ground.

"You have an extensive criminal record," Jett said. "Care to tell me about it?"

"What's the use?" Kevin exploded. "You've already made up your mind. You think I did it, don't you? Isn't that why you're here?"

Jett eyed him solemnly. "If I thought you'd done it, Kevin, you'd already be cuffed by now. I'm here to talk to you, to find out the truth. Now, are you going to remove that chip on your shoulder and tell me what the hell happened that day?"

The bravado suddenly went out of Kevin and his shoulders slumped on a heavy sigh. "I don't know what happened," he muttered. "That poor woman and her baby..." His voice trembled and Jett caught the glint of tears in his eyes.

Forcing any feelings of sympathy aside, Jett continued his interrogation. "You were seen outside the Cooks' condominium. What were you doing there?"

"Mrs Cook had put in a call to the super. She had a blocked drain. I was there to repair it."

"What time was this?" Jett asked.

"About twelve."

Jett nodded. The time coincided with what Marcia Willis had recalled. "Did you go inside?"

Kevin lowered his gaze and shook his head slowly back and forth. "No. I knocked on the door, but nobody answered. I knocked again and called out, yelled my name. I could hear the sound of water runnin'. Mrs Cook shouted back at me from somewhere inside. She said she was takin' a bath and could I come back a bit later. So I left."

"How did you know it was her?" Jett asked, making a note.

"I recognized her voice."

"Did you come back later?"

"No. I didn't get the chance. Before I went back Mr Cook came home and found them and..." Thompson's voice faded away again. His lips compressed.

"Why did you run, Kevin?"

Anger flickered in the black man's face. He stared hard at Jett. "You *know* why I ran. I ran because of *this*. I ran because I'd been outside that condominium not long before. It would only be a matter of time before the police discovered my record. I'm a black man who's seen the inside of a jail on more than one occasion. I knew I'd be the first suspect on your list." He threw Jett another hard look. "And I was right."

Jett refused to be intimidated. The truth was, the man had been seen outside the Cooks' condominium. According to the autopsy reports, death had occurred sometime within the hour prior to the arrival of emergency services. That put Kevin Thompson squarely within the frame, whether he liked it or not.

"Don't play that race card bullshit with me," Jett growled. "I won't buy it. I don't care if you're black, white or brindle. I'm investigating a brutal double homicide. You're on the suspect list because you were seen in the vicinity of the crime scene shortly before it happened. That is the *only* reason we're talking."

Thompson's expression remained belligerent, but a little of the anger and tension eased from his tall frame. He shrugged. "So, we've talked. Now what are you gonna do?"

Jett eyeballed him. "I want the clothes that you

were wearing the day Sabrina and Marnie Cook were murdered."

Kevin's eyes flared with anger, but he turned and disappeared into the house. A short time later, he reappeared, carrying a set of dark green work clothes.

"Here," he said and shoved them toward Jett.

"How do I know these were the ones you were wearing that day?"

"You don't," Thompson growled. "But it's the only set I have. I work Monday to Friday. They get washed at the end of the week. I haven't worn them since the Monday it happened. They weren't dirty enough to wash."

Jett acknowledged Kevin's explanation with a nod. "Fair enough." He tucked the clothes under his arm.

All of a sudden Thompson's expression turned fierce. "It wasn't me, Detective. I swear. I know it looks bad. I was there, outside their unit, right before it happened. But they were still alive then. At least, Mrs Cook was. I left, like she asked me to. I didn't get time to go back. When I heard about what happened..." He shook his head, looking a little bewildered. "I couldn't believe it. I'd been up there and spoken to her not long before. I got scared, Detective. I panicked. That's why I ran."

Jett held Thompson's gaze. The man appeared to be sincere. Still, Jett would take the clothing and have it analyzed. There was no way the killer could have murdered the mother and child so violently and not be covered in blood.

Acknowledging Kevin's words with a brief nod,

Jett tucked his notebook back in the pocket of his shirt. "Thanks for talking to me, Kevin. I appreciate your time. Don't go leaving town, all right?"

"You still think I done it?" Kevin said, his voice tinged with desperation. "I swear, it wasn't me!"

"I'm not sure what to think right now, Kevin. We'll see what the evidence shows." He held up Kevin's clothing. "Starting with these."

"You're wastin' your time. You won't find nothin' on them."

"Then you have nothing to worry about," Jett replied.

Turning on his heel, he made his way back down the cracked pavement that led to the street. He tossed the clothing into a plastic evidence bag he found on the back seat of the squad car and then climbed behind the wheel and headed in the direction of the office.

Dropping Thompson's clothing on his desk, he checked through his email messages. A call had come in from Franklin Cook. With all the guy had going on that day, Jett was surprised to hear from the man. He'd only spoken to him a few hours earlier, at the cemetery. Tugging the phone out of his pocket, Jett called him.

"Detective Craigdon, thanks for returning my call."

"Of course. What can I do for you?"

"I was just wondering if there have been any new developments. Have they found the maintenance man, yet?"

"Yes. I just came from his apartment," Jett replied.

"So, you arrested him?" Franklin's voice was filled with sudden hope.

"No, I'm sorry, Mr Cook. It doesn't quite work that way."

"What are you waiting for? He was seen outside our condominium right before it happened."

Jett drew in a deep breath and forced himself to remain calm. "You're right, but you're a smart guy. You know how this works. We need more than just the testimony of an eyewitness placing him in the vicinity. After all, the building super confirmed he was there to unblock a drain."

"Sabrina never mentioned anything to me." Franklin's tone held a belligerent edge.

"Was that normal for her to apprise you of such things?"

"Yes. Well, sometimes. It depends what it was."

"Is it possible she might not have considered a blocked drain important enough to mention to you, given how busy you were with the Al-Jabiri case?"

Jett heard Franklin sigh heavily on the other end of the phone. "Yes, you're right, Detective. She wouldn't have bothered me with something like that. Not at that time."

"She would have simply picked up the phone and reported the problem to the super, right?" Jett asked.

"Yes," came the reluctant reply.

Jett remained silent. He knew how Franklin felt. Helpless, frustrated, angry... The same way the family of crime victims usually felt. He decided to cut the man some slack.

"Look, Mr Cook, I understand how you're feeling. We want to find the person responsible, too. We're doing everything we can, but so far, we don't have much to go on. I've collected the clothes Kevin Thompson was wearing the day of the murders, but a cursory examination doesn't show any evidence of blood. No perp could have done what they did without being covered in it."

"How do you know he's given you the clothes he was wearing that day?" Cook demanded.

"I put that very question to him," Jett responded calmly. "He told me he only owns one set of work clothes."

"And you believed him?" Cook's voice was filled with disbelief.

Jett understood his reaction. He doubted if Cook had worn the same thing twice in his life. "I'll check with his supervisor, of course, but yes, I believe him. And that reminds me," he added. "Did anyone collect *your* clothes?"

"My clothes? Don't tell me you still regard *me* as a suspect?"

Ignoring Franklin's question, Jett replied, "It's standard procedure. We need the clothing you were wearing the day of the murders."

The man blustered a little more, but eventually sighed. "Of course, Detective. They're... They're not in the best of shape. I got blood on them when I tried to pull Sabrina out of the bath. Keep them for as long as you need. I don't want them back."

"Thank you. I'll drop by after work. Is six okay?"

"Sure. I'll make sure I have them ready."

"Are you still at your condominium?"

Franklin sighed again. "Yes, I'm here. Dani's staying with me. Neither of us want to be alone tonight."

Jett nodded. Images of Sabrina's beautiful sister surfaced in his mind. A sudden unwelcoming thought intruded. *Could there be something going on between Franklin and Danielle? Could that be a possible motive? One he hadn't thought of?* It wouldn't be the first time such a thing had happened and it could have provided enough incentive to do away with the woman standing in their way...

Jett shook his head. Danielle Porter appeared distraught at the deaths. *Surely she wasn't that good an actress?* Jett didn't think so, but how could he be so sure? After all, he'd known her less than a week.

Chapter 7

Dear Diary,

Today I buried my little sister and her gorgeous baby girl. It was the hardest thing I've ever done, even harder than walking away from the only life I'd known and starting again.

I'll never see their faces, never again feel the joy from their laughter. The pain of loss tears me to pieces. How will I bear it?

Franklin's curled up on the sofa, salty tears long dried on his cheeks. He's suffering just as badly as me. He loved them with everything that he was.

I'm glad I was able to reassure him that Sabrina loved him till the end; that she didn't blame him for his hurtful accusation. It brought him a measure of comfort—and after all, it was the truth.

Dani sipped from her Coke and for the first time in a decade, wished it were something stronger. What she wouldn't give for the blissful numbness a bottle of scotch would bring. But that was the wish of old Dani, a woman she never wanted to be again; a woman she no longer recognized inside her. And she was glad.

She'd come a long way since the car wreck that was her childhood. If it hadn't been for Sabrina's love and encouragement, Dani might still be living that life. Drinking every night to obliterate the memories; picking up strangers and inviting them home. She was lucky she hadn't picked up some awful STD, or worse.

It was bad enough she'd been arrested for prostitution. Twice. She didn't blame the police officers. One of them, at least, was merely doing their job. In fact, she ought to be grateful for their intervention. She'd been sixteen and more or less living on the streets. Her parents had long since given up caring—if they'd ever cared at all.

Try as she might, she couldn't summon a single memory of feeling loved and cherished by her mom and dad. The only person who'd loved her was Sabrina and now Dani's beautiful, gentle sister was dead.

Dani's chest tightened painfully and tears burned behind her eyes. She thought she was done crying. Over the past five days, she'd shed enough tears to flood Sydney Harbour. She didn't think she had any left. And yet, they kept coming.

Franklin sat at the other end of the modular

sofa. Apart from a couple of phone calls he'd taken in another room, he'd stayed mostly in the same spot, curled up in fetal position or bent over with his head between his knees. She watched as he tugged out a monogrammed handkerchief and delicately blew his nose. A knock sounded on the door, startling her. Her gaze flew to Franklin.

He grimaced. "It's probably the detective. I spoke to him earlier."

Butterflies swarmed in her stomach. She quickly looked away and tried to tell herself her reaction was merely because the officer might have news, rather than because she was coming face to face with the man again.

She'd been taken aback to see him at the funeral. She hadn't given any thought to the fact he might come. And then he was there, beside the grave, offering condolences and asking questions—questions that had annoyed the hell out of her.

She guessed she ought to be grateful he was doing all that he could to solve the crimes, even if they were in the middle of burying their loved ones and he still seemed fixed on the possibility that the killer was close to home.

"He's come for my clothes," Franklin muttered, hoisting himself off the couch. "I'm assuming he's checking for blood."

Dani blinked to clear her thoughts and then frowned in confusion. "Why would he need to do that? I get that spouses are always the first suspects, but he can't honestly believe you capable of murdering your wife and child?"

"Stranger things have happened, Dani," Franklin replied quietly. "You see it on the news all the time."

"Yes, but not to *your* family. That kind of thing doesn't happen to *you*."

Franklin shrugged and headed across the open concept living and dining room. He opened the door to the detective. Dani heard the officer greet her brother-in-law, his voice deep and solemn.

"Mr Cook, thank you for seeing me."

Dani stood and made her way over to the men. She nodded to the detective.

"Ms Porter, it's nice to see you again," he said quietly.

A lock of his black hair had fallen across his eyes, lending him a boyish air, but there was nothing immature about the chiseled jawline, the broad shoulders that tapered to a narrow waist and the long legs that put him at least a head above her. Despite the gravity of the situation, her stomach clenched with nerves that had nothing to do with the reasons for his visit.

When his eyes suddenly widened and his nostrils flared, Dani realized she'd been staring. A blush raced across her face, heating her cheeks. She hurriedly averted her gaze.

"I'll go and fetch those clothes for you," Franklin said, seeming oblivious to the silent exchange.

Detective Craigdon nodded and cleared his throat. "Thank you. I'm sorry to trouble you, especially today, but time is of the essence. I'm sure you understand."

"Yes, of course," Franklin agreed. "I'm happy to

do whatever I can to help you find the person responsible. I just hope it's soon."

"We're all hoping for that, Mr Cook. I want you to know, we're doing everything that we can."

The detective glanced down. His attention was drawn to the white bandage that covered Franklin's right hand.

"Tell me again how you cut yourself, Mr Cook. I'm afraid with all that was happening that day, I've forgotten what you said."

Dani waited for Franklin to reply. She'd noticed the bandage earlier in the week, but hadn't gotten around to asking him about it.

"It was stupid," Franklin replied with a wry smile. "I was chopping vegetables and trying to watch the National Basketball League game on TV. The knife slipped and I cut my hand." He grimaced and offered another slight smile. "Like I said, stupid."

"Who was playing?" the detective asked, his tone only mildly curious.

"Playing?" Franklin asked.

"Yes, you said you were watching a basketball game. I was wondering who was playing."

Franklin flushed under the detective's perusal. He frowned and averted his gaze. Dani stared at him. He was talking about a game that had happened less than a week ago. *Surely he could remember?*

"Um... I... I think it was the Sydney Kings and the Perth Wildcats. Yes, that's right. Sabrina follows the NBL. She used to play in high school. She just loves Josh Childress. The Kings were way out in front. She was ecstatic."

The detective regarded Franklin closely, but seemed satisfied by his answer. With his hands in the pockets of his suit pants, he wandered over to the floor-to-ceiling plate glass windows that framed the spectacular view of Sydney Harbour.

Night had softly fallen, catching Dani unawares. A thousand golden lights twinkled in the distance from yachts and houseboats and tall buildings on the other side of the harbor. A ferry passed far below them, lit up like a Christmas tree, reminding her that the festive season wasn't far away. She wondered fleetingly about its occupants, all heading home after a busy, uneventful day. She wished she were one of them.

The detective stared out the window at the darkness far below. "Did you go to the emergency department for treatment?" he asked, keeping his back to them.

Franklin cleared his throat and moved to lean against the couch. "Sabrina wanted me to, but I brushed off her concerns. I didn't think it was too bad, but a couple of days later, I was in agony. The cut was infected." He grimaced. "I should have listened to Sabrina. She always knew best."

His voice broke and Dani was flooded with another wave of sadness. She still couldn't believe her sister and baby niece were gone and that she'd never see their beloved faces again.

"When did you cut your hand?" the detective asked, turning to face them. His gaze remained fixed on Franklin.

Franklin frowned. "I guess it must have been Friday or Saturday afternoon. I'd gone into the office on Sunday to get a head start on the week. I was there until late."

"I met you on the Monday," Detective Craigdon murmured. "The wound looked pretty fresh back then. Certainly not infected."

Franklin flushed. "Then it must have happened on Saturday."

The detective stilled. He stared at Franklin. "You're sure?"

"Yes, yes, of course," Franklin hurriedly replied, his gaze fixed on some point above Dani's head. "It was Saturday. I remember now. Sabrina had suggested we order take-out, but I'd already started to cook."

The detective moved with panther-like grace, his large strides eating up the distance as he crossed the living room and came to a halt near Franklin. Dani held her breath. There was something about the man that commanded attention.

"You know," he said to no one in particular, "I'm a pretty big fan of the NBL and in particular, the Sydney Kings. When I'm not working, I try hard to catch their games."

Franklin offered a nervous smile. Dani tensed. She wasn't sure what was going on, but all of a sudden, the air around them was charged.

"I've never known them to play on a Saturday afternoon."

The quiet statement fell from the detective's lips as if they were of no consequence, but disquiet stirred in Dani's stomach. She stared at Franklin.

Franklin chuckled, as if in amusement, but the

humor didn't reach his eyes. The detective's expression remained grim.

"How about you find those clothes for me?" the detective murmured, his voice laced with steel.

Franklin offered a jerky nod and headed straight toward the corridor that led to the bedrooms. The detective turned to her and all of a sudden, her chest tightened so much, she wasn't sure if she could breathe.

He was even better looking than she'd remembered. A dark stubble shadowed his cheeks, thicker than the last time, as if he hadn't shaved all week. She wondered if he was growing a beard or if he simply hadn't found the time. His eyes studied her, a clear and honest blue that contrasted with the golden tan of his skin. His black hair gleamed under the myriad of downlights.

"Your brother-in-law tells me you're staying with him for a while."

His words broke the spell that had held her enthralled for an infinitesimal moment. She blinked and regathered her thoughts.

"Yes. I... We... We didn't want to be alone. At least, not tonight. I live by myself in North Sydney. Franklin's...also alone."

The detective eyed her curiously. "You and Franklin get along well."

It wasn't a question. Dani stared at him, trying to see if there was anything behind his statement, but his eyes revealed nothing.

"Yes, I guess we do. He adored my sister as much as I did. I guess I love him for that alone."

The detective raised one silky, dark eyebrow. "You love him?"

She blushed. "Not like that, Detective. Franklin's the brother I never had. He met Sabrina when she was still in her final year of high school. I'm only two years older."

The detective nodded. "You've known him a long time."

"Yes."

"And are you a Sydney Kings fan, too?"

She smiled sadly, beset with memories. "No. Sabrina was the one who loved following the NBL. I'm more of a football girl."

The same dark eyebrow arched in amusement. "Who's your team?"

"The Melbourne Storm."

His face flooded with surprise. A smile played around his lips. "Traitor."

"Hey," she protested, smiling back at him. "Just because I live in Sydney, doesn't mean I can't barrack for an interstate team."

He shook his head. Humor glinted in his eyes. "Uh, oh. Don't try and justify your decision. Nothing you say can will make it any better. You barrack for Melbourne. Our arch-rival. It's nothing short of a betrayal."

"They're on the top of the table," she shot back.

"They were caught cheating a couple of seasons ago."

She narrowed her eyes in mock annoyance. "They exceeded the salary cap. It's not exactly cheating."

His eyes widened in surprise. "Oh, so there are degrees of deceit, are there?"

She chuckled and the sound of it shocked her. She hadn't laughed since he'd brought her the awful news. Their gazes caught and held. Time stood still. Dani's breath halted in her chest. A second later, her heartbeat took off at a gallop.

He stood so close she could see the tiny, dark flecks in his eyes. Her fingers itched to reach out and touch the whiskers on his chin. The faint smell of male cologne wafted in the air, crisp and cool and masculine. Her pulse thundered in her ears.

"Here you go."

Franklin appeared beside them carrying an armful of clothing and Dani jumped like she'd been burned. Heat crept up her neck and flooded her cheeks. She moved away, stumbling in her haste to put some distance between her and the detective.

"Thanks," the detective replied calmly and accepted Franklin's bundle.

Franklin flashed him a look filled with derision. "What, you're not going to ask me if these are the same clothes I wore the day my wife and daughter were murdered?"

Detective Craigdon's gaze narrowed on her brother-in-law's. "Do you want me to?"

Franklin shrugged, as if what the detective did or didn't do no longer mattered. "Suit yourself."

Dani frowned, bewildered by Franklin's attitude. *Why was he going out of his way to antagonize the detective?* They needed the officer to be totally committed to finding Sabrina and Marnie's killer. He'd hardly feel inclined to go the extra mile if Franklin treated him like a second-class citizen.

She shot her brother-in-law a questioning look and was irritated when he ignored her. She'd been just as affected as he was by the deaths of his wife and baby. They were *her* family, too. It was only right that he acknowledge that.

"Are we done?" Franklin asked, his tone not in the least repentant.

Dani glared at him again, but the detective appeared unaffected by her brother-in-law's rudeness.

"Not quite. I still haven't received a copy of those paternity tests. You were meant to send them in."

Franklin's tone lost some of its edge. "I... I'm not sure what happened to them. I remember bringing them home from the office, but it was the same day Sabrina and Marnie were murdered. At the time, I had much more important matters to deal with. I must have put them down somewhere, but I'm not sure where. As soon as I find them, I'll give you a copy."

"You do that," the officer replied, giving Franklin a hard look. "We're done. For now."

Chapter 8

Jett threw the squad car into gear and headed out into the traffic, his thoughts on the two people he'd just left behind. While he continued to warm toward Danielle Porter, her brother-in-law was a different matter.

After interviewing the man on the day of the murders and observing him at the funeral, Jett had been convinced the man didn't have anything to do with the awful events that had taken place in his luxurious condominium and was nothing more than a man grieving deeply for the tragic loss of his family. Now, he wasn't so sure.

A few moments ago, Cook had come across as surly and belligerent, not at all like the broken and desolate man in evidence earlier in the day. Okay, he'd just buried his wife and baby. It was enough to put anyone in a churlish mood. Jett couldn't imagine what that would feel like and he hoped he never had to experience it, but he wondered now if Franklin's devastation had been nothing more than an act. *Had it all been for show? Put on for the cameras? And what was with the paternity results? Had he really misplaced them, like he claimed?*

Jett glanced at the clothes on the front seat, now contained in a clear plastic evidence bag. Large, dark stains were visible on the pale blue business shirt. It was more difficult to ascertain if the charcoal-gray suit was similarly marked, but the lab would be able to tell. The stains that were visible appeared to be blood stains, but their existence didn't get Jett excited. He'd noticed them during his initial interview with Franklin, when Jett and Lane had first attended the crime scene and Franklin had told him that he'd gotten covered in blood while trying to haul his wife out of the bath. It was a reasonable explanation and could be the truth. Proper analysis would tell them for sure.

Pulling close to the curb outside the State Crime Command headquarters, he killed the engine and leaned back against the seat with a heavy sigh. For all the hours he'd spent on the investigation, he had nothing to show for his efforts. Kevin Thompson had looked like a promising suspect, but Jett's suspicions had gone off him for now. Call him an idiot, but he believed Kevin's protestations of innocence. No doubt his work clothing would tell the tale.

Franklin Cook, on the other hand, was an enigma. Jett didn't want to admit his growing dislike for the guy had more than a little do with the obvious love and respect Danielle had for him. The jury was still out on whether she felt more than sisterly affection for her brother-in-law, despite her assurances to the contrary. And if that were so, Jett could understand her attraction.

Cook was a prominent, wealthy lawyer. Some women would probably find him attractive—if they were into the brown-haired, brown-eyed, glasses-wearing office type who looked like they didn't get enough sun. He wasn't Jett's idea of sexy, but then again, Jett wasn't a woman.

With an impatient growl in the back of his throat, he threw off his seatbelt. *Why the hell was he wasting his thoughts on such stupidity?* It was late and he was tired. He couldn't care less if women found Franklin Cook attractive. Reaching across the gear stick, he retrieved the bag of clothes. Opening the car door, he climbed out and made his way up to his office. He'd drop off the evidence, check his emails and head for home. He'd be thankful to finally put the day behind him.

Franklin stared out through the plate glass window that formed the back wall of the living room. The place was in darkness. He wasn't sure what time it was, but it was way past late. Dani had retired to the guest room hours ago. She'd shuddered as she'd passed Marnie's room and had steadfastly refused to use the bathroom where her sister had been found, but the small sounds she'd made as she'd prepared for bed, in what was known fondly as "Dani's room," had stopped some time ago and he assumed she'd finally succumbed to sleep.

He wished he could do the same. He hadn't slept properly since it happened. Right now, he couldn't imagine ever sleeping soundly again. The very thought was ludicrous. His wife and child were lying dead and buried beneath the ground. In an instant, his life had been transformed into a nightmare.

One moment, he'd been on top of the world, working hard at a successful career and a loving, stable home life and the next, everything that had been warm and familiar was ripped apart at the seams. And now, judging by Detective Craigdon's reaction, he was back firmly on the suspect list.

He cursed aloud. His voice sounded harsh in the stillness. It was his own fault the detective's suspicions had been raised. Franklin should never have lost his temper. He was a defense lawyer. He, of all people, knew the power of self-control and yet, he'd let the detective rattle him.

It was the man's dig about the NBL game that had done it. So, national basketball games weren't televised on a Saturday. How was he meant to know? He was sure he'd seen Sabrina watching them at that time of day in the past. Maybe it was a replay? Then again, perhaps he was mistaken? After all, it had been a long time since he'd been home on a Saturday afternoon. It appeared his mistake might have cost him dearly, if the detective's sudden change in attitude was anything to go by. That and the stupid lab test.

It annoyed him that his actions would divert the police's attention from the other potential suspects. Kevin Thompson, for one. The man had been seen outside the condo shortly before Franklin arrived home. He didn't want to believe the friendly maintenance man could be capable of such atrocities, but how well did anyone know the people they came into contact with?

Then there was the Islamic angle. For weeks, there had been a number of protestors outside his office. Tensions had been running high. It was possible some fanatic had discovered his home address and caught Sabrina unawares. He needed to remind the detective who the real suspects were. First thing in the morning, he'd make the call.

———

Jett took a sip of his morning coffee. He leaned forward in his chair and stared at the footage he'd received from the CCTV cameras installed in the foyer of the building where the Cook family lived. The screen showed grainy, black-and-white images, but they were still clear enough to be able to identify faces. One of the junior detectives had already reviewed it and had reported that nothing suspicious had been seen, but Jett had just taken another call from Sabrina's husband.

It appeared that Franklin Cook had convinced himself that the intruder was related to his current court case. He'd insisted Jett review the footage again and make certain no one untoward had entered the building. When Jett queried the likelihood of his wife letting a stranger into her home, he'd assured Jett that Sabrina trusted everyone and never gave thought to possible dangers. Especially not while she was in the safety and security of her home.

Now Jett stared at the screen and watched the residents of the condominium complex come and go the morning of the murders. He saw Franklin leave for work at seven, like he'd told them, dressed in a suit and tie. Kevin Thompson and his boss entered the building a short while later. Other people exited, many between the hours of seven-thirty and eight, most of them looking harried as they rushed out the door.

By eight-thirty, the crowd had thinned. There was a gap of a few hours where almost nobody entered or left. Apart from a postal worker delivering mail and a mother pushing a pram, the security visual remained void of people.

And then Franklin Cook's image once again filled the screen. The time on the camera recorded twelve forty-three. Jett frowned. Something niggled at his memory. Tugging out his notebook, he flipped through it until he found the entries made the day he attended the crime scene. *And there it was.*

Franklin had told Detective Bennett he'd arrived home that afternoon at about one-thirty. Almost an hour after the cameras showed him arriving there. The emergency call he made from his condo was received at one thirty-six. The difference being more than forty-five minutes... *What had he been doing all that time?* Surely the first thing anyone would do upon discovering their loved ones had been attacked was call the police? Jett shook his head. Something didn't make sense.

Dragging the phone on his desk toward him, he found Franklin's number and dialed it. It rang out until it was picked up by a machine. Jett cleared his throat and left a message.

"Mr Cook, it's Detective Craigdon. I—"

"Detective, it's Franklin Cook."

"Oh, I was just leaving you a message."

"Yes, I'm sorry. I'm screening my calls. The media have been calling non stop. It's driving me crazy."

"I understand."

"Yes, well, how did you do? I'm assuming you've had time to review the footage. Have you identified any suspects? Anyone who might have gained access and done this?"

"No," Jett replied, "but I have another question. You told one of the detectives at the scene that you'd arrived home for lunch at one-thirty, right?"

"Yes, I think it was somewhere around that time. I didn't check my watch." The man laughed a little nervously. "I didn't realize I'd need to pinpoint my exact movements."

"Of course not. The thing is though, most of us can usually make a good estimation, within ten or fifteen minutes, of where we were at a certain time. You were on your lunch break. I assume you had some idea of the time. The security cameras show you entering your building at twelve forty-three. That's some forty-seven minutes ahead of the time you gave the officer."

Jett paused and wondered if Franklin would rush in with an explanation. The man had to know his actions would put him squarely under suspicion. When he remained silent, Jett prompted him.

"According to the CCTV footage, you were in the condominium nearly an hour before you made the emergency call. What were you doing in there, Mr Cook? Why did it take so long?"

Still, the man remained silent. Jett cursed quietly under his breath. *Did the man* want *Jett to suspect him?* He was certainly going about it the right way. First the attitude the night before and now this. Unconsciously, Jett fingered his handcuffs.

"Mr Cook...?"

"Um... I'm sorry, Detective. I... I... The truth is..."

Jett's heart skipped a beat and blood thundered through his ears. *Was the man about to confess?*

"I was...on the phone," Franklin murmured.

Jett blew out his breath. It wasn't exactly the revelation he'd expected. "To whom?"

"My... My mother. She's been having a hard time of it lately regarding her health. She wanted to share all the details with me." Franklin gave a half laugh. "You know how mothers are."

"Yeah," Jett agreed, slightly disappointed. It wasn't like he *wanted* the killer to be Franklin, but it would have made his job easier and his chances for promotion a helluva lot better if he were to wrap up the double homicide inside a week. Of course, it was possible Franklin wasn't telling the truth.

"So, you talked to your mother. Where was that?"

"I stayed in the lobby."

"Did anyone see you?" Jett asked, making a note on the pad before him.

"N-no. I don't think so."

"What time did you go up to your condominium?"

"It must have been around one-thirty, like I told the officer. I caught the elevator upstairs, went into the condo, put down my briefcase and keys. I called out for Sabrina. She...she didn't answer." His voice cracked, but he managed to add, "That's when I found them."

Jett grimaced at the pain and agony that flooded the man's voice. While Franklin was still a suspect, he wasn't at the top of the list and if he were innocent of any wrongdoing...

Jett couldn't imagine what it would be like to come home and confront such a situation. Most people would never get over it. He certainly wouldn't and he'd seen his fair share of awful things.

"Was it normal for you to come home for lunch, Franklin?" Jett asked quietly.

Franklin cleared his throat. "No, I'm usually too busy at work to do more than grab a sandwich from the deli in my building. When the lab results arrived, I decided to go home and open them with Sabrina. I knew the results would reassure me that I was Marnie's father and I wanted to apologize again to Sabrina for doubting her."

He paused and then added, "I'm glad you called, Detective Craigdon. I... I was about to pick up the phone. I was going through my briefcase and I found something. I received it a few days before...before the murders. I'd forgotten about it."

"What is it?" Jett asked.

"It's a threatening letter."

Jett tensed and his senses came alert. He sat up straighter in his chair. "What does it contain?"

"It references the case against Bilal Al-Jabiri. It's signed 'anonymous,' but whoever sent it was clearly angry at me for representing the boy."

A sense of urgency rushed through Jett's veins. "I need to see it. I'll send someone over to collect it right away. Don't touch it. We'll check it for fingerprints. We might even get some DNA."

"I've already handled it. I opened it the first time I received it and again now, when I found it in my briefcase. The only fingerprints on it will likely be mine."

"That might be so, but we'll check it just the same. You never know what we might find. Do you have any idea who sent it?" Jett asked.

"No. Though there have been protests outside the courthouse every time the Bilal's case is heard. It could be anyone."

"Have you received this kind of letter before?"

"Unfortunately, yes. I represent some very high-profile defendants. It's not the first time I've put people off side. I believe in our justice system and I believe everyone has the right to the presumption of innocence until proven otherwise in a court of law. It's why I do what I do."

Jett thought back to the numerous times Franklin Cook had appeared on the six o'clock news, defending one high-profile criminal after another. He'd gained a reputation for being one of the best defense lawyers in the country.

"And you're good at it," Jett murmured.

"Thank you," Franklin replied, his tone low and humble.

"If you think of anything else, please call me right away," Jett urged.

"I will, Detective. And I'm sorry for not remembering about this letter earlier. As I mentioned, it wasn't the first threat I'd received, so I guess I didn't pay it all that much attention when it arrived and with all that went on after I got home... To tell you the truth, it was the last thing on my mind."

"I understand," Jett replied. "While you're at it," he added, "give the officer a copy of those lab results."

"The thing is, Detective, I've been looking for them. I... I seem to have misplaced them. Perhaps the police took them from the crime scene. Could you check? Otherwise, I'll get them to you as soon as I find them. I can assure you, they contain nothing of relevance and had absolutely nothing to do with what happened to my wife and daughter."

"I get what you're saying, Franklin, but I'm sure you understand I'm just being thorough. You received the results the day of the murders. Until we know who did this, everything is relevant."

"Of course, Detective. I'll keep looking."

"What lab did you use? I can call them and get a copy from there."

"The Life Biologistics Lab. It's on George Street."

Jett noted the information and ended the call. A part of him wondered how the threatening letter could slip the man's mind. Franklin had been asked on more than one occasion in the immediate aftermath of the deaths if he knew who might be responsible and even if he'd received death threats in the past. At the time, he'd offered up nothing.

Perhaps the man had been too distraught to think clearly? It wasn't beyond the scope of possibility. It was easy for Jett to say he'd remember any infinitesimal detail that could assist the police. He was a detective, trained to remain calm in stressful situations and to observe things other people didn't. That he didn't share the information sooner didn't mean Franklin was lying. So far, everything the man had told them had panned out.

Lane had looked into the insurance policy owned by Sabrina Cook's husband. Sure enough, her life had been insured for the sum of one hundred thousand. A reasonable amount for some, but not for the Cook family. In Jett's considered opinion, it wasn't enough for Franklin to murder his wife and child.

No, but still, thirty-seven stab wounds was personal. Forty, if you counted the three wounds inflicted upon the baby. This wasn't a random break-in. Nor was it about money. Of that, he was certain.

The threatening letter might just be the break they were looking for. All along, there had been a real possibility that the attacks had resulted from Franklin's decision to defend Bilal Al-Jabiri. The actions of the fifteen-year-old student had divided opinions across the state.

Jett had watched the frenzied demonstrations outside the courthouse on television. They'd angered him. It didn't matter how one felt about terrorism, they lived in a country where everyone was entitled to the benefit of the doubt. It was up to the courts to decide the guilt or innocence of a defendant, not members of the public who were, no doubt, ill informed and charged with their own agenda.

Of course, he'd check Franklin's mother's phone records and verify that she had, in fact, called him at the relevant time, but again, Franklin was a smart man. He'd hardly offer up a story that couldn't be verified. It would be plain stupid and that was one word Jett wouldn't apply to the lawyer.

He'd also gone through every scrap of evidence collected at the scene, and the DNA test results were not among the items at the police station.

Picking up the phone, he spoke to one of the junior detectives and asked them to drop by Franklin's place and collect the letter. Pulling up a file on his computer, he went through the evidence log on the Cook murders. The DNA test results were not among the items taken from the condominium. They must have been left at the scene.

He glanced up in time to see Lane stride into the squad room, looking grim and determined. He came to a halt beside Jett's desk.

"What is it?" Jett asked.

"I've just heard back from the fingerprint guys. They lifted partial fingerprints and part of a palm print off the wall outside the front door to the Cooks' condominium. The technician stated at the time that it looked like someone had put their hand out to lean on the wall."

"Did they find a match?" Jett asked.

"Yes."

His heart skipped a beat. "Who was it?"

"Roger Barber."

Jett frowned. The name sounded familiar, but he couldn't place it.

"He's the self-proclaimed leader of an anti-Islamic group in western Sydney," Lane explained. "He and his followers have been instrumental in organizing the demonstrations outside the courthouse each time the Al-Jabiri case is brought before the judge."

Jett's heartbeat took off at a gallop. Coming so soon after Franklin's call about the threatening letter, all of a sudden, things felt like they were falling into place. He quickly brought Lane up to speed.

"Why the hell didn't he say something about it on Monday?" Lane exploded. "We could have already had this prick behind bars."

Jett nodded grimly. "Yeah. Well, he said it

slipped his mind. It's not the first time he's received threatening letters. Given his job and the number of high-profile clients..." Jett's voice drifted off. He didn't need to spell it out.

Lane grimaced. "Yeah, he's just one of those guys who seems to go out of his way to piss people off."

Jett shrugged. "Somebody has to do it and you believe in our justice system as strongly as I do. Innocent until proven guilty, right? It's the way of the civilized world and thank God for it. I can't even imagine what it must be like to live in a society where one person gets to make and break the rules at will."

"Yeah, it's why so many of them risk their lives to hop on a boat and do their best to make it to our sunny shores."

A thought suddenly struck Jett and he dragged his keyboard closer. A sense of urgency flooded through him. As if noticing the tension in Jett's face, Lane frowned down at him.

"What is it?"

Jett compressed his lips and typed commands into the computer until the CCTV footage from the Cooks' complex was once again displayed across the screen.

"You said Roger Barber's fingerprints were found at the scene. I just finished reviewing the security tapes. I didn't see him enter or exit the building. I must have missed it."

"Do you know what he looks like?" Lane asked, pulling up a seat.

"No."

Lane threw him a droll look. "Then don't beat yourself up about it."

Jett nodded and rewound the footage to the morning, when groups of people in twos and threes and sometimes more, streamed out of the elevators, presumably heading for work. He paused on the image of Franklin, dressed in a dark-colored suit and tie and carrying a briefcase.

"That's Franklin," Lane murmured.

"Yes. Leaving at seven, like he said."

They continued to watch the footage. Like the first time, the number of people coming and going slowed after eight-thirty. The mother with the pram appeared about ten-fifteen. The mailman and a delivery guy. Two twenty-something women of Asian descent departed the building around eleven, laughing and swinging their tote bags.

The mother with the pram re-entered a little over an hour later and then there was nothing until Franklin returned.

"There he is," Lane murmured, staring at the screen.

"Yes. See the time?"

Lane noted the time on the security footage and frowned. "Twelve forty-three? I thought he told us he got there at one-thirty?"

Jett grimaced. "Right you are, Detective. Mr Cook did indeed tell us that. I called him about it just a few minutes ago. He told me he received a phone call from his mother just as he stepped into the foyer. According to the time record on the security footage, he spoke to her for around forty minutes before going up to his condo."

"Are there any cameras in the foyer? Can we see him on the phone?"

"No. There are only two cameras. One gives us vision of the front yard area, out into the street. The other one takes pictures from a closer angle, of people entering and exiting the building. Unfortunately, as soon as they're inside, we lose them."

"Dammit," Lane cursed softly.

"Yeah, but we can verify Franklin's alibi by speaking with his mom in the first instance and of course, checking her phone records."

"Do we have her details?"

"Not yet," Jett replied. "But I'm sure they won't be hard to track down. I'll call Franklin again."

"Stop the camera!" Lane shouted, pointing to the screen.

Jett clicked on the pause button and frowned. "What is it?"

"There," Lane said, pointing again. "Behind those girls. That's Roger Barber. I'm sure of it."

Jett peered closely at the screen and cursed softly under his breath. He hadn't noticed the girls' return the first time. He looked at the time displayed on the security footage: one-twenty, and then realized why.

He'd stopped viewing not long after Franklin entered the building. At the time, he'd been focused on the fact Sabrina's husband had arrived home more than forty-five minutes before he'd said he had. Jett wasn't expecting the killer to walk in afterwards. After all, Jett had been working on the supposition that Franklin had entered the building and gone immediately to his condominium and shortly after, found his family dead.

Jett stared at the back of a tall, brawny-looking male with closely cropped, light-colored hair. The man wore long dark pants and a dark-colored T-shirt. He appeared to be carrying nothing in his hands.

Lane pulled out his phone and a moment later, shoved it toward Jett. "Here. I just did a search on Roger Barber. You can see him in the front row, here."

Jett took the phone and looked at the picture on the screen. The rowdy crowd were shouting and held up signs that protested against Islam, terrorism and everything else in between. Standing shoulder to shoulder with the demonstrators stood a tall, fair-haired, heavyset man who bore a striking resemblance to the man in the CCTV footage who entered the Cooks' building.

"You're right," Jett said grimly. "It's him, all right. Coupled with the fingerprint evidence, it's time we paid Mr Barber a visit."

Lane nodded, his face filling with determination. "I already found his details in the system. He lives out at Mount Druitt."

"We'll get onto the boys out there. Get them to bring him in. They can call us when they locate him."

"Good idea," Lane said, pushing away from Jett's desk.

"Where did you get that image?" Jett asked, pointing toward Lane's phone.

"Off a clip on YouTube. It was footage taken by a news crew the morning of the murders. Barber and his buddies were outside the courthouse, expressing their concerns in a rather loud, explicit way. It proved to be a good sound bite. The clip's had over one hundred thousand views."

Jett shook his head in disgust. He was all for freedom of speech, but more often than not, it felt like a minority of people expressing minority viewpoints got the most airplay. It annoyed him no end.

"Keep that clip handy. I want to show it to Mr Barber if he decides to play dumb. It provides him with a pretty strong motive. Along with the letter, CCTV footage and fingerprints, he's going to find it a challenge to prove to us why we shouldn't arrest him on the spot."

Lane nodded, his expression grim. "Let's hope he doesn't lawyer up."

Jett shrugged. "There's nothing we can do about it if he refuses to talk, but at least we get to rattle his cage. He's our best bet yet."

"How'd things go with the sister?" Lane asked.

Jett's gut tightened involuntarily at his words. Images of the beautiful Danielle Porter flooded his mind.

"She has an alibi for the time in question and we haven't seen her leave or enter the building. Unless she got someone else to do her dirty work and so far, I haven't been able to uncover a motive, it's my guess she's not involved."

Lane nodded, accepting his explanation. "What about the maintenance man? He was seen outside the condominium during the relevant time."

"Yeah and I finally managed to track him down at his sister's place. He certainly had opportunity and according to his criminal record, he's been violent in the past, but as yet, I haven't found a motive for him, either. I've taken his clothes for analysis. We'll see what they show."

"You don't sound too enthusiastic," Lane drawled.

"Kevin Thompson sounds good in theory, but he comes across as way too sincere." Jett looked up at Lane and shook his head. "I believe it when he tells me he's innocent. I don't think he's our man."

"Fair enough," Lane agreed. "Many would question your gut instinct, but I'm not one of them. I've seen it hit the money too many times to discredit it. Call me when you hear back from the Mount Druitt guys."

"Yeah, I will and thanks," Jett said to Lane's departing back. Lane lifted his hand in acknowledgement, but didn't break stride.

Jett leaned back against his chair with a sigh, but this time, it wasn't a sigh of defeat. They were making progress. At least, it felt that way.

"Detective Craigdon?"

Jett looked up and nodded in acknowledgement toward the junior officer who approached Jett's desk.

"Yes?"

"I have the letter from Franklin Cook." He handed Jett a piece of paper, clearly visible through the plastic evidence bag. Jett took it from him.

"Thanks." Tugging on a pair of gloves, he pulled the letter out of the bag and scanned the contents.

It had been typed on a computer and was in standard twelve point Times New Roman font. While there was no direct threat against Cook's family, the letter left the recipient in no doubt that if he didn't stop acting for Bilal Al-Jabiri, he'd live to regret it.

It must have come from Barber, or at the very least, at his direction. Adrenaline surged through Jett at the thought of confronting the man. Perhaps they'd wrap up the investigation inside a week, after all. The possibility brought with it a smile.

CHAPTER 9

Jett glared at Roger Barber who was seated beside his lawyer. Barber merely smirked, as if he was well aware of Jett's irritation. Along with Lane, the four of them sat across from each other in an interview room in the Mount Druitt Police Station.

It had taken the local police a few hours to locate Barber, but finally, the call had come in. Jett and Lane had made the drive out west to the station and were in the process of interviewing the man they'd both begun to suspect had murdered Sabrina Cook and her daughter.

Lane had obtained a copy of the news footage and Jett had watched the entire clip more than four times. Each time, he'd paused on Barber's angry features and was more and more convinced Barber was their man. That near certainty was the reason why he was so irritated by Barber's arrogance. If Jett had his way, the prick would shortly be behind bars, facing a string of charges and unlikely to see his family for quite some years.

"What were you doing at the Cook building?" Jett demanded, his voice hard.

"I don't know what you're talking about," Barber smirked.

Jett's blood boiled. It was time to wipe the smirk clean off the asshole's face. "Wrong answer, Roger. We have your fingerprints right outside the door."

Barber paled and his cockiness dissolved. A moment later, two spots of angry color appeared on his cheeks. "Bullshit."

"There's no bullshit about it, Roger," Lane said, his tone mild. "Our fingerprint guys are among the best in the world. They identified all five of your fingerprints and a partial print of your palm. Unless you're going to tell us someone else is walking around with your hand, you'd better ditch the attitude and start answering our questions."

Barber shot a quick look at his lawyer, his expression tinged with panic. The lawyer looked at him with a questioning expression on his face.

Jett dragged a laptop toward him and clicked on the CCTV footage he'd loaded onto the device. He turned the screen around so that Barber and his lawyer could see.

"This is security footage taken from outside the Cooks' building the day of the murders. Here's you entering the building at one-twenty in the afternoon." Jett tapped the screen, his eyes narrowed on Barber's.

Barber's eyes widened and panic flashed across his face. Once again, he turned to his lawyer.

"And here you are exiting the building, seven minutes later," Jett added. He glared across at Barber. "Plenty of time to stab a woman and her baby to death."

The four of them watched as the figure of Barber reappeared on the screen, this time hurrying away from the building. He looked frazzled, glancing more than once over his shoulder. The dark clothing he wore didn't reveal evidence of any blood spatter in the black-and-white footage, but a routine analysis of his clothes from that day would put the issue to rest.

"I didn't do it! I swear! I don't even know the people!" Barber cried, his eyes now full of distress.

"Roger! Don't say anything," the lawyer intervened, shooting his client a stern look.

"There's more, Roger," Lane drawled, once again maintaining a casual tone. Lane nodded toward Jett.

With a few clicks of the mouse, Jett pulled up the YouTube video Lane had shown him earlier. The clip clearly showed Barber in the front row. His face was a mask of anger as he shouted and incited the crowd. He held up a placard that was succinct and demeaning of the Islamic race.

"Look a little familiar?" Jett growled and Barber's panic appeared to know no bounds. He stared at the screen and then back to his lawyer, his gaze becoming more and more frantic.

"That's you, isn't it, Mr Barber?" Jett asked, his eyes narrowed on the man opposite. "This was taken outside the courthouse where Franklin Cook was inside with his client. Bilal Al-Jabiri. You know that name well. This isn't the first time you've demonstrated against Mr Cook and his client. A few hours later, Mr Cook's wife and child were dead." Jett's voice rose with his anger. "The two of them were brutally murdered. An innocent woman and her baby. Together, they were stabbed a total of forty times. And you're the one who did it."

"No!" The word was torn from Barber's mouth. His skin had gone deathly pale. Sweat popped out on his forehead. His frantic gaze moved between the officers and his lawyer.

"That's enough, Detectives. Mr Barber will not be saying anything more," the lawyer stated, pushing himself to his feet.

"In that case," Jett replied, tugging out his handcuffs, "we're going to arrest Mr Barber for two counts of murder and that's just the start of it."

"*No, please! You have to believe me! It wasn't me!*" Barber protested, his eyes now wide with fear.

The lawyer frowned down at his client. "Mr Barber, please. Stop talking."

"I want to tell them what happened," Barber pleaded, his gaze filled with desperation. All signs of the arrogant asshole had long since disappeared.

The lawyer looked at Jett. "I'd like a few moments to confer with my client."

Jett glanced at Lane and then gave the lawyer a brief nod. "Okay, but don't take too long. We'll be waiting outside." Gathering his laptop and notepad, Jett followed Lane out of the room.

"What do you think?" Jett asked as soon as they were outside.

Lane's lips compressed. He looked thoughtful. "There's a lot of evidence against Barber and his prints put him at least outside the door. He also has motive. He looked pretty angry outside the courthouse and that footage was taken only hours before. He'd need to have a good explanation and even then, I won't buy it without absolute proof."

"You're talking about his clothing," Jett guessed.

"Yeah. It was impossible to tell if they were bloodstained, but we can find out easily enough."

"I'll make sure I remember to ask for it. Given that we have him on camera, it will be hard for him to hand over anything but what he wore."

"Unless he just happens to own another pair of dark pants and a dark T-shirt," Lane replied, his lips twisting into a wry smile.

Jett grimaced. "Yeah, you're right. Let's hope he thinks we'll be able to tell the difference and comes up with the goods."

Lane nodded and indicated the door to the interview room. "Shall we?"

Jett smiled, filled with anticipation of what was to come. "I think they've had long enough."

Jett pushed open the door with his shoulder and the two officers regained their seats. Barber stared at the scarred Formica table, his hands twisted in front of him.

"What did you decide?" Jett asked, directing his question to the lawyer.

The lawyer's expression was stoic. "Against my advice, my client has decided to participate fully in an interview for the record. We're ready to proceed."

Jett ignored the shaft of elation that surged through him and concentrated on the matter at hand. Asking the right questions to shore up a confession was one of the most important things to do. Without one, or with one that wouldn't stand up in court, they were often left scrambling for enough evidence for a conviction. Jett didn't intend for that to happen. After advising Barber that the interview would be videoed and recording the man's personal details, Jett took him to the day in question, careful to follow the rulebook every step of the way.

"Mr Barber, tell us about your presence outside the courtroom on the day Sabrina Cook and her baby were murdered."

In a halting voice, Barber told them how he'd organized a group of likeminded individuals to stage a protest outside the courtroom every time Bilal Al-Jabiri's case came before the judge. As he talked about the fifteen-year-old Islamic boy, some of his confidence returned. Jett was stunned at the man's self-righteous and narrow-minded attitude. Roger Barber was a racist and a bigot, but was he a murderer?

Jett kept peppering the man with questions until Barber's anger rose. It was exactly what Jett intended. Angry men usually spoke without thinking. It was easier to discover the truth that way.

"Mr Barber, why were you at the Cooks' condominium?" he asked, pitching his voice low and firm.

Barber glanced at his lawyer. The lawyer shook his head. "You know how I feel, Roger. I advised you at the outset not to answer their questions. My advice still stands. It's not too late to bring this interview to an end. In fact, I strongly advise you to do just that."

Barber stared at him and shook his head. "No, I want to finish it. Let's just get it over with." He turned back to face Jett.

"Okay, I was there. It's me in that footage. But I only went there to scare her."

"Why?" Jett asked, his gaze fixed on Barber's.

"You saw that lawyer on the TV. You heard him defending that piece of shit. The boy was found with explosives, timers and everything else he needed. He was planning to walk into the Penrith Westfield and blow himself and everyone else to pieces. He should be in jail already, not being paraded before us. If it wasn't for that lawyer, that's exactly where he'd be."

"So, you found out where Franklin Cook lived and you decided to pay him a visit," Jett supplied. "Only, you knew he wouldn't be home, right? Because it was obvious he was at work. You'd seen him on the steps of the courthouse a few hours earlier."

"Right. I knew he had a wife and child. I'd seen them in the papers. At some social event. I can't remember what. I guessed his family might be home, given that it was the middle of the day. I was pretty certain the lawyer wouldn't be with them. As you said, I figured he'd still be at work."

"How did you know where he lived?" Lane asked.

"I followed the prick home one night. I waited for him outside his office. He hopped on the bus, headed for Hunters Hill. I got on behind him and sat a few seats back. He didn't even notice me. He had his head stuck in the paper the entire way. It was easy enough to get off at his bus stop and follow him to his door."

"How did you know what floor he lived on?" Jett asked.

"I guessed he'd probably live at the top, but I didn't know for sure. I waited until he got into the elevator. Lucky for me, he got in alone. He asked me if I was going up, but I told him I was waiting for someone. As the elevator rose, I watched the numbers and saw where it stopped."

"Didn't he recognize you?" Lane asked, frowning.

"No, that's the funny thing. I've been in the news almost as much as he has these past weeks. He looked right at me, but I didn't see any hint of recognition. I'm guessing his head's so far up his ass, he doesn't notice anything but him."

"What happened when you got to the condo?" Jett asked, making a few notes on his pad.

"Lucky for me, his was the only one on that floor. I tried the door, expecting to find it locked, but it wasn't. That must have been when I leaned against the wall. I opened the door and went inside. Everything was quiet, not even the TV was on. I headed down the corridor, intent on checking rooms. I wasn't sure exactly what I intended to do, but finding the wife was my first priority."

The man paused. Jett looked up at him. "Keep going."

Barber drew in a deep breath and blew out on a heavy sigh. "The first room I came across was the bathroom. The door was open. I could see something red all over the floor. I looked at it and thought it looked like blood, but that didn't seem right. Why would there be blood all over the floor?

"I walked closer. That's when I saw the woman. She was in the bath. The water was crimson. She had her throat slit. There was no doubt she was dead." Barber shuddered at the memory and scrubbed his hands across his face.

"What happened next?" Lane asked.

"I got the hell out of there," Barber said. "I swear, I had nothing to do with it. Yes, I was there in the condo, but by the time I got there, she was already dead."

"What about the child?" Jett questioned, his gaze still focused on Barber.

"I didn't know anything about the child. The first I heard of that was on the news. I knew she had one, but that was all. I didn't see another soul. Like I said, I bolted straight after I found the wife."

"What about the note, Roger?" Lane asked.

Barber frowned in confusion. "What note?"

"The threatening letter you sent Franklin Cook. He received it at his office a few days before the murders. I'm sure you know where he works."

Barber continued to look bewildered. "I don't know anything about a letter. I don't know what you're talking about."

Lane shot Jett a look and Jett replied with an imperceptible movement of his head. They were getting nothing. They'd revisit the letter another time.

"Why didn't you come forward, Roger?" Jett asked. "You could have saved everyone a lot of trouble."

"Because I knew how it would look. I was there, in the unit, with a woman who'd just been murdered. My face was all over the television, protesting against her husband and I didn't even know about the cameras outside their building. It turned out just like I imagined. Here I am, being questioned on suspicion of murder."

"Did you see anyone or hear anything?" Lane asked, glancing at Jett.

Jett acknowledged Lane's question with a nod. According to the security footage and Franklin Cook's own evidence, Franklin was also inside the condo by then.

"No, I didn't see or hear anything," Barber replied. "I just got the hell out of there."

"What about going down, in the elevator?"

Barber shook his head. "No, I went down alone."

Jett swallowed a sigh. It was possible Barber was telling the truth. They could very well be back to square one.

"We'll need the clothing you were wearing on

the day of the murders," he said and Barber nodded.

"My old lady's probably already put it through the wash, but I'll get it to you, one way or the other."

"Good," Jett said. "We'll send a constable with you. He can bring it back to the station." He brought the interview to an end and switched off the recording.

Hope flared in Barber's eyes. He looked from Jett and Lane to his lawyer and back again. "Does this mean I can go?"

As much as it pained him, Jett nodded. "Yes, but you'd better find that clothing and don't try anything stupid. We know what you were wearing on the day of the murders. If there's so much as a speck of blood on it that doesn't belong to you, we're going to haul your ass off to jail so quickly you won't even know it's happened. Got it?"

"Got it," Barber replied eagerly, pushing back his chair. The lawyer gathered his papers and briefcase and followed suit.

Jett stood and opened the door. "I want those clothes brought to the station within the hour," he growled and received an answering nod. "Wait outside. I'll find a uniform to accompany you."

Barber and his lawyer departed. Lane stared solemnly at the laptop screen. "What do you think?"

Jett stared back at him grimly. "Barber has means, motive and opportunity. He admits he was there. We only have his word that Sabrina Cook was dead by the time he arrived."

"Yeah, for all we know, he could be feeding us a crock of shit," Lane replied.

"He could be," Jett agreed. "But I'm just not sensing it. Earlier, I was as good as convinced we had our killer, but now, I'm not so sure."

"I guess we see what forensics comes back with after his clothing is analyzed. Even if it's been laundered, there's no way that amount of blood wouldn't have left some stains behind and surely his wife would have asked questions."

"Yeah," Jett replied, "unless he's lying about that, too. We don't even know if he's married."

Lane blew out his breath on a sigh. "That's one thing we can check easily. As for the rest, I guess we'll just have to wait and see."

CHAPTER 10

Dear Diary,

The weeks go by in a blur. My life will never be the same again. My beautiful sister, the light of my world, is gone. She was my yardstick, my conscience. Without Sabrina, I might never have dragged myself out of the muck. My life was a mess before she gave me the support and confidence and unconditional love to change direction and wrest back some control. She did that for me. I owe her my life and everything that I've become. And now she's dead and no one can tell me why.

I must find who did this to her, who destroyed her perfect life. She was an angel, a gift from God. A woman who had never done anyone harm. I owe this to her and her baby. I won't rest until it's done...

The howl of an emergency vehicle's siren sounded outside the open window of Ben Fitzgerald's inner city apartment. Dani normally took the time to appreciate the tasteful, sleek wood and glass furniture that filled the spaces of her sponsor's bachelor pad, but tonight, she was feeling tired and lethargic. Some days, the world was just too damn hard.

Her head dropped back against the soft cushion of Ben's expensive couch and she sighed. Squeezing her eyes shut, she did her best to block out the world. The days since the death of Sabrina and Marnie had morphed into weeks, and still the police had no clue who had murdered them. Every time she thought of it, her heart was weighed down with a grief so immense, she couldn't see a way out of it.

"Would you like another iced tea, honey?" Ben asked, his voice soft and gentle.

Dani opened her eyes and looked at him where he sat across from her in the matching armchair. She held out her empty glass, wishing, not for the first time, that it was something stronger.

"Thanks, Ben. That would be nice." Ben took the glass from her and headed toward the kitchen.

She'd lost count of the number of evenings she'd found herself in Ben's apartment since the murders. She didn't know how she would have coped without him. She'd known him since she was eighteen. He was one of the first people she'd met at the AA meeting she'd grudgingly agreed to attend.

Sabrina had been with her. Her sister had been the only reason Dani was there, having finally managed to convince Dani she needed help. Ben was only a few years older than Dani and right away, the two of them hit it off. They had a lot in common; both knew what it was like to hit rock bottom and have to claw their way back to the top. When he offered to be her sponsor, she'd readily agreed.

It hadn't taken long for them to develop a strong friendship that had deepened into mutual love, admiration and respect. For a fleeting moment in time they'd been lovers, but it hadn't taken them long to figure out they were much more comfortable as friends. Ben saw her as a little sister and Dani regarded him as the brother she'd never had. They shared a comfortable, supportive relationship that had become warm and familiar and necessary over the years.

Like she'd told the detective, it had been Ben she'd met with over her lunch break the day Sabrina and Marnie were murdered. The two of them often got together for coffee or lunch and caught up on what was happening in their lives. Ben was a successful lawyer in a large and prestigious law firm in the city. Dani's job at the Sydney Harbour Hospital was only a short bus ride away.

He'd been the first person she'd called after receiving the terrible news and he'd immediately rushed to her side. Ben knew better than anyone how much Sabrina had meant to her and he'd shared in her shock and grief.

"Here you go, honey," Ben murmured and offered her a fresh glass of iced tea.

Dani sat upright and reached for it gratefully. Wearily, she nodded her thanks.

"How are you holding up, sweetie?" he asked quietly, regaining his seat across from her and taking a sip from his drink.

Dani heaved another sigh. It was all she could do to get herself to work each day and home again. Even the pleasure of finally living in a home of her own hadn't managed to lift her from her dark mood.

"Not so good," she admitted.

Ben regarded her somberly. "Give it time, Dani. It's only been a few weeks. No one would expect you to be back to normal. There's nothing normal about what happened."

A familiar wave of anger and frustration flooded through her veins. "It's because the police still haven't found the person responsible," she cried. "It's bad enough that the lives of my sister and niece were taken so violently, but for nobody to be held accountable—it's eating me up inside!

"I can't sleep. I can barely think. I can't concentrate at work. All I can see is my beautiful Sabrina and her innocent baby lying in pools of blood. I didn't go to the scene of the crime and I didn't see any photos, but I didn't need to. Franklin told me what happened. I see them, Ben," she whimpered. "I see them every time I close my eyes and there's nothing I can do to help!"

Her voice cracked with emotion and tears spilled down her cheeks. She'd cried so long and so hard since the tragedy, she was surprised there were any tears left, but it seemed where Sabrina and Marnie were concerned, the supply was endless.

"Oh, honey." Ben stood and moved to sit beside her. Putting his arm around her shoulders, he gathered her close. As if finding their release, the sobs came harder and once again tears flooded her eyes. She buried her face in Ben's soft cotton shirt.

What she'd told him was true. The fact the police hadn't captured the killer only exacerbated her suffering and pain. Grieving over the unexpected loss of family members was one thing, but to know that the person responsible for their deaths was still out there, free to live their life as they pleased, was like rubbing salt into an open wound.

"Where are the police with their investigation?" Ben asked quietly, stroking her hair.

"I haven't spoken to them since the evening of the funeral." Unbidden, an image of the darkly handsome detective filled her mind.

"Perhaps you need to call them," Ben suggested. "They might have something to share, something that might help you through those times when you feel so helpless."

She half sat and turned to look at him. "Wouldn't they have called me and told me if they'd had a breakthrough?"

Ben shrugged. "I'm not sure. Franklin's the next

of kin. I'm guessing he's the one they'll keep up to date."

"Franklin hasn't called me, either," Dani admitted. "I've kept my distance since the night after the funeral. I... I wanted to give him time to grieve. He doesn't need me in his face, sad and depressed all the time. It would only make him feel worse."

"Well, if you don't want to phone Franklin and ask him for a progress report, you're going to have to call the detectives." Ben paused. "What was the name of the one who spoke to both of us? He found me right after he broke the news to you. I assume he was checking out your story, given that I was your alibi."

"Detective Jett Craigdon," Dani murmured.

Once again, the detective's image filled her mind and her heart skipped a beat. In another lifetime, she'd be more than interested in the good-looking officer. Right now, she couldn't think past the murders.

"He wore a suit well, I'll give him that," Ben said, his expression neutral, but she caught a glint of mischief in his wide green eyes.

Irritated that Ben had somehow picked up on her confused feelings, she flopped back against the couch and blew out her breath on a sigh of frustration. "I couldn't care less what he looks like. It's been almost three weeks. I *have* to know what's going on. Even if they've made no ground, I need answers—for Sabrina's sake and for my own."

Ben glanced at his watch. "It's barely eight. Not too late. You could call right now."

Dani's stomach clenched. Her pulse picked up its pace. Despite her brash words, the thought of speaking to Detective Craigdon sent a rush of nerves running through her. With determination, she pushed them away. She wanted to know what was happening with the investigation, didn't she? Calling the detective was the best way to find out.

Dani lifted her chin and met Ben's steady gaze. She accepted his challenge with her eyes. "All right," she said. "I will."

"That's my girl," Ben replied, shooting her an encouraging smile.

Setting her glass down on the wood-and-glass coffee table that stood between them, Dani reached for her phone. She'd put the detective's number into her contacts. Within moments, his number was on the screen.

A fresh flutter of nerves filled her stomach and worked their way up her throat. She glanced at Ben and then swallowed and dialed the number before her courage deserted her.

It was answered on the second ring.

Jett stared at the screen in front of him and cursed quietly under his breath. The weeks were passing and they were no closer to finding the "penthouse killer." The name had been coined by a tabloid newspaper and much to Jett's chagrin, it stuck. Now, even the detectives used the term.

The sound of his cell ringing interrupted his dark thoughts and he welcomed the distraction. Tugging the phone out of his pocket, he glanced at the screen.

The number wasn't familiar, but that was normal. This was his work phone. He gave the number out to a lot of people, including potential witnesses. Even the fact it was ringing at eight o'clock on a Saturday night wasn't uncommon. People often found the courage to tell him things—when the world was dark and shadowy— things they hadn't been able to share in the light of day. It was just the way it was.

"Detective Craigdon," he said. His greeting was met with silence. He tried again. "This is Detective Craigdon. May I help you?" This time, he heard the faintest sound of indrawn breath and then a woman stammered out a reply.

"D-Detective Craigdon. This is… This is Danielle Porter. I'm Sabrina Cook's—"

"Ms Porter. I know who you are," he interrupted, working hard to hide his surprise. He hadn't spoken to her since the evening he'd attended Franklin's condominium, after the funeral and though Jett and his team had been working hard behind the scenes, she'd kept herself out of the limelight.

It was a pity her brother-in-law wasn't quite so reticent. Franklin Cook had nearly driven everyone at the station mad with his twice daily phone calls for updates. The man had insinuated himself so far into their investigation, the mere mention of his name on the other end of the phone was enough to cause a chorus of groans in the office.

It was as if Franklin refused to accept Jett's word that he'd call him the instant they had a breakthrough. The man's insistence on knowing every aspect of their investigation was not only irritating, Jett had begun to question Franklin's motives.

Most grieving relatives accepted the police knew how to do their job and would do that job to the best of their ability. Though the victim's family was almost always willing to assist the police in whatever way they could, their enthusiasm usually fell short of needing to be kept informed on every move the police made. There was an implicit level of trust that seemed to be missing between him and Franklin Cook. Jett guessed it had something to do with Sabrina Cook's husband being a defense lawyer.

"I... I need to know what's happening with your investigation into the murder of my niece and sister," Danielle Porter continued, breaking into Jett's thoughts. He cleared his throat and answered her.

"Of course, Ms Porter. What would you like to know?"

"I want to know if you've found the person who did this."

"We have several strong leads, Ms Porter. I—"

"It's been three *weeks*, Detective. I don't want to hear about your *leads*. I want to know if you've found the killer. I want you to tell me you've arrested and charged the person responsible for these terrible crimes and that even now, he's sitting in jail."

"I'm sorry, Ms Porter. I wish I had better news. I—"

Once again, she interrupted him. "You aren't listening, Detective." Her words were clipped and her tone had built in volume.

All of a sudden, Jett's temper got the better of him. He and the rest of the members of the taskforce were working their asses off. He didn't need the constant phone calls from the victims' husband and father demanding hourly updates and he sure as hell could do without the attitude from the woman on the other end of the phone.

He got that she was grieving and as the sister and aunt of the deceased, she was as close as relatives got, but the police were doing everything they could. Didn't she understand they wanted to find the killer as much as she did? That he was just as frustrated as she was that they hadn't? He told her as much.

"Don't *tell* me, Detective. *Show* me. *Show* me how hard you've been working, what you've managed to achieve. I want to see what my tax dollars have bought me these past few weeks."

Her sarcasm drew blood and his anger ratcheted up another notch. With a supreme effort, he kept his tone civil.

"You're welcome to come down here, Ms Porter. I'm at the office right now. I'll be here until midnight. You want to know what I've been doing. Come on down and see for yourself."

The words were out before he could stop them. He cursed under his breath. *What the hell was he doing?* The last thing he needed was the dead woman's sister looking over his shoulder, breathing down his neck. It would be worse than her husband's way-too-frequent phone calls. At least Franklin didn't stir his blood.

The unwelcome thought popped into his head and he frowned. Try as he might, he couldn't deny he found Danielle Porter attractive. *Very* attractive. It wasn't just in a physical sense, although she was a beautiful woman. There was something about her that drew him. He couldn't put it into words and the very fact it existed was annoying and vastly inconvenient, but he couldn't deny there was something there.

If circumstances were different, he might even ask her out. It had been a long time since he'd felt like pursuing a potential relationship. He wasn't sure that he'd ever felt as interested as he did with Danielle. But she was a relative of the victims of a terrible double homicide and as such, she was off limits. At least until after the investigation had come to an end. Just another reason why he needed to make an arrest as soon as possible.

"All right." Her voice was sure and firm.

He blinked back his surprise and did his best to ignore the jolt her words gave him. Anticipation surged through him at the thought of seeing her again.

"Give me fifteen minutes to get to the station," she added. "Will there be someone around to let me in?"

Ben stared at Dani and shook his head.

Feeling self-conscious, she averted her gaze. "What?"

"You know what. Did I just hear you say you're going to the station? At this time of night? Are you mad?"

Irritation stirred inside her, along with the residual anger left over from her phone conversation. She looked back at Ben. "You were the one who told me to call him, to find out what the hell was going on."

"Yes, but I didn't mean for you to go charging out in the middle of the night, demanding answers. There's nothing he can tell you tonight that he can't tell you in the morning."

Stubbornness surged through her. She clenched her teeth and glared at her friend. He knew her well enough to know he wasn't going to change her mind. "You said yourself it wasn't too late. It's barely eight-fifteen."

"I wasn't talking about making house calls," Ben replied, his voice dry.

"I'm not making house calls. I'm going to his office."

"The police station," Ben said.

Dani shrugged. "I guess. He called it his office."

"Do you even know how to get there?"

"No, but he works at the State Crime Command in Chatswood. How hard can it be to find? I'm sure I can plug it into a search engine and come up with an address."

Ben sighed and rubbed a hand through his thick, dark hair, leaving it standing on end. Her tension eased. She moved to sit beside him and put a reassuring hand on his arm.

"I'll be fine, Ben. I'm going there to get some answers. The detective invited me down. He's going to show me what progress they've made on the investigation."

He opened his mouth on another protest, but she held up her hand. "I *need* to see it, Ben," she said quietly, pleading with him to understand. "For once, I need to go to bed comforted by the fact the investigation into who killed my sister and niece is in good hands."

"Okay, honey, I understand." Ben's voice was gentle.

Tears pricked the back of her eyes. He *did* understand. He understood like no one else could. He knew all about her tawdry past and how Sabrina had saved her from it. Her sister had given Dani back her self-respect.

And now, Sabrina was dead and there was nothing Dani could do about it, except make sure the person responsible was made to pay for their crimes. If that meant marching on down to the police station on a Saturday night, then so be it.

She'd predicted locating the building that housed the State Crime Command would be easy, and it was. Dani parked her Prius on the side of the road opposite and waited for a gap in the traffic to cross. Even at this time of night, there was a reasonable amount of traffic passing by in both directions. She could have walked a little further up and crossed at the lights, but just as the thought formed, a gap opened in the traffic and she hurried across.

In deference to the fact it was a Saturday night and she'd gone over to Ben's for dinner, she'd traded her usual sensible flats for something slightly more glamorous. Her three-inch heels clattered against the pavement. She looked around her, grateful that the street was well lit. Chatswood was one of the nicer parts of Sydney, but she wasn't a fool. Nowhere was completely safe for a woman to be walking on her own at that time of night, even a woman headed toward a police station.

The automatic double glass sliding doors remained closed upon Dani's approach. Spying an intercom off to one side, she pressed the button and waited. Almost immediately, it crackled to life.

"Can I help you?"

The familiar voice, rich and well-modulated, came through the speaker. She cleared her throat of a sudden rush of nerves.

"Yes, it's Danielle Porter. We spoke on the phone."

"I'll be out in a minute."

The intercom crackled again and went silent. Less than thirty seconds later, the glass doors of the State Crime Command headquarters swished open and Detective Jett Craigdon stood before her, looking every bit as tall and good looking as he had the first time they'd met.

He was dressed in another dark-colored suit, though this time, his tie was loosened and the top two buttons of his white shirt were undone. He looked mussed just enough to be sexy and her heart skipped a beat.

"Danielle, it's good to see you again. Thank you for stopping by." His voice was dry as sandpaper and she immediately went on the defensive.

"You invited me, remember?" she snapped.

His expression didn't alter. His gaze remained steady on her. "You're right. I did. I guess you'd better come in."

And with that, he indicated that she precede him. The glass doors slid open at her approach and he paused to relock them as he passed through. Inside, the only illumination came from the occasional security light.

"Are you working solo?" she asked, looking around the reception area which was dim and deserted.

"Yes. I've been putting in extra hours on your family's murder case. As you said, it's been three weeks." His pointed stare seemed to last a lifetime, but finally he turned away. "The rest of the crew left hours ago," he tossed over his shoulder as he made his way across the darkened foyer. "Follow me. I'm upstairs."

In silence, they climbed the stairs to the next floor and entered an open concept office space with numerous workstations divided by partitions spread across the floor. Jett led her to a desk that was cluttered with loose papers, photographs and files. He indicated a chair and without waiting for her to be seated, he sat in its twin across from her and crossed his arms over his chest.

"All right, you wanted an update. Here's what I

have so far." He pointed toward the spread of files and other documents on his desk and then reached for a sheaf of papers.

"Here's the interview we conducted with Kevin Thompson, the maintenance man. He was seen outside the door to your sister's condominium in the hour prior to her death."

Dani was shaking her head even before he'd finished. "I know Kevin. There's no way he did this."

Jett eyed her steadily. "After speaking with him, I tend to agree with you. Nevertheless, we collected the clothes he was wearing on the day in question and sent them to the lab."

"What are you testing for?" Dani asked.

"Blood. Whoever murdered your niece and your sister didn't do it without getting soaked in the process. And not only blood, but a particular kind of blood spatter that only being in close proximity to a stabbing such as this would achieve."

As he spoke, Dani's stomach churned. She didn't want to think about the suffering her family members had endured, but at times like this it was so difficult to ignore. She'd known that her demand to be brought up to date on the investigation would more than likely entail listening to information she didn't want to hear, but there was nothing else for it.

She needed to know what was happening. She wasn't exaggerating when she'd told Ben she hadn't slept properly since the day of the murders and wouldn't until the perpetrator had been caught. With an effort, she forced herself to remain still and kept her gaze steady on the detective.

He picked up another sheaf of papers and tossed them back on the desk. "And here is the interview I conducted with Roger Barber."

Dani frowned. "Who's Roger Barber?"

Jett's mouth compressed into a grim line. "Roger Barber is a builder's laborer most of the time. At least, that's the way he earns a living. But in his spare time, he's the self-appointed leader of a group of anti-Islamic supporters and goes out of his way to protest all things Islam that cross his path. His latest vendetta is against your brother-in-law. I'm afraid for the past six weeks, he's had Franklin firmly in his sights. His fingerprints and palm print were found on the wall outside the door to your sister's condominium."

Dani's mouth gaped open in surprise. "Oh, my God! He was there? *Why?*" The very thought horrified her.

"He told us he wanted to scare your sister. It was meant to be a warning to Franklin."

Dani shook her head, speechless. She'd had no idea someone had taken such a personal campaign against Sabrina's husband. She struggled to understand it. "You mean, this Barber has a vendetta against Franklin because he's representing that teenager—the one who was planning a terrorist attack?"

Jett nodded.

"Does Franklin know about this Barber guy?"

"I'm not sure. He was certainly aware of the protestors who've targeted his law firm and the courthouse ever since he took on the Al-Jabiri case. In fact, he'd received a threatening letter at his office only a few days before the murders. Though the letter was anonymous, it appears likely it originated from Barber, or one of his supporters."

Another wave of shock ricocheted through Dani. "Franklin received a death threat only days before my sister and niece were murdered? Did he *tell* anyone? Call the *police*?"

"I'm not sure if he told anyone. He certainly didn't call the police. He said he put it in his briefcase and forgot about it until a couple of weeks ago."

Dani stared at the detective in disbelief. "How does anyone forget about something like that?"

Jett shrugged nonchalantly. "Apparently it's not the first time he's received such a letter. He didn't put much stock in it."

"But with everything going on—the protestors, the anger, the media hype... He must have had some concerns the threat could be legitimate."

"I can't say, Ms Porter. You'll have to take that up with your brother-in-law. The truth is, I don't think Roger Barber's responsible."

She blinked in surprise. "You said his fingerprints were found outside the condominium."

"Yes. I also told you Kevin Thompson was seen outside the door and yet, neither of us think he's the man we're looking for, either."

Dani held his gaze. "What makes you think it wasn't Barber?"

"I interviewed him. Though he initially denied any involvement, we were able to prove through security camera footage that he was there. Along with the fingerprints, we were able to bring a fair degree of pressure on the man. We didn't get a confession, but my gut tells me we got the truth."

"Which was?" Dani asked quietly.

"He said Sabrina was already dead when he entered the condo. He found her in the bath. When we questioned him about your niece, he claimed not to know anything about the child. I believe him."

She opened her mouth to protest. There were so many other possibilities. *The man could be lying. He could—*

The detective held up his hand as if to ward off her thoughts. "I get it. My gut could be way off. It's why we asked for the clothing he wore on the day of the murders. It's also at the lab, along with your brother-in-law's."

Dani closed her mouth and nodded. She'd been there when Franklin had handed over his clothes.

"Do you have any results?"

"No, but even without the lab results, I have renewed interest in your brother-in-law."

Dani started in surprise. "You mean, as a suspect? No, I refuse to believe Franklin's capable of such a thing. He loved Sabrina and Marnie. He couldn't possibly be the killer."

"There's a discrepancy in his story."

Dani stared at the man who sat across from her. Her heart skipped a beat and then took off at a gallop. "What are you talking about?"

"When we spoke to him at the crime scene, he told us he'd arrived home about one-thirty. The security camera footage shows him arriving at the building at twelve forty-three."

Dani frowned and did the math. A forty-seven

minute discrepancy. It was a fair amount of time. Franklin had gone home for lunch. She would have thought he'd have been more aware of the time. Still, she refused to believe he had anything to do with the death of his wife and daughter.

"It doesn't prove—"

"No, it doesn't," the detective interrupted. "That's why I asked him about it."

"What did he say?"

"He told me he'd received a phone call on his way inside the building. He said he remained in the foyer, talking to his mother, for more than forty minutes—which would put him upstairs around one-thirty. Of course, his phone records don't record incoming calls, only the calls he makes. We'll check the phone records of his mother to determine if he's telling the truth."

Dani's mind snagged on Jett's words. She frowned in bewilderment. "Did... Did you say Franklin was talking to his mother?"

"Yes. That's what he said."

"No, you must be mistaken."

Jett lifted a single dark eyebrow. "I don't think so."

Dani shook her head vehemently, needing to make the detective see. "No, I'm telling you. You must have misunderstood. Franklin has no mother. She died before he and Sabrina met."

Jett stared at the woman before him. Her

cheeks were flushed and her breath came fast.

"Excuse me?" he said.

"Franklin's an orphan. His parents were killed in a car accident when he was twenty. Like I said, you must have misheard."

Jett's eyes narrowed and his pulse picked up its pace. There was no way he'd misheard. He'd even left a message for Franklin only a few days earlier requesting further details about his mother so that Jett could track down her phone records.

He leaned forward, holding his gaze steady on Danielle's. "Are you sure?"

"Yes, of course I'm sure. I've known Franklin for years. He and Sabrina started dating when she was only eighteen."

Jett sat back, his mind reeling. *Why would Franklin tell him he'd talked to his mother when it was obvious he hadn't?* Surely he would have realized, sooner or later, Jett would discover his deceit? And there was a gap of more than forty-five minutes. That kind of anomaly would never be overlooked. Franklin must have known the police would check his story.

Jett stared at the papers scattered on the desk in front of him, trying to get his head around it. If Franklin were responsible for the death of his wife and child, why wouldn't he have come up with an airtight alibi? It didn't make sense. Unless Danielle Porter was the one who wasn't telling the truth.

He lifted his gaze and stared hard at Sabrina's sister, dread forming a cold, hard lump in his gut. "Tell me again where you were the day your sister was murdered."

CHAPTER 11

Franklin stared at the happy images that filled his computer screen. Sabrina laughing at the camera, smiling, clowning around. Earlier pictures, of baby Marnie, all wrinkled and red and screaming as she greeted the world. He remembered her birth like it was yesterday. And there was their wedding, with Sabrina beautiful and glowing in a sparkling white dress. It was the happiest day of his life.

Tears burned behind his eyes and leaked down his cheeks. They were gone... His angels, dead and buried, now watching over him from above. Never again would he hear their laughter or see the love and happiness in their eyes. Never again would he hold his wife close or make silly faces at his daughter. In a few fatal moments, his perfect life was over and there was no way to get it back. The very thought brought forth another round of tears.

Giving in to the overwhelming sadness, he hunched forward, holding his head in his hands.

The tears came faster, pouring out. Sobs wracked his body. He gulped and gasped and howled out his pain and then cursed out his grief and anger.

How had it happened? *Why* did it happen? He didn't know and the knowledge only exacerbated his suffering. What was worse, he wasn't the only one without answers.

The police investigation was going nowhere. It was obvious they were clueless. They were chasing their tails, going after this one and that one. First it was the maintenance man, then Roger Barber. Even *he* was in their sights. The last message from the detective was a request for further information about Franklin's mother. His mother! What a joke.

———————————

Jett scanned his emails with eyes that were gritty and tired. It was barely eight in the morning, but he was already weighed down with frustration and fatigue. He'd worked late, for a few hours after Danielle left and when he finally headed for home, his mind had given him no rest.

Upon Danielle's abrupt departure the night before, he'd gone online to research Franklin's parents. Sure enough, they'd died in a car crash in 2008, just as Danielle had said. The discovery that Franklin had lied about his phone call filled Jett with disquiet. He had no direct evidence linking Sabrina's husband to the crimes, but his gut still insisted the man should remain on the suspect list.

There were anomalies in his story and there was something about him that didn't sit right.

His thoughts drifted to Franklin's beautiful sister-in-law and he wondered again if it were possible she'd been involved in the brutal crimes. Last night, after refusing to answer his question, she'd stormed out. At the time he'd wondered if she lied about Franklin's mother to shift the blame from herself, but her story had been corroborated again by several newspaper reports. Indeed, Franklin's parents were dead.

Jett rubbed a hand across his eyes and blew out his breath on a heavy sigh. It was time to pay Franklin Cook another visit.

"Jesus, Craigdon, you look like shit. Did you even go home last night?"

Jett looked up in time to see Lane descending upon him, carrying two jumbo sized Styrofoam cups.

"I hope that's coffee you have there," Jett muttered, ignoring Lane's question.

Lane offered him one of the cups. "I drove past the office late last night and saw your light on. I figured you might be needing it."

"Thanks," Jett replied and took a grateful sip.

"What were you working on?" Lane asked, propping a hip against Jett's desk.

"The Cook murders. What else?"

Lane's lips compressed into a grim line. "I thought you might be."

Jett cursed. "I keep going round and round in circles. We find a viable suspect and then the lead just dissolves in front of us and we're back to square one. Thompson, Barber, even Cook. We don't have enough on any of them." He sighed again and took another sip of coffee, enjoying the strong, hot brew.

Lane grimaced. "I'm afraid it's about to get worse."

"What do you mean?"

"Fiona called me from the lab this morning. She had results on the clothing we submitted. I stopped by there on the way to work and collected them."

Jett sat up straighter in his seat, his gaze narrowed on Lane's. "What did they say?"

Lane shook his head slowly back and forth. "Nothing that's going to help us. Neither Kevin nor Roger's clothing had any trace of blood. Franklin's clothing had some, but not the right kind."

"No blood spatter," Jett guessed.

"Right. None of them are our guy."

A wave of frustration surged through Jett and he cursed long and loudly. Lane shot him an understanding look.

"I wish I had better news for you, buddy."

"Yeah," Jett replied sourly. "I just can't understand why the hell Franklin Cook would lie."

"About what?" Lane asked, curiosity filling his gaze.

"About the phone call. When I questioned him about the discrepancy in time between his arrival at his building and the time he said he found his wife and child, he told me he'd remained downstairs, talking to his mother on the phone. But I met with Danielle Porter last night and she told me both Franklin's parents were dead."

Lane's eyebrows rose in surprise. Jett acknowledged his reaction with a grim nod before continuing.

"I wasn't sure I believed her, but I did some research online after she left and sure enough, they died when Franklin was twenty, just like Danielle said."

Lane looked bemused. "So, was there even a call, and if there was, who was he talking to for over forty minutes?"

Jett stared back at his colleague. "There's no way of knowing he was talking to anyone. We only have his word that he received a call. But if he did, why would he give us the name of his mother? He must have known we couldn't verify that call. I remember thinking at the time it had to be right because it would be plain stupid to offer a name that could easily prove he was lying. Franklin Cook's a smart guy. It doesn't make sense."

"Perhaps he panicked?" Lane suggested. "Perhaps he was hoping you'd accept the information in exactly the way you did. If you hadn't followed it up with further enquires, none of us would be any the wiser."

Jett stared at Lane. "Could it really be as simple as that? A fatal lapse in judgement? A stupid answer he gave by mistake? It sounds ludicrous."

"And yet, Al Capone was put away on charges of tax evasion. The most infamous gangster in American history got caught for something as basic as that. Stupid."

Jett nodded, still unsure he was convinced.

"So, you met with the sister-in-law again?" Lane asked, his tone casual.

Jett picked up his coffee cup and took another sip. "Yep."

"She's a looker, I'll give her that. How did it come about?"

"What?" Jett asked, playing for time.

At the mere mention of Danielle, he felt a blush creep up his neck. Soon it would spread over his face for everyone to see. He turned away and busied himself with the paperwork spread across his desk.

"Your meeting with Danielle Porter. Did you call her in an effort to find out more information?"

"No, actually. She called me."

Lane's expression reflected his surprise. "Oh, all right. So she just called you out of the blue and offered up the titbit about Franklin's mother?"

"Yes. No. Sort of." Jett's blush deepened and he cursed softly beneath his breath.

This was ridiculous. What did it matter that Danielle Porter was the most exquisite looking creature he'd met? She was just a woman, the sister and aunt of his murder victims. Nothing more, nothing less.

Lane continued to look bemused. "Okay, which one is it?"

Jett gritted his teeth and then forced himself to relax. There was nothing untoward going on between him and his witness. He had nothing to hide.

"She called me, all riled up about the investigation, that we hadn't made an arrest. I was still at the office. She demanded to know what was going on. She implied we weren't working hard enough to find the killer. I guess I lost my temper. I invited her to come down and see for herself."

Lane frowned. "She came *here*? Last night?"

"Yes. As you know, I stayed back late, going over things, trying to see if there was another angle, something we'd missed."

"So you told her about Franklin's alleged phone call?"

"Yes. I hadn't planned on it. I just wanted to give her an update on where we were, but then she insisted Franklin's parents were both dead."

"Which they are," Lane stated.

"And now we're back to square one," Jett finished with a grimace.

"What's your take on the sister?" Lane asked slowly. "You didn't think she was involved in the early days, but what about now? Could she have had anything to do with it? She was quick to cast doubt on Franklin's alibi—"

"Her concerns turned out to be true," Jett interrupted.

"Yes, they did. Which brings us back to the question of why Franklin lied. Unless he was confused, and mixed up one conversation with another. I mean, he was talking on the phone about whatever, goes upstairs and walks smack bang into a gruesome double murder scene. It's not beyond reasonable to accept his memory became a little scattered."

"Right," Jett agreed. "But he remembered

what clothes he was wearing the day it happened and it was nearly a week later that I spoke to him about them. And how could he forget his mother died years ago?"

"His clothing had his wife's blood all over them," Lane replied. "Not so difficult to recall, I suspect."

Silence fell between them. Lane finally broke it. "You shouldn't have told the Porter woman about that phone call. She's still not off the suspect list."

Jett felt an instinctive denial forming on his lips. "Everything she's told us has checked out. I'm certain she wasn't involved."

"Are you sure you're not discounting the sister because she looks like a Hollywood starlet? Toss in the fact her boobs could double as airbags—"

"Stop!" Jett shouted, unwilling to listen to Lane's disrespectful comments. Pushing away from his desk, he stood and rounded on his colleague. "You don't know what the hell you're talking about. Her looks have nothing to do with it. You ought to know me better than that."

Lane stood his ground. "What I know is that you were very quick to discount her as a potential suspect. I think right from the first meeting with her, you'd already made up your mind."

"That's not true," Jett replied, glaring at him. "She provided me with an alibi for the time of the deaths. It checked out."

"The guy is her AA sponsor," Lane scoffed. "How reliable is that?"

Jett clenched his fists and with a mammoth effort, clung to his temper. Any more signs of annoyance would only confirm Lane's suspicions: that where Danielle Porter was concerned, Jett wasn't thinking clearly.

"All right," Jett said, his tone almost conversational. "I'll reinterview the sponsor. If you like, you can come along, see for yourself."

"I might just do that," Lane quipped.

"Good."

"Good."

The two of them stood nose to nose. Eventually, Lane lowered his gaze and stepped away. "Let me know when you've set it up."

Jett continued to eyeball him, feeling grim. "I will and straight afterwards, I'm going to have another chat with Franklin Cook."

———

Jett was surprised to discover Ben Fitzgerald worked as a lawyer in a busy, downtown office. Harton & Wentworth was a well respected law firm with a reputation for success. The first time Jett had interviewed him, he'd found Fitzgerald lying on the freshly mown grass of Sydney University's No.1 Oval. He'd said he was enjoying the sun.

With Lane in tow, Jett sat on the couch outside Fitzgerald's office, tapping impatiently on his knee as he waited for the lawyer to see them. Fitzgerald's secretary sat behind a desk across the way, ignoring them. The phone rang constantly. Jett could only assume the defense lawyer was in demand after the weekend. Eventually, the secretary answered a phone call and a moment later, she hung up and invited them to go in.

In place of the Levis and T-shirt Fitzgerald wore the first time Jett had met him, the lawyer was dressed in a dark-gray suit and equally somber tie. He greeted them with an expression almost as serious.

"Detectives, what can I do for you?"

"We're here to talk to you about the murders of Sabrina and Marnie Cook. We understand you know Danielle Porter, the sister of Sabrina?"

A frown creased the broad, tanned forehead of the man who sat across from them. "Yes, I'm a friend of Danielle's. I also know—knew—Sabrina." Fitzgerald's gaze landed on Jett. "I've already told you everything I know."

"We have some more questions," Lane replied, keeping his gaze on the lawyer.

Fitzgerald looked like he was going to argue, but instead, leaned back in his chair and sighed. "All right, ask away."

"How long have you known Danielle Porter?" Lane asked.

"I met her ten years ago. She was eighteen. I was twenty-two."

"You told Detective Craigdon you met at a meeting for Alcoholics Anonymous. Is that correct?"

Fitzgerald's gaze remained steady on Lane's. "Yes, that's correct."

"So, you were an alcoholic," Lane stated.

"Yes," Fitzgerald agreed. "I still am. We refer to ourselves as recovering alcoholics. We never make the mistake of believing that we're cured. Just one drink is all it takes to fall off the wagon. None of us want to go there again."

"So, you met Danielle Porter at an AA meeting and eventually became her sponsor," Jett continued. "That's what you told me, right?"

Fitzgerald studied Jett, his expression neutral. "Yes, that's right."

"And you're still her sponsor, correct?" Jett continued.

"Yes, that's correct."

"How well do you know Danielle, Mr Fitzgerald?" Lane asked.

"As I said, I've known her since she was a teenager. We've shared many stories, bonded over our past. She's a woman I think very highly of and I'd trust her with my life."

"Are you lovers?" Lane asked bluntly.

Jett coughed loudly in surprise and then strained to hear the lawyer's answer. A flicker of irritation passed across Fitzgerald's face.

"How is that relevant, Detective?"

Lane's gaze narrowed. "You've provided Ms Porter with an alibi at the time her niece and sister were murdered. I'm curious to know how close you are to Ms Porter and whether you have additional incentive to lend support to her story."

Fitzgerald held Lane's gaze and then a moment later, looked away. "I still don't see how it's relevant, but yes, Detective. We were lovers."

Jett's gut clenched and disappointment flooded his veins.

"Were?" Lane questioned. "As in, in the past tense?"

"Yes," Fitzgerald replied. "We got together not long after we met. At the time, it seemed a natural progression of our relationship. She liked me and I liked her. We were both doing our best to come to terms with our addictions. She was helping me as much as I was helping her. We spent a lot of time together."

"What happened?" Lane asked.

Fitzgerald shrugged. "We realized we loved each other more as a brother and sister. We ended the relationship. Fortunately, our friendship survived."

"How long were you sleeping with each other?" Lane asked.

Once again, Fitzgerald turned his bemused gaze on Lane. "How is that relevant, Detective?"

"I'm trying to piece together a picture of your relationship, Mr Fitzgerald. Everything is relevant."

"It might have been three weeks, maybe even a month," came the impatient reply. "Not long, Detective. We've been friends for all the time since then. Whatever you're thinking, Danielle didn't do it. She loved Sabrina and Marnie more than anyone."

"More than Sabrina's husband?" Jett asked, curious.

Fitzgerald shrugged. "Love isn't like that, Detective. There's more than enough to go around. Let's just say Sabrina and Marnie Cook were well loved by those around them. I can't imagine who could have done this."

After jotting some points in his notebook, Jett

brought the interview to an end. He and Lane stood and Jett thanked the lawyer for his time. The man was tall and broad shouldered with the kind of looks that would make both men and women look twice. It was no surprise Danielle had found him attractive. Knowing the relationship hadn't lasted long gave Jett a modicum of relief.

"What do you think?" he asked Lane as they headed outside into the sunshine.

Lane shrugged. "He appears legitimate and his occupation will have sway with the jury, but he's her ex-lover and close friend. He's not exactly impartial."

Jett wanted to protest, but what Lane said was true. Still, Jett's gut was still telling him she wasn't the monster responsible. It was time to pay another visit to Sabrina's husband.

———————

Ben Fitzgerald closed the door behind the detectives and returned to his seat. He hated that Dani was being dragged into this. She'd already suffered enough. He hadn't been lying when he'd told the officers there was no way she was responsible for the gruesome deaths. The very idea was preposterous. Still, he had to warn her that the detectives were once again looking in her direction.

Tugging his cell phone out of his pocket, he dialed her number and was relieved when she answered.

"Ben! How are you?"

Quickly, he apprised her of the reasons for his call.

"Why the hell would they want to know about that?" she exploded, as he knew she would.

"They said they needed more information about our relationship. I'm sorry, Dani. I admitted we used to be lovers. They left thinking I might have good reason to cover for you, to back your story."

"You mean, my alibi?"

"Yes," he replied.

"I can't believe they're still looking to me as a suspect!" she shouted. "What kind of dumb-assed, incompetent cops are they?"

"I don't know, but I got the distinct impression both of them were doubting you were with me when the murders happened."

"Shit!" Dani cursed, her voice filled with frustration. "Why the hell are they wasting their time? Franklin's the one telling stories, not me."

Ben frowned. He knew Franklin Cook on a professional level and had met him a couple of times at social occasions at Dani's place, but he didn't really know him.

"What are you talking about?" he asked.

"Detective Craigdon told me on Saturday night that there was a discrepancy in the time line of Franklin's statement. He told them he arrived home at one-thirty, but footage from the security camera outside the building shows him entering the foyer at twelve forty-something. When the detective questioned Franklin about it, he said he was talking on the phone to his mother."

"But—"

"Exactly," Dani interrupted. "Doreen and Lionel Cook died years ago."

"Did you tell the detective?"

"Yes." Dani's voice was grim.

"Didn't he trust your word?" Ben asked in disbelief.

Dani's voice turned grimmer. "I don't know what he believed, but I'm sure as hell not going to take this lying down. Detective Craigdon has some explaining to do."

CHAPTER 12

The mid-afternoon sun beat down on Jett's head as he and Lane made their way across the busy Pitt Street Mall toward their parked squad car. The glass windows of the storefronts were strung with brightly colored Christmas baubles and other decorations. The holiday season would soon be upon them.

"It's warmed up out here," Lane muttered, swiping at the thin sheen of perspiration on his upper lip.

"Yeah. Thank God for air conditioning," Jett responded with a smile.

"Where to?" Lane asked as he climbed behind the wheel.

Jett took a seat adjacent to him and buckled up. "The Cook penthouse."

"Hunters Hill, right?"

Jett nodded and turned to stare out the window. With a determined effort, he pushed aside thoughts of Danielle and Fitzgerald and concentrated on the interview ahead.

The bright summer sunlight glinted off the deep blue ocean as they crossed the Harbour Bridge. Far below, the pristine white sails of a smattering of yachts snapped soundlessly in the light breeze. A ferry on its way back from Manly chugged across the waves, its outside decks filled with commuters enjoying the afternoon. Jett swallowed a sigh at their carefree existence in that snapshot of time, longing to be among them.

Ever since he'd caught sight of Sabrina Cook lying butchered in the bath, he hadn't been sleeping well. That was always the way when he was in the middle of an important and complicated murder case. He took his work seriously and wouldn't relax until they had the killer behind bars.

Lane swung the squad car into Franklin's street and came to a halt opposite the up-scale building. The carefully tended lawn was green and inviting. The flowers bloomed in manicured beds. The smell of frangipani and orange blossom permeated the hot summer air. Lane stepped out of the vehicle and Jett followed suit, inhaling deeply.

"I see you don't suffer from hay fever," Lane chuckled.

Jett shook his head. "Never. I love summer with all the trees and flowers in bloom. I don't even mind the heat."

Lane rolled his eyes. "You wax so lyrical, Craigdon. I never pegged you for a poet."

Jett stuck up his middle finger in a rude gesture, but Lane merely laughed. The two men fell silent as they approached the complex.

"How do you want to handle this?" Lane asked, pitching his voice low.

"Softly, softly," Jett replied. "Let's not scare him off."

"Do you think he could have done it?"

"Who knows? Maybe. He's the husband, after all. Our number one suspect straight out of the gate. After speaking with him the day of the murders, I was convinced it couldn't be him, but he was almost rude and belligerent the night I came back and asked for his clothing and now he's lied about a phone call. I don't know what to think."

"Yeah. He said he stayed down here, in the foyer. Too bad the cameras didn't reach inside."

Jett frowned. "What about Roger Barber? If he told us the truth, he must have nearly passed Franklin, and yet, he said he saw no one."

Lane nodded, his expression grim. "I guess we should go and see what Mr Cook has to say."

As Jett stepped off the elevator at the top floor of the condominium building, he checked his watch.

"Twenty-one seconds," he said.

Lane shot him a curious look. "Excuse me?"

"I said, twenty-one seconds. It took twenty-one seconds to reach the penthouse floor without a stop."

"Okay..." Lane replied slowly, still not comprehending.

"Barber arrived at the complex at one-twenty. The footage shows him leaving the building at one twenty-seven. Franklin Cook told us he was in the foyer, talking on the phone until one-thirty. If he didn't stop on the way up to his condo, he must have still been in the foyer when Barber stepped off the elevator."

Lane's eyes lit up with sudden comprehension. "Except Barber says he saw no one."

"Exactly," Jett replied, feeling grim. "I'm very interested to hear what our grieving husband has to say about that."

———————

Franklin heard the sound of his doorbell and couldn't prevent the rush of nerves. Detective Craigdon had called earlier and told him they were on their way over. He'd have thought, after all the years he'd come into contact with police officers in the course of his job and met with clients in jail cells, the thought of speaking with a couple of detectives wouldn't raise a sweat. But it was different when he was the one in the spotlight. Much different.

The doorbell sounded a second time and he drew in a deep breath and hurried across the polished marble tiles to open it. Some of his neighbors wondered how he could bear to stay in the place where his wife and daughter had been so brutally slain, but he loved the place and couldn't imagine living anywhere else.

A professional cleaning crew had come through and removed any evidence of the crimes. Though he hadn't been able to bring himself to enter the bathroom where there had been blood sprayed in every direction, there were many nights he found himself in Marnie's room, cuddling her favorite soft toy.

It still smelled of her, her sweet baby scent and it brought back bittersweet memories of his little girl. He often left the room in tears, but somehow, he kept going back. It was almost like he was punishing himself.

Shaking his head in an effort to dislodge the sad memories, Franklin opened the door. The two detectives he'd spoken to the day of the murders stood side by side, identical expressions of grim expectation on their faces.

"Mr Cook, do you mind if we come in?"

It was the younger detective who spoke, the one who'd introduced himself earlier as Detective Jett Craigdon. He couldn't remember the name of the other one.

Franklin stood back to allow them to enter. They followed him into the open concept kitchen, dining and living area. Like most guests, their eyes were immediately drawn to the spectacular view, but the visitors remained silent.

"Can I get you something to drink?" he offered. Both detectives declined. Craigdon cleared his throat.

"Franklin, we wanted to ask you a few more questions. Do you remember telling me about the phone call you received from your mother?"

Franklin stared at the detective, his heart kicking up a gear. "Yes, of course. We spoke about it last Friday."

"Right," Craigdon replied. "See, it's like this. I'm a little curious why you told me she called you that day, given that your mother's dead."

Fear congealed in the pit of Franklin's stomach, but he steadfastly ignored it. So, he'd made a mistake, a lapse of memory. It wasn't enough to charge him with a crime.

"Oh, did I tell you I'd been speaking with my mother?" He managed a self-deprecating chuckle. "I have no idea why I said that, Detective. Of course, my mother's dead. She's been dead for years. A car accident. It killed both of my parents."

"Yes, that's what Danielle told me."

Franklin was taken aback. Anger and hurt surged through him. He hadn't expected Sabrina's sister to betray him like that. He wondered what else she'd told them. Aware of the detectives' close scrutiny, he forced a smile.

"Really? How did that come about? Dani and Sabrina didn't even know my parents."

"Yes, that's what she said," Detective Craigdon replied. "She attended the office last Saturday. She wanted an update on the case. I think she's a little frustrated we haven't arrested anyone, yet."

"As we all are, Detective," Franklin answered in a much less amiable tone than a few moments earlier.

"So, if it wasn't your mother you were speaking with, who was it?"

The question came from the older detective. Heat rushed across Franklin's cheeks. He forced himself to turn to face him.

"I... I'd rather not say."

His answer was met with a bark of disbelief. "You're kidding, right?" the detective replied. "You have a forty-seven minute window of opportunity where you could have taken a knife to your wife and child and you'd rather not provide us with an explanation? Are you really that obtuse?"

Obtuse? Franklin's anger morphed into fury. He glared at both of them. He couldn't care less what they thought. He wouldn't stand for this. He opened his mouth to order them out of his house and then caught the knowing look in the older detective's eyes. They wanted him to lose his cool. They wanted him to throw them out. It would give them further ammunition against him and that was one thing he didn't need.

Drawing in a deep breath, he eased it out between taut lips. Slowly, he regained control of his temper. Striding across the polished tiles, he poured himself a drink. Throwing back the scotch neat, he squared his shoulders and turned to face the detectives, bracing himself for what he was about to reveal.

"I received a phone call from Angel Lockhart while I was waiting for the elevator. The call was private. I didn't want anyone to overhear, especially Sabrina. So, I stayed in the foyer until I was finished."

"Who's Angel Lockhart?" Craigdon asked.

Franklin sighed and walked slowly over to his ten-thousand-dollar couch. Seating himself upon the butter-soft leather, he leaned his head back and closed his eyes.

"Angel Lockhart is an escort. I see her a couple times a week."

His announcement was met with silence. He opened his eyes and caught identical looks of surprise on the faces of the detectives. Almost immediately, their expressions changed and became grim and calculating. He could almost see the questions racing around their heads.

"You're wondering why a man married to a beautiful woman like Sabrina would have need of a mistress, right?"

The older detective remained silent. Craigdon shrugged. "Why don't you tell us?"

"Sabrina and I have a good marriage, loving and respectful. We've been together since she was eighteen. Barely an adult. I was her first lover. She was sweet and tender and willing whenever we made love, but sometimes, I craved just a little bit more."

Another wave of heat rushed up from his neck and turned his cheeks to fire. He averted his gaze from the detectives and stared out at the harbor below.

"Keep going," the older detective said.

Franklin cleared his throat. "The thing is, I have a few fetishes, things I couldn't share with my sweet, innocent wife. I like certain…things in the bedroom that I wouldn't expect Sabrina to participate in. So, I found Angel and she fulfilled that need. It worked out well for everyone."

Craigdon snorted, his eyes hard. "Well, for you at least. Did Sabrina know you were cheating? And did Angel recognize those boundaries, or had she wanted more?"

Irritation surged through Franklin. He turned his glare on the detective. "It wasn't *cheating*, Detective. Angel filled a void. It was sex. Nothing more. She understood that. It had nothing to do with the way I felt about my wife. We had a good marriage. I loved Sabrina with everything that I was. The time I spent with Angel didn't change anything."

"I wonder if Sabrina felt that way," the older detective murmured, his expression harsh.

"You have no right to judge me," Franklin cried, his anger once again coming to the fore.

"Why didn't you tell me about this earlier?" Craigdon asked. "Why give me that bullshit about your mother?"

Franklin lowered his gaze and shrugged. "Because I knew how you'd react. I'd already told you how much I loved my wife. And I knew you'd wonder how I could be sleeping with another, if that were true. You would have immediately discounted my feelings for Sabrina. It wouldn't be much of a leap for you to apportion that relationship as a motive for killing my family. I'd have been arrested and your investigation would have come to an end—until the trial, that is, when your sloppy police work would have been exposed and your flimsy evidence tossed out on its ear. But by then, it would be too late. The real killer would have disappeared, along with any evidence. I couldn't take that risk. So, I lied."

His shoulders slumped on a heavy sigh. He bowed his head. "When you first asked me about it, I panicked. Telling you I was speaking to my mother seemed a reasonable thing to do. Most of us take calls from our mothers and most of us are caught talking to them far longer than we want to. I didn't know you'd talk to Dani about it and I didn't know she'd tell you different."

He suddenly lifted his head and stared at the younger detective. "You're not going to tell her about Angel, are you? Dani will kill me. She'll...kill me." His voice drifted off. A moment later, his lip curled up in a sneer and he added, "As if she has a right to judge."

Detective Craigdon tensed and his expression became alert. He moved closer to where Franklin sat on the couch.

"What do you mean by that?" Craigdon asked, his tone a low rumble.

"I mean, she's hardly the perfect angel. She comes across all Miss Goody Two-Shoes, but I know different. Sabrina told me all about it."

"What are you talking about?" Craigdon asked.

"Dani and her dubious past. That's what I'm talking about. She was a real wild child in her younger days. Fucked anything with a dick. She was even arrested for prostitution. Sabrina filled me in on all the details. It broke her heart to talk about it, but the story had a happy ending. Somehow, Dani pulled herself out of the gutter and made something of her life. Sabrina was so proud."

Franklin glanced in Craigdon's direction. His expression could have been carved from stone. He felt a spurt of guilt. Perhaps he shouldn't have spoken so meanly about Dani. After all, she'd only ever shown him kindness and acceptance in the past.

But, it was her fault the police were standing in his living room this time, gazing at him with questions and accusation in their eyes. If disclosing her sordid past was what it took to take the heat off him, then so be it. He'd deal with his guilt later.

"How long have you been seeing Ms Lockhart?" the older detective asked.

Franklin paused and then answered. "A few years. Before Sabrina and I were married. I realized I needed to look elsewhere to fulfil some of my...needs."

"And Sabrina knew about it?" Craigdon asked, his voice brusque.

He held the detective's hard gaze and lied. "Yes."

"Tell us about Ben Fitzgerald," the older detective asked, moving slightly away.

Franklin blinked at the change of subject and took a few moments to gather his thoughts. "What do you want to know?"

"He's known your sister-in-law even longer than you have, right?" the same detective asked.

Franklin shrugged. "I think so. Like I said, Dani's life was in a bit of a mess during her teenage years—drugs, sex, alcohol. She was still fairly young when she decided to get help. She met Ben at AA."

"He became her sponsor," Craigdon stated, rejoining the conversation.

"Yes."

"How long were they lovers?" the older detective asked.

Franklin bit back a sound of surprise. So, the police had already spoken to Fitzgerald. Or maybe Dani had offered that piece of information, too? No, she wasn't the kind of person to talk freely about her personal life. Too bad she hadn't been so reticent about discussing his.

"I'm not sure," he finally answered. "I've only met the guy a few times."

"He's a lawyer," Craigdon stated. "You ever come across him in court?"

Franklin suppressed a grin. "No."

"Why not? You're both criminal lawyers working in large city firms. Sydney isn't that big."

"You're right. Of course, I've heard about him through the traps, but let's just say his usual clientele have budgets far inferior to mine."

"You mean he represents your average Joe criminal. Is that what you're saying?" Craigdon's expression remained neutral, but Franklin was certain he detected a sneer.

"He takes on his fair share of pro bono cases, or cases near enough to it," Franklin said.

"Unlike you?" the other detective said.

Franklin's anger stirred, but he forced himself to keep it in check. It wasn't wise to antagonize them.

"I make no excuses for the fact I'm choosy about who I offer representation, Detective."

"You mean the very few who can afford to pay your exorbitant fees," Craigdon replied, his voice dry.

Franklin shrugged. They could believe what they wanted about the way he ran his practice. He couldn't care less. The truth was, his hard work and top-shelf pricing had bought him a very comfortable life. He wouldn't change it for anyone.

"The day of the murders, while you were on the phone to your mistress, did you see anyone else in the foyer?" Craigdon asked.

Franklin frowned. Once again, the detectives had changed the subject. He thought back to that day, the day that was forever embedded in his brain. "No."

"Are you sure?" This from the older detective.

He thought about it again and nodded. "Yes, I'm sure."

"What about in the elevator, on the way up?" Craigdon asked. "Did anyone share the ride?"

Again, Franklin took a moment to consider the question, but once again, he replied in the negative and once again, the detective asked him if he was sure.

"Yes, I'm sure. I would have remembered. I saw no one."

The detectives shared a look between them and Franklin felt a twinge of concern. *What was that all about? Did they know something he didn't?* All of a sudden, he felt the need to take control of the questions.

"How did you do with that letter I received? Were you able to lift any prints?"

"No," Craigdon replied. "But we took a guess

and checked the television footage taken on the day of the murders. There was an anti-Islamic protest held outside the courthouse. Your client's matter was listed for mention. Do you remember seeing the demonstrators?"

Franklin nodded. "Yes. They've been showing up every time Bilal's matter comes to court. It's a nuisance and quite frightening for my client. After all, he's just a kid. He shouldn't be subjected to shit like that."

"You're right, but I guess we live in a lucky country. Freedom of speech and all that," Craigdon replied.

"Do you know a man by the name of Roger Barber?" the older detective asked.

"No, I don't know him, but I've heard him mentioned in the media. He's the ring leader of that band of thugs, isn't he?"

"Well, he's the self-appointed leader of the group of demonstrators," the detective corrected. "None of them are actually doing anything illegal."

Franklin scoffed. "Does that make it acceptable?"

Both detectives remained silent. Craigdon wandered over to the floor-to-ceiling plate glass window and stared out at the water below. It was a view Franklin never tired of.

"I caught up with Roger Barber last Saturday," Craigdon murmured, keeping his back to Franklin. Franklin's heart skipped a beat as he waited for the detective to speak again.

"The three of us had a very interesting

conversation, didn't we, Detective Black?" Craigdon continued.

"Four of us, actually," Black replied. "Barber had his lawyer there."

"Of course. How could I forget?" Craigdon replied with a derisive laugh. "The man kept advising Barber to keep his mouth shut. He was beside himself when his client paid him no attention and began to talk."

Franklin's breath caught. He leaned forward, anxious to hear what Barber had said. As if sensing his keen anticipation, Craigdon turned around to face him, a wry smile playing around his lips.

"Barber proved quite talkative and for a while, we wondered if we had our man, but he denied any involvement and—"

"Of course he did!" Franklin exploded, getting to his feet. "What did you expect? A confession?"

"And then we analyzed the clothing he was wearing on the day of the murders and it came back clean," Craigdon added, staring at him with a hard expression in his eyes.

Franklin lowered his gaze. A shiver of unease ran down his spine. He looked for his drink and found it on the low table beside the couch. Taking a healthy mouthful, he breathed a sigh of relief, grateful for the burn of alcohol and the way it helped calm his nerves.

"What about Thompson's?" he asked quietly. "Have you received those results?"

"Yes," Black replied. "They were also clean."

"In fact," Craigdon added, rounding on

Franklin. "Yours were the only ones that came back positive for your wife's blood."

Panic fluttered inside Franklin's gut and turned his mouth dry. "But, of course there was blood on my clothing," he spluttered. "I tried to haul Sabrina out of the bath. I told you that already. She had so many wounds. The blood was everywhere. I'm surprised I wasn't covered in it."

"Yes," Craigdon murmured, his eyes still narrowed on Franklin. "So were we."

Franklin bristled at the implied threat that glinted in the detective's eyes. The gall of the man. Franklin decided to call his bluff. If the police truly had enough on him to arrest him, they'd have done it by now. There would have been no pussyfooting around with questions about his mother and Ben and Dani. The handcuffs would have come out the moment he'd opened the door.

"What's that supposed to mean, Detective? If you have something to say to me, I suggest you say it now."

The two men faced off with each other. As each moment passed, Franklin's temper rose. He was a partner at Sydney's most prestigious law firm. He represented only the best. People paid thousands of dollars for his services and they were more than happy to do it. In fact, they felt *privileged* to do it; honored to be among the chosen few. He'd be damned if some upstart of a detective, out to make a name for himself, would intimidate him.

The sound of a phone ringing broke the tension.

Craigdon glanced at his colleague, who tugged out a cell phone. Turning away from them, he answered the call. Franklin returned to the couch and finished his drink. A few moments, later, Black turned back to them.

"We have to go," he said to Craigdon and then turned to Franklin. "Thank you for your time."

"I need Angel Lockhart's contact details," Craigdon said and handed Franklin a notepad and pen.

"I only have a cell number," he said.

"That's fine," Craigdon replied.

Franklin jotted down the number and handed the notepad and pen back to the detective. The fact that he was able to give them the number from memory earned him another narrow-eyed look.

He cursed silently under his breath. It was another stupid mistake. He should have at least made a show of having to look it up. Once again, he'd put the detectives off side. He clenched his jaw and hoped his lapse wouldn't prove fatal.

"We'll be in touch, Mr Cook," Detective Black murmured as both men let themselves out.

"You know where to find me," Franklin replied, keeping up the show of bravado.

The door closed behind them and he collapsed against the couch in relief. The interrogation was over.

CHAPTER 13

Dani glanced at the clock on the wall opposite her workstation and tugged off her latex gloves. It was time for her break and she intended to make good use of it by phoning Detective Craigdon. She was still fuming over the knowledge he'd questioned Ben a second time about her alibi. As if she could even *contemplate* murdering her sister and baby niece, let alone carry through with it! The very thought was unthinkable and utterly repulsive.

Slipping out of the lab, she headed downstairs to the coffee shop situated on the ground floor of her building. She grabbed a cappuccino and continued past the information desk, waved to the elderly volunteers manning the area and then walked out into the afternoon sunshine. Finding a spot beneath the shade of a large magnolia tree, she stretched out on the grass. She tugged out her cell, taking care not to spill her coffee. The anger she'd felt when Ben told her about Jett Craigdon's recent visit reignited the moment the detective answered the phone.

"Detective Craigdon."

"Detective, it's Danielle Porter."

"Danielle. What can I do for you?"

His tone was polite, if not a little distant. Her anger boiled over. "This is not a social call, Detective Craigdon." In contrast to the heat that flooded her every pore, her tone was as cold as ice.

"Okay," came the far more cautious reply.

"Ben Fitzgerald told me about your visit. It seems as though I'm once again on your suspect list."

"You're assuming you were ever actually off it," came the mild response.

Her eyes burned with anger. "How can you be so dense?" she cried. "You're wasting precious time! I'm not the one who did this! I could *never* do something so awful! She was my *sister!* My baby sister!"

Her voice cracked with the force of her emotions and she cursed beneath her breath. She didn't want to sound distressed and out of control. She wanted to be the voice of reason. No matter what she said, he didn't understand and it was tearing her up inside. He was wasting time double checking her alibi when the real killer was walking free. She wanted to scream out her frustration, pound her fists against something hard. Anything, to take away this feeling of helplessness and dread she'd been carrying around since the murders.

As if sensing her precarious emotional state, the detective's voice gentled. "We're working around the clock on this, Ms Porter. I'm sorry that, so far, it hasn't been enough, but we're making progress. My colleague felt it necessary to reinterview Mr Fitzgerald. We've also spoken to your brother-in-law again."

She couldn't keep the sarcasm from her voice. "About the phone call he apparently made to his mother?"

"Yes, that and other things."

"What did he say?"

"He told us he panicked and gave us what he thought would pass by unnoticed. He was a little upset when I told him you were the one who told us his mother was dead."

Dani closed her eyes briefly on a quiet sigh. *Great.* Now Franklin was pissed at her. Just what she needed. Still, he shouldn't have said something so stupid. He should have told the truth.

"What was he feeling panicked about? Who was he speaking to?" she asked, curious.

There was a brief pause, as if the detective was debating about what to tell her. A moment later, he replied. "He received a call from his mistress. At least, that's what he said."

Shock rendered her momentarily speechless. Her mouth opened and closed. She blinked rapidly, trying to take it in. The very thought seemed unbelievable.

"Bullshit," she replied. "I don't believe it."

"That's up to you," the detective murmured. "We got the information directly from your brother-in-law. He gave us her name and her cell phone number."

"Have you called her? Spoken to her to verify what he said?"

"We've tried. The number's currently not in service. We went back to your brother-in-law. He told us she must be out of credit on her phone."

Dani shook her head slowly back and forth, still stunned at the revelation. A mistress seemed so out of character for Franklin. Dani didn't want to believe it, but according to the detective, it was true. She thought of Franklin's demands for a paternity test and her anger flared back to life.

"How long's it been going on?" she said.

"Your brother-in-law said he'd been seeing Ms Lockhart since before he and Sabrina were married. Of course, until we speak to the woman, we won't know if that's the truth."

Another wave of fury surged through her. "The bastard! I don't believe it! To think he had the hide to accuse Sabrina of cheating! What an asshole!"

She shook her head again, her anger at Franklin far from done. "His accusation devastated my sister. She was overwrought that he could think her capable of such deceit. And all this time, the asshole's been keeping a mistress. The dishonesty of it! The hypocrisy! I'm just grateful Sabrina isn't alive to hear it."

"He said your sister knew about the arrangement. Besides, you're not exactly in a position to judge him," the detective said in a cool voice.

Dani's heart skipped a beat and then galloped hard against the wall of her chest. "What the hell does that mean?"

"I put your name into the system. It came up with a hit. Two separate charges for prostitution. Not exactly the clean-living, girl-next-door image you portray. Does your employer know about your past?"

Another wall of shock crashed into her. She gasped and tried to respond, but no words were forthcoming. It was like her brain had forgotten how to function. She didn't know what to say.

The detective's quiet announcement hammered inside her mind. She bowed her head, awash with embarrassment and shame.

"You are Danielle Veronica Porter, born June eighteen, 1988, aren't you?"

"Yes," she whispered, all the fight gone out of her.

"So, there's no mistake. It's you."

The disappointment in the detective's voice made her feel even worse. She didn't know why she cared what he thought, but the truth was, she did. He was the first man who'd ever stirred something inside her, something that made her yearn to get to know him better.

She'd lost count of the number of men she'd been with as a teen, searching for something she hadn't received at home, but none of them had touched her heart. She'd used them as much as they'd used her. They might have known her body, but none of them got inside her head...or her heart.

It was different with the detective. There was a goodness and kindness in him she'd sensed right from their first meeting and he was sinfully good looking. For all his crazy ideas, including her being responsible for the murders, he was only doing his job, investigating every possibility. She couldn't blame him for that. In fact, she admired his dedication. He was just the kind of officer she wanted looking into the murders of her sister and niece.

"Is there somewhere we can meet to talk about this?"

The quiet words were out of her mouth before she realized, but she didn't take them back. All of a sudden, she wanted to explain to him about the charges, about her unsavory past. She didn't want him continuing to think what he no doubt already was. Whether her explanation would change his mind, she wouldn't know, but she wanted the chance to try.

"I guess so," came the uncertain reply. "My shift finishes at six. I was planning to put in some overtime, but I guess I can spare you an hour or two. How does that sound?"

"That sounds great," she replied, breathing a silent sigh of relief. At the same time, her heart skipped a beat at the thought of being in his company again.

"I could meet you at the Commodore Hotel in North Sydney. Would that be all right?"

"That's fine."

"Good. I'll see you then."

Dani slipped her phone back in her pocket with a hand that wasn't quite steady. In a couple of hours, she'd be facing Jett Craigdon across a table and disclosing the sordid details of her past.

The sudden urge to call him back and cancel was almost overwhelming, but she drew in a deep breath and resisted.

The upmarket bar was not far from where she lived. She finished work in an hour. It would take her another thirty minutes to get home. If she hurried, she'd have time to shower and change before the appointed time.

Her heart tripped over in anticipation and she frowned. The sexy detective had given her no indication he found her attractive or that he had even the slightest interest. She needed to rein in her excitement. After he heard what she had to say, he'd probably want nothing to do with her. Any possible interest would be snuffed out before it sparked.

The thought was depressing, but now that she'd set things in motion, she was determined to see it through. She liked him and if there were even the slightest chance there might one day be something between them, he needed to know the truth.

———————

Jett glanced at his watch and swiveled on the barstool to check the entrance to the Commodore Hotel. He'd arrived at the bar right on the dot of six, but Danielle was nowhere in sight.

The barman placed a Budweiser in front of him and Jett turned back to the bar. Handing over some money, he murmured his thanks and lifted the bottle to his lips, relishing the icy cold brew. The December day had brought with it warm summer temperatures and he sweated beneath his suit. He'd come straight from work, not wanting to be late and he only hoped he didn't stink.

Looking around, he noted the other patrons scattered around the hotel. The building had been refurbished and the curved, brightly lit lime green bar and dark wooden furniture gave the place a modern, classy feel. There were plenty of other professional types in suits, filling tables and standing in groups of twos and threes, all talking and laughing and drinking, winding down after a long day at work.

The doors to the hotel opened and he glanced over his shoulder and saw her. She looked to the left and then to the right, searching for him. He took the time to study her and was pleased with what he saw.

She wore a halter dress that was knotted behind her neck. The soft, filmy fabric floated over her rounded hips and kissed the tops of her knees. She wore red high heels that matched the color of her dress and set off her dark hair and olive-toned skin. Her small waist was made even tinier with the assistance of a wide gold belt that also had the effect of emphasizing her more than generous breasts.

She turned in his direction and caught sight of him at the bar. Her eyes widened with recognition and her mouth turned up in a nervous smile. A swarm of butterflies fluttered in his gut and all of a sudden, he felt like a teenager on his first date.

He made a sound of annoyance in the back of his throat. This was ridiculous. They weren't on a date. This wasn't anything like a date. They'd met through horrible circumstances. The person who'd killed her sister and niece was still on the loose and he was responsible for finding him. They'd agreed to meet so that she could explain her past. That was all. As if two separate charges of prostitution didn't say it all.

"H-hi," she stammered.

A blush crept up her cheeks. Her nervousness helped ease his and he indicated the empty seat beside him. "What are you drinking?"

"Um, I'll have a lime and soda," she said and then murmured her thanks to the barman when he placed the drink before her.

She reached for her purse, but Jett stayed her movement and handed over a few more bills.

"Thank you," she murmured again, this time in his direction. She took a sip of her drink.

She was even more beautiful up close and did his best not to stare. She wore eye shadow and mascara and her lips were a bright cherry red. Her hair was loose and flowed in curly waves around her shoulders. He'd only ever seen her in person with her hair up on her head, secured in an uncompromising bun. Though the severe hairstyle hadn't detracted from her beauty, he liked the relaxed look better.

As if sensing his scrutiny, she turned and offered him another shaky smile. Awareness shot through him and heat centered in his groin. His hand tightened around the Budweiser and he took a quick gulp, needing the distraction and fortification the alcohol could bring.

"Should we get a table?" she asked, looking around.

"Sure," Jett agreed. Given that she was here to explain her past, a little privacy was called for. "Follow me."

He picked up his beer and threaded his way through the throng of people. Danielle followed close behind. He found a vacant table in a far corner of the room, partly concealed by a large potted plant, and pulled out a chair. She murmured her thanks, and took a seat.

Now that the moment was upon them, nerves once again swarmed in his gut. Her brother-in-law had spoken about her past in less than flattering terms and two decade-old charges for prostitution didn't bode well, but it was obvious she'd turned her life around. She was a university graduate and held down a responsible job. He wanted to hear from *her* how her life had once been so far off course.

She lifted her glass and in three quick swallows, emptied the rest of her drink. He made no comment, merely braced himself for what he was about to hear.

"I was born to drunken, no-good parents who never earned the right to be called Mom and Dad. Jim and Gladys Porter couldn't care less about their kids. Thank God they stopped at me and Sabrina. It was bad enough for the two of us. Why they bothered with any kids at all, is beyond me. They did nothing but yell and shout and criticize. As the oldest, I bore the brunt of their discontent."

Jett saw the pain and anger in her eyes and remained silent. After a moment, she continued.

"My parents were drunk more times than they were sober. There were always debt collectors at our door. I began to spend more and more time away from home, walking the train line, wishing I was somewhere else. Then I went through puberty and my life took another turn."

Jett's fingers tightened around the neck of his beer, but he forced himself to show no outward sign of his turmoil. She'd grown up in a household that was the antithesis of his. He struggled to imagine what it must have been like to be raised without love, respect and acceptance.

"Almost overnight, I grew hips, buttocks and boobs," she continued in a voice that was calm and detached. "Boys flocked to me at school. They wanted to ask me out. Before then, I'd been nothing more than the poor white trash that lived on the wrong side of town.

"I was flattered by the attention. It was the first time I'd ever received praise. It didn't matter to me that their comments were directed at my physical attributes. I craved attention of any kind. And so, I learned to encourage it and pretty soon, I was hanging out in bars on the edge of town. I was fifteen but could pass for much older. Nobody cared too much for ID."

She paused and stared down at her hands where they were clenched on the table in front of her. When she spoke again, he had to strain over the noise of the other patrons to hear.

"The man who took my virginity had long gray whiskers and smelled of stale beer. It happened on the seat of his pickup. I told him it was my first time and I guess he tried to be gentle, but in the end, it hurt like hell and when it was over, I left in tears. The sad thing was, any love and attention was better than none and I kept going back, time and again."

Jett envisaged the young teen, putting on a show for the men. She should have been safe and secure at home, swaddled and protected and loved by her family, valued like the treasure she was. Instead, she'd been forced to seek comfort in the arms of strangers; men old enough to be her father. Helpless anger stirred in his veins.

"How were you brought up on charges?" he asked, keeping his tone non-judgemental.

She grimaced. "Let's just say we had an over zealous sergeant who didn't take kindly to being refused. I might have had the morals of an alley cat, but I still got to pick and choose. The sergeant felt he should have had the right to demand my attentions. When I turned him down, he brought me up on prostitution charges."

"What about the second time?" he asked calmly.

Her lips compressed into a thin line. "The second time it was a young constable, eager to make his mark. He caught me climbing out of the back of a pickup. I was still adjusting my clothing. I had some money tucked into the pocket of my skirt that I'd stolen from the cookie jar at home. I was going to use it to buy some food. Unfortunately, the constable saw me with the wad of bills about the same time I left the truck and he was certain I'd just earned it on my back."

She shook her head. "There was nothing I could say to convince him otherwise. He arrested me and took me down to the station."

"But the charges were dropped," Jett said.

"Yes," she replied. "I was lucky enough to get the ear of the kindly local area commander. He'd known me since I was a little kid. On both occasions, he came into the cells and asked me what had happened. I told him the truth. Neither matter went any further."

She drew in a long breath and let it out on a heavy sigh. Tears glinted in her eyes. Without thinking, Jett reached over and squeezed her hand. She tensed, but didn't move away.

He thought about her childhood and fresh anger flooded through his veins. The adults charged with seeing to her protection, offering her guidance and love, had failed her. If it hadn't been for the local area commander, she could have done time in jail. It would have affected her job options and might have been the end of any career aspirations, but it hadn't worked out like that. Somehow, she'd turned her life around. He was curious to know more.

"Where was Sabrina in all this?" he said. "She was only a couple of years younger. She couldn't have been oblivious to what was going on."

Dani glanced up at him and then stared at the

table again. Slowly, she offered him a nod. "You're right. Of course she knew and it broke her heart, but there was nothing she could do about it. I lost count of the number of times she begged me to stay home, to not go out at night. She'd heard all the rumors; she knew what happened on the edge of town.

"I wouldn't listen. I didn't *want* to listen. I didn't think she understood. She'd been born beautiful, inside and out—all serene and kind and golden. For some reason, our parents treated her better. I think they were a little in awe of her, of this exquisite creature with the long blond hair and sunny smile that lived with them. Whatever scraps of affection they had, they gave to her."

"That must have been hard on you," Jett murmured, his heart breaking at the thought of the young Danielle, unloved and unwanted.

Dani shrugged. "I guess, but I didn't blame Sabrina. It wasn't her fault. She didn't have a nasty bone in her body. She treated everyone with kindness and respect. I never saw her get angry or say anything mean. She was good and kind and beautiful, an angel, until the day she died."

Her voice caught and more tears welled up in her eyes. Jett's heart tightened with emotion. He wanted to take her in his arms and comfort her. He wanted to hold her close and promise her that everything would be all right; that she'd never be sad again.

But of course, he could do none of those things. They'd only met three weeks ago. They barely knew each other. She was part of his murder investigation. Even worse, she'd been on and off his suspect list. The fact that he'd never seriously entertained the possibility she was the killer wasn't relevant.

"It was Sabrina who finally made me realize I was on a fast track to nowhere and that if I didn't do something to bring a halt to the way I was living my life, I might never find my way back. She convinced me I could do it, that I deserved better. She *believed* in me, she *loved* me. She gave me the courage to do what had to be done."

She made a soft sound of distress and once again, Jett restrained the urge to hold her. When she looked up at him, her eyes glistened with tears.

"She found the AA meeting in a nearby suburb. She even came along. She was there when I met Ben. We clicked right away and Sabrina was so pleased. I'd found someone who not only cared, but who understood what I'd been through."

At the mention of Ben Fitzgerald, Jett compressed his lips, but he reminded himself the two of them were no longer a couple and his tension eased. He gazed at Dani and realized she looked exhausted. She'd spent the day at work and had just gone through a rollercoaster of emotions. It couldn't have been easy recounting her past. She'd had no idea how he was going to react.

He couldn't deny he was shocked at the previous life she'd led, but he didn't blame her. No one was perfect. Everyone made bad choices and decisions they lived to regret. What was important was that she'd risen above it and had worked hard to turn her life around. No one meeting her today would have an inkling of where she'd been. She was a beautiful vibrant woman and... He could understand her sister's pride. He was proud of her, too.

"Thank you for sharing your story," he said quietly and once again, squeezed her hand. He wanted to do so much more, but he wasn't sure how she felt about him—about them. Hell, what was he thinking? There was no *them* and there probably never would be.

"Do you...think Franklin...might have had...something to do with...the deaths of Marnie and Sabrina?"

The question was voiced so softly and hesitantly, he wasn't sure that he'd heard right. He stared at her.

"Do I think Franklin...?" He let the question hang. She stared at her hands where they clenched and unclenched in her lap. A long moment later, she nodded.

Her head came up and she caught his gaze, her eyes wide and dark and shadowed with pain. "Yes," she whispered, her voice ragged. "Do you think it was Franklin?"

Jett reared back, his mind awhirl. There were aspects of Franklin's responses that he found unsettling and there'd been moments when he definitely didn't like the man, but did he really think Dani's brother-in-law was a murderer? He wasn't sure. Holding her gaze, he told her as much.

"Is there some reason you felt the need to put this to me?" he asked, feeling a little confused. "The first time I asked you about Franklin, you were adamant he couldn't be responsible. What happened to change your mind?"

She toyed with a paper napkin that was folded near her place. Her gaze remained fixed on the table.

"I don't know," she said quietly. "It's just that he lied about talking to his mother and then confessed to having a long-term affair. I would have sworn he loved my sister with every fiber of his being, but how can someone love another person like that and be sleeping with someone else? It's made me rethink everything I thought about him and I can't help but question everything I believed. I mean, what if Sabrina found out about this other woman? What if they had a terrible fight and it ended with Sabrina's and Marnie's deaths?"

"I told you your sister knew about the affair, remember?" Jett replied, keeping his tone neutral.

She frowned at him and then shook her head, frustration evident in her eyes. "Yes, you did, but that was according to Franklin. What if he lied about that, too? He's already lied once. What's to stop him lying again? I can't help thinking his little dig about Sabrina being unfaithful and demanding the paternity test was his way of removing the heat from him."

Jett nodded thoughtfully. "I asked him about the paternity test."

"Yes, at the funeral and then later, when you

came by the condominium. He said he never opened the letter. He hadn't seen the results. Did he give you a copy?"

"No," he said slowly. With all that had been going on, the lab test had slipped his mind. He had yet to phone the lab that had conducted the testing.

"No one will convince me Sabrina was unfaithful," Dani said, her expression fierce.

Jett regarded her solemnly, admiring her loyalty. "There's only one way of knowing for sure," he murmured and glanced at his watch. "I'll phone the lab now and see if they're still open."

"You know who conducted the tests?" she asked in surprise.

"Yes, Franklin told me. He was having trouble finding his copy. At least, that's what he said."

Jett pulled out his phone and found a number for Life Biologistics. A moment later, the call connected and was answered on the third ring. Jett introduced himself to the female on the other end of the phone and explained the reason for his call.

"I'm sorry, Detective Craigdon, I won't be able to release any information to you without written consent from Franklin Cook."

Jett gritted his teeth in frustration. "Could you at least confirm that Franklin and Marnie Cook are clients?"

There was a moment of silence and Jett could hear the sound of fingernails tapping on a keyboard before the woman replied.

"What were the names again?"

Jett gave her the information.

"I'm sorry, Detective. I don't have any record for either of those names."

Jett frowned. "Are you sure?"

"Yes, I'm sure. They're not in our system. I think you've made a mistake."

After thanking the woman for her time, Jett ended the call. He stared across at Dani in confusion.

"The lab doesn't have any record of Franklin and Marnie," he said.

Dani frowned. "I thought you said Franklin—"

"I did. Franklin gave me the name of the lab. Only, the information wasn't correct."

Dani's eyes widened. "Do you think he made a mistake?"

Jett stared at her. "Either that, or he lied."

Dani reared back. Jett couldn't tell if she was shocked or simply unwilling to accept the possibility. She shook her head slowly back and forth.

"Why would he do that? I refuse to believe those results had anything to do with the deaths."

"I understand you don't want to hear this, Dani, but I'm convinced those test results are connected. I'm not sure how, but every which way I turn, those results come back to haunt me. Franklin received them the day your sister and niece were murdered. Strangely enough, he's misplaced the envelope with the documents; he lied about the lab where I could obtain a copy. There's something going on. I feel it in my gut."

She remained silent, but he refused to be put off. "There might be another way we can get hold of a copy. Franklin said he brought the results home from his office that day. They must have been in the house. I wonder if he left the mail somewhere on his way inside?" The faintest stirring of excitement started in Jett's gut.

"I could check the crime scene photos," he added. "You never know your luck. If he left the mail on a table or the counter, we might have captured it in a frame. It's worth a second look."

Dani nodded. "I agree, but you're surmising the results indicated Franklin wasn't Marnie's father." She shot him a pointed look. "That *is* what you're getting at, right? That my sister was unfaithful, got pregnant by another guy and tried to pass Marnie off as the baby of her husband?"

Jett shifted in his seat, but was able to hold her gaze. "Yes, that's what I'm getting at. If Franklin *did* open the letter and saw the results, it's possible he then went home and attacked his wife and daughter in a jealous rage."

Dani's expression turned bleak and she shuddered as if tasting something distasteful. "I just can't imagine it happening like that. Franklin..." Her voice drifted off and she shook her head slowly back and forth, shadows of helplessness in her eyes.

A moment later, her shoulders squared and she met his gaze, a new light of determination replacing the shadows.

"For me to believe it happened the way you suggest, I have to accept Sabrina was unfaithful, that Franklin wasn't Marnie's dad and I... I just can't... I can't believe Sabrina capable of such deception. It isn't possible. Anyone else, maybe, but we're talking about my little sister! You didn't know her. I refuse to believe she cheated on her husband."

Jett stared at her, his heart flooding with compassion. He'd come across his fair share of shocked relatives who struggled to accept what their loved ones were capable of. Even some serial killers had families who loved them.

"I'm sorry," he said, "I didn't know Sabrina, and I accept that you knew her well, but you wouldn't be the first relative to be duped by someone they love."

She tensed and her face closed. He sat forward, hoping to make her understand. "Everyone has secrets, Dani and they're called secrets for a reason. I don't want to make this any more difficult for you, but, I don't think either of us can say with certainty that your sister did or didn't cheat on her husband."

Her eyes flared with anger. She glared across at him. "You were right the first time," she said coldly. "You *didn't* know my sister. You didn't know anything about her. So don't presume to categorize her with all the other victims you've come across. I won't have it. And for your information, Sabrina didn't have any secrets. We told each other everything."

Anger stirred in his gut. *Didn't she get it?* He was on her side! He was trying to help her!

"You didn't know about Franklin's mistress."

She glared at him. "We've already established my brother-in-law is less than truthful at times."

Jett's temper rose to the surface. "For Christ's

sake, Dani! Your sister was stabbed a total of thirty-seven times."

Dani flinched in horror and her face lost most of its color. Jett felt a stab of guilt for being so harsh, but he needed to make her see.

"The attack on Sabrina was personal. Very personal. When we see this kind of overkill, any detective worth his salt will look to those closest to the victim and unfortunately, most of the time, that's where we find the murderer. It's an awful statistic. I can't force you to believe it, but it's the truth."

He drew in a deep breath and let it out on a heavy sigh. She continued to stare at him with equal parts anger and desolation. She looked so vulnerable and alone. Though he wanted to comfort her, he maintained control and remained seated with his hands firmly at his sides.

"When someone is murdered the way Sabrina was murdered, the first people we look at are the family. You've told me you weren't the killer; neither of your parents are in your lives. We also looked into the maintenance man and the anti-Islamic protester. They've both been cleared."

Her shoulders slumped and once again, she looked despondent. She picked up her glass and realized it was empty so put it down again. He signaled the waiter for another.

"That leaves Franklin," she whispered, her voice hoarse.

He stared at her and slowly nodded. "Yes, that leaves Franklin."

CHAPTER 14

The next day, Jett was the first to arrive at his office. Switching on the lights and the air conditioning, he threaded his way through the rows of empty workstations until he came to his. Dumping his briefcase on his desk, he leaned over and booted up his computer.

After buying Dani another drink the night before, he'd invited her to dinner, but she'd declined. He'd been disappointed. Though their conversation had traversed some heavy topics, he'd felt a connection to her throughout and was almost certain she felt it, too.

But she'd accepted his offer to drive her home to her tiny bedsit and had walked her to the door. She'd stared at him for a few endless seconds and he wondered if she would kiss him. But she turned away and fumbled for her keys, muttered a brief thank you and goodnight—and with that, she was gone.

Still, he refused to be put off. Whether Danielle Porter liked it or not, there was something between them—a spark, a connection—he didn't know what to call it, but it existed and he wanted to explore it further.

She was the antithesis of every woman he'd dreamed about. For years, he'd pictured himself with a sweet, loving blonde. Quiet and shy, with a pure heart and body, she'd be keenly intelligent with a good sense of humor, and modest about her accomplishments.

He realized with a start he was describing what he knew about Sabrina Cook and yet, it was her sister who'd captured his thoughts. Dark and sexy and fiercely determined, she couldn't be more different from her sister if she'd tried—and yet, he was drawn to her.

He was a virgin who believed in love and remaining pure until he was married and she... Well, she...wasn't. But she was strong and smart and loyal and beneath her tough exterior was the heart of a woman with a warm and generous soul. He wondered if she was even aware of her good qualities.

He'd spent a restless night, tossing and turning over the case as one scenario after another paraded themselves through his mind. The more he thought about it, the further up his suspect list Franklin Cook climbed. Even without the paternity results, Sabrina and her husband could have argued over something else—his mistress, for example.

But there was still a glaring problem: Franklin's clothing had failed to disclose any blood spatter and there was no way he could have instigated the vicious attack without having that kind of blood pattern on them.

Jett threw himself in his chair with an irritable grunt, already out of sorts. The lack of blood spatter bugged him. It wasn't just him. Everyone working the case agreed, the killer couldn't have escaped such a bloodbath unscathed. At the back of his mind, he knew he was missing something obvious. Yet, Jett had been over the security camera footage again. No one who'd left the building during the relevant time period appeared to be covered in blood.

What was he missing?

The thud of several packages landing on his desk startled him from his heavy thoughts. With a frown of annoyance, he stared at the clear plastic bags in front of him and then looked up. Lane stared back at him.

"You're in nice and early," Jett's colleague commented with a smile.

"What are these?" Jett replied, pointing to the bags that looked to contain clothing.

"I stopped by the lab on my way into work. It's the clothes from our suspects. The pathologist who ran the tests asked me to collect them now that their analyses are done."

Jett picked up the bag that lay on top of the pile and glanced at the label that sealed the opening. COOK—Franklin James File Reference 6653/2016. A jolt of awareness went through him. They were the clothes Sabrina's husband had worn the day of the murders. It was a shame they hadn't found anything to assist the investigation.

Half-heartedly, Jett broke the seal with his fingernail and tugged out the jacket of a charcoal-gray suit. It was stained with patches of blood. The suit pants were relatively clean, but the pale blue shirt was ruined. A large, dark red stain covered most of the front of it. The bright yellow silk tie had fared even worse. It looked like it had been dipped in blood. The image turned Jett's stomach.

He looked away, but as he did so, something stirred in his memory. He turned back and stared at Franklin's clothing, trying to figure out what it was. He remembered seeing Franklin wearing the blue shirt and tie at the crime scene. The yellow had been hard to miss. Coated in bright red blood, it had provided a stark reminder of why they were there but was there something he was missing?

"What is it?" Lane asked, noticing Jett's narrow-eyed look of concentration.

Jett shook his head, nonplussed. "I'm not sure. I just got a weird feeling when I looked at Cook's clothing, like I should be noticing something I'm not."

"Well, that's definitely what he was wearing on the day of the murders. I'll never forget that tie. It looks a like a canary went a few rounds with a Tom cat. There's no guessing who came off second best."

Lane chuckled at his own joke, but Jett's mind stayed focused on the clothing in front of him. A moment later, it hit him. Franklin's own words suddenly echoed in Jett's head: *How do you know he's given you the clothes he was wearing that day?*

"That's it! The clothing! We know Franklin Cook wore these clothes at the crime scene. We both saw him in it. But are we sure this is the same clothing he wore prior to our arrival?"

Lane shrugged. "I guess so."

"A guess, isn't good enough," Jett responded thinking how Franklin might have given himself away. "Lucky for us, we can find out for sure."

"How?"

"The television footage. Remember? You got it for the purposes of canvassing the crowd of demonstrators. We found Barber looking angry and menacing. It provided him with motive. Coupled with his fingerprints, we thought he was our man."

Lane grimaced. "Yeah, until he wasn't."

"It doesn't matter," Jett replied a little impatiently, tugging his keyboard toward him. "What matters is that the TV camera crew filmed Franklin leaving the courthouse with his client in tow. It was taken on the day of the murders. We can compare Cook's clothing then with these clothes, the ones he wore when we arrived at the penthouse."

Tapping on his keyboard, Jett brought up the file containing the TV footage and clicked on it. A few moments later, the scene outside the courthouse erupted on Jett's computer screen in noisy Technicolor detail. He fast-forwarded to the part where the courthouse doors swung open and Franklin and his young client were standing at the top of the stairs. Hitting pause, he stared at Sabrina's husband.

"Holy shit," Lane breathed and Jett's gut tightened with excitement.

Franklin Cook stood beside Bilal Al-Jabiri. Looking every bit the distinguished lawyer who was prepared for a fight, Franklin stared arrogantly into the crowd of protestors. He wore a navy-blue suit and a white shirt. Around his neck was an expensive looking navy-and-white striped tie.

"It's him," Jett breathed, his heart racing.

With his breath coming fast, Jett worked quickly to bring up the footage taken outside the Cooks' building. Once again, he fast-forwarded until he found the place where Franklin entered the complex. Hitting pause once again, both officers stared at Franklin's clothing. Though the images were grainier and in black and white, there was no mistaking the man wore a striped, dark-colored tie.

"We've got him," Lane said, his voice filled with grim satisfaction.

Jett let out a *whoop* of glee. "I don't believe it. The bastard argued with his wife, came home and murdered her and their infant daughter, cleaned up, changed his clothes and then staged it to look like the clothes he wore when we arrived were what he'd been wearing all along. We got there and, of course, we didn't know any different."

"Do we know what triggered the argument?" Lane asked.

"No, but there are a couple of possibilities. Sabrina could have found out about the mistress.

Franklin told us she knew about it, but it's possible she didn't. Then there's the paternity test. I'm betting Franklin lied when he said he didn't open the envelope to read the results. I'm betting he did just that and the results showed he wasn't the dad.

"We know Sabrina was in the bath. Not only was she found there, but when Kevin Thompson arrived to carry out some plumbing repairs he said she'd told him she was going to take a bath. She asked him to come back later.

"That was about twelve o'clock. According to the security camera, Franklin arrived home at twelve forty-three. He didn't make the emergency call until one thirty-six. If we run with the idea his phone call from his mistress didn't happen, he had plenty of time to complete the murders, shower, change and get the blood on the second set of clothes."

Lane shook his head in disbelief. "Barber arrived at the complex at one-twenty. By that time, Sabrina was already dead. Franklin was no doubt in the shower by then and didn't see or hear Barber come in. It could also explain why Barber didn't see anyone, either."

"And it also explains why neither Barber nor Franklin saw each other in the elevator or downstairs," Jett added. "According to the evidence provided by the time indicated on the security tapes, their paths should have crossed, and yet they didn't."

"Because Franklin was never in the foyer on the phone," Lane finished. "The prick came home in a blind fury and went straight upstairs. The problem is, how do we prove it?"

Jett stared at the computer screen, his thoughts racing. "The lab results," he said.

"What about them?" Lane asked.

"I've been asking for them since the funeral. Franklin said he couldn't find them. When I pressed him, he gave me the name of the lab, but he lied. Again. I called the lab. They had no record of him or his daughter. I meant to check the crime scene photos as soon as I came in this morning."

"What do they have to do with the lab test?" Lane asked.

"Franklin said he brought the lab results home from the office unopened. He even suggested we'd taken it along as evidence. If he's like most of us, he probably tosses the mail and house keys on the table, or maybe a kitchen counter. Even wild with fury, it's possible old habits kicked in. With a bit of luck, the police photographer might have inadvertently captured a picture of the mail."

Lane nodded his agreement. "It's worth a shot. Let me know how that goes." He turned away and then turned back to Jett. "Good work on this one, Craigdon. The boss will be pleased. You'll make detective sergeant before you know it." Lane gave him a wink and then headed toward his desk.

Jett drew in a deep breath and eased it out. His chest was still tight with excitement and the adrenaline that had poured through his veins. He was sure they were on the right track. It all fit together far too well. Franklin Cook had murdered his wife and daughter. Jett was now certain of it.

He thought of Danielle and his spirits sunk. Dread formed a hard knot in his gut. The knowledge that her brother-in-law was responsible would devastate her and when the time came, it would be up to Jett to tell her.

With a heavy sigh, he opened the file on Sabrina and Marnie Cook and retrieved the packet containing the crime scene photos. Flicking through them, his gut churned with remembered horror. Anger, sharp and icy, bit into his gut. Franklin Cook was a monster who had shown no mercy.

Pictures of the luxurious condominium followed those of Sabrina in the bath. The expensive furniture, the picture-perfect view—all that meant nothing because Jett knew what had happened inside those gilded walls.

A close-up had been taken of a sideboard where a bloody handprint could be seen. Jett recalled it had come back to Franklin. They'd assumed he'd rested his hand there at some point after discovering the carnage.

Right next to the handprint was a pile of mail. On the top was a sheet of paper with a letterhead. The contents of the letter weren't visible, but it was a computer printout, not handwritten.

Jett's heart skipped a beat and then took off at a gallop. Using special enhancement software, he managed to enlarge the image. Slowly, the letterhead became visible: DNA Tracker— Biological Testing Laboratory.

The lab test. That had to be the results. And as Jett guessed, the letter was open. The argument that Franklin had opened it before he arrived home was no longer purely circumstantial, and coupled with the other evidence, Jett was prepared to go with it.

Taking note of the laboratory's details, he reached for the phone to confirm what he suspected. His call connected to a message bank and he cursed silently and then left a message requesting that someone call him back as a matter of urgency.

He glanced at his watch and noted it wasn't even seven. The lab probably didn't open until nine. He gritted his teeth against a surge of impatience and pushed away from his desk. Right now, he needed caffeine and plenty of it.

Two hours and several cups of coffee later, a friendly technician from DNA Tracker returned his call.

"Detective Craigdon, it's Mary Peterson. What can I do for you?"

As quickly as he could, Jett explained the situation and asked for a copy of the lab results.

"I'm sorry, Detective. Those results are confidential. I can't release them to you without Mr Cook's consent and if that's not forthcoming, I'll need a subpoena."

Jett cursed silently under his breath. He'd known a subpoena was more than likely in the cards. He could hardly approach Franklin for permission to access the results and chance revealing his hand. The man wasn't stupid. He'd immediately realize the significance of Jett's request.

"A subpoena it is, then," he replied with a sigh.

"I'm really sorry, Detective, but rules are rules."

After thanking her for her time, Jett ended the call and got on with it. A couple hours later and a quick visit to the court registry, he had a subpoena in his hand. Lane accompanied him to the laboratory to serve it.

He'd called ahead and had given Mary a heads-up and was grateful when she met him in reception with a copy of the Cook results. Wasting no time, Jett scanned the single page. It was as he'd guessed. Franklin Cook was not Marnie Cook's biological father.

CHAPTER 15

With the back of her forearm, Dani pushed a wayward strand of hair out of her eyes and once again leaned over to peer through the lenses of her microscope. The tiny sample of breast tissue on the slide contained malignant cells. It saddened her to know that somewhere there was a woman who would shortly be given the bad news. Dani could only hope the tumor hadn't metastasized, reducing the woman's chances of survival.

Like they had, a hundred times a day since the murders, Dani's thoughts drifted to Sabrina. She wondered what her sister had felt in those final moments before death. *Had she looked into the face of her killer? Had she tried to fight back?*

Franklin had told her the police report had indicated there were no defensive wounds. Dani knew what that meant. More than likely, Sabrina was taken by surprise. She'd been found in the bath in the middle of the day. The water had still been warm. Dani could almost see her sister putting Marnie down for a nap and then taking the opportunity to relax. To think that perfect scene of serenity had been so violently destroyed. It weighed Dani down with sadness.

Memories of Sabrina inevitably brought forth thoughts of Franklin and she wondered uncomfortably about the possibility he could have been responsible for the deaths. When the detective had first raised the idea, Dani had been quick and vehement in her denial, but after learning about her brother-in-law's dishonesty to the police and about the mistress he'd kept all these years, her faith in him had been irrevocably shaken.

She hadn't expected Jett Craigdon to share the information with her. He hadn't exactly been forthcoming during the previous occasions they'd met. She guessed his reticence had something to do with the fact she'd been a potential suspect and she hoped that his show of confidence indicated she was finally off his list.

From their conversation the night before, it appeared almost certain that Jett regarded her brother-in-law as the prime suspect, despite the fact, as far as she knew, the police had no concrete evidence. Though she was anxious to find the killer, a part of her hoped desperately that Franklin wasn't the person who'd done this terrible deed.

A shaft of pain stabbed through her chest at the possibility and she gasped and clenched her fist. She didn't know how she would cope if it turned out to be Franklin. Though she hadn't been as enamored of him as Sabrina had been, Dani liked him well enough. He'd been a good brother-in-law, caring and polite. He'd opened his home to her whenever she felt the need for company and always appeared genuinely pleased to see her.

He'd known from the earliest days of his courtship of her sister how close she and Sabrina were and he accepted their closeness with equanimity, even encouraged it. He'd once told her how special he regarded their sisterly relationship. As an only child, he'd never had the chance to bond with a sibling. Not once had he voiced any jealousy, or even intimated as much. It had only served to endear him to her. Over the years, she'd come to care for him very much.

Now, if Detective Craigdon's instincts were correct, she might very well have to face the reality that the brother-in-law she respected and admired was a cold-hearted killer who had brutally stolen the lives of her beautiful sister and niece. The possibility filled her with a fresh wave of horror.

In an effort to distract herself, she focused on something else, like how good looking the detective was. He'd arrived at the bar still dressed in work clothes, though he was minus the jacket of his suit. The top couple of buttons on his blue-and-white striped shirt had been undone and his dark green tie had been loosened. The exposed column of his throat looked tanned and strong. She'd glimpsed a scattering of dark hair.

The sight of his bare skin had done funny things

to her insides and she'd become flustered. She wasn't used to the feeling. For more than a decade, she'd been strong and resilient, staunch in her independence and her vow to steer clear of men.

Apart from her brief fling with Ben, over the last ten years she hadn't allowed another man to get close—and over that time it hadn't once been as hard as she was finding it now, to keep the detective at a distance. She'd been with countless men in her youth, but none of them had made her feel what the detective did—all warm and fluttery and achy inside.

And they hadn't even kissed.

Of course, she'd been tempted. When he'd walked her to her door and had thanked her for the evening, it was all she could do not to lean over and press her mouth to his. The faint illumination from a nearby street light had accentuated the dark five o'clock shadow on his cheeks and gilded his hard male profile.

She'd been reluctant to accept his dinner invitation for the very same reason she'd refrained from kissing him. He unsettled her, made her feel things she couldn't define, made her feel cut loose from her moorings and she was terrified she wouldn't be able to find her way home.

For too many years, she'd kept up her vigilance, desperate and determined not to fall back in her old ways. Not that she worried she'd turn sluttish, but the feeling of being worthless, the damaged self-esteem—she never wanted to feel that way again and was scared that by giving in to her burgeoning feelings, she'd lose herself in the process. What was worse, she no longer had Sabrina to help her.

The very idea of dropping her guard terrified her, but the thought of spending the rest of her life alone was depressing. What if this thing with the detective—whatever it was—was real? What if it could help her heal? Even after a decade of therapy, she hadn't forgiven herself for the waywardness of her youth and she wasn't sure if she'd ever get to the point where she could.

The buzz of her cell phone interrupted her musings. She tugged the phone out of the pocket of her lab coat and glanced at the screen.

Jett.

Her heart skipped a beat. It was almost like he knew her thoughts had been centered on him. Taking a deep breath, she answered the call.

Jett glanced around him at the people walking by, all heading to various destinations. He hadn't wanted to break the news of Franklin's culpability to Dani over the phone and had asked her to meet him on the Sydney University No.1 Oval, situated within walking distance of the hospital.

The feeling of dread and resignation that had filled his gut upon realizing the murders had more likely than not occurred the way he'd imagined, continued to grow inside him. Dani would be devastated. He panicked at the thought of finding the right words to tell her. He couldn't just blurt it out, but neither could he pretend they hadn't figured out what happened.

While the police had been back to the condo earlier that day with a search warrant and had turned the place upside down, they hadn't found the clothes Franklin had worn earlier on the fateful day. But that didn't mean the terrible murders hadn't happened the way he surmised. He had to tell her. She had a right to know.

He checked his watch and his panic increased. She'd be there any minute. He'd been trained for this very thing. He'd done it many times before and yet, with Dani, everything was different. It was because he cared for her and he cared how she felt. The thought of burdening her with the truth made him sick.

An arrest team was being put together at that very moment. By the end of the day, news of Franklin's arrest would be broadcast from every television station and Internet service in town. He had to tell her before she found out some other way. He owed her that much.

He turned and caught sight of her making her way across the paved walkway to where he sat on a bench near a stand of gums, overlooking the oval. It wasn't exactly secluded, but the trees provided a modicum of privacy.

Another wave of nervousness rushed through him. Last night, they'd touched on the possibility of Franklin being involved, but even then, it was pure speculation. Now Jett had proof that his theory had been right.

She came closer and smiled, though he noticed it didn't reach her eyes. Her gaze glanced off his and her cheeks were tinged with pink. It was hot beneath the afternoon sun, but he was guessing it wasn't the sun's heat that had her color up.

"H-hi," she stammered and he was immediately transported back to the night before. He resisted the urge to lean over and kiss her, like he'd wanted to outside her house. Instead, he satisfied himself with a much more subdued greeting.

"Thank you for coming," he said and then indicated the bench seat. "Would you like to sit?"

"Um, I'm... I'm not sure," she replied and then perched on the very edge. She looked up at him, her expression grave. "What's this about, Jett?"

It was the first time she'd used his Christian name and a surge of warmth rushed through him. He quickly tamped it down. The news he bore was far from happy. Her life was about to be torn apart. Again. He took a seat beside her. The scent of her perfume—spicy and exotic—wafted toward him in the air. He tried to ignore how good it smelled.

"There've been some new developments in the investigation," he started. "I... I wanted to tell you about them in person."

She frowned, but her gaze remained steady on his. It was as if she'd gotten over her initial bout of nervousness and was now totally focused on their conversation.

"What kind of developments?"

"Firstly, I've had access to the paternity test results."

She lowered her gaze and he caught her quick indrawn breath. Her face paled. "I don't know that I can bear to hear what it revealed," she whispered, her voice hoarse.

His chest tightened, making it difficult to breathe. This was going to be awful. "The results were negative, Dani. Franklin was not Marnie's father."

"*No!*" The word of denial burst out of her. Her eyes widened, filled with an agony of shock and disbelief. She leaped up from the bench, her hands fisted at her sides.

"I don't believe it! I *won't* believe it! You didn't know Sabrina like I did. The results must be wrong."

His heart went out to her and he could no longer stand by helplessly and ignore her pain. He came to his feet and closed the distance between them. Putting his arms around her shoulders, he pulled her in against him. She tensed momentarily and then her body went limp. She buried her face against his shirt.

She cried out her pain like her heart was broken. The force of her sobs shook her slight frame. He could only imagine her bewilderment. Sabrina had been the golden-haired child, the woman who could do no wrong; an angel who loved everyone and everything and who everyone loved in return. How utterly debilitating it must be for Dani to accept her perfect sister had had secrets, faults and failings, like everyone else.

The worst of it was, he had yet to tell her the rest. That Franklin had changed his clothing before calling the police. That he was now their number one suspect and was about to be arrested for the murder of his wife and child. That his face would be plastered all over the news, and along with it, the images of Marnie and Sabrina. Dani would be forced to endure the nightmare all over again and this time, the horror would be worse. For instead of some faceless stranger, the perpetrator was none other than the man entrusted with their safety.

At the thought of what lay ahead, his arms tightened about her and he bit back a groan of distress. Pressing his lips against the softness of her hair, he murmured mindless words of comfort. Finally, her sobs subsided to an occasional hiccup and sniffle. She lifted her head and stared at him, her eyes red and swollen from her tears. Her lips trembled.

"It was Franklin, wasn't it?" Her voice cracked with emotion. Fresh tears slid down her cheeks.

He nodded. Though he was relieved he hadn't actually had to say the words, he struggled just the same. With a gentle hand, he reached up and wiped the moisture from her eyes. Her breath caught and her mouth parted in surprise. She held his gaze for the longest time.

The air crackled between them, charged with emotions neither of them were brave enough to voice. Her eyes darkened with need and fire catapulted its way through his veins. Heat centered in his groin and it was all he could do not to crush her against him and never let her go.

Instead, he lowered his head until his lips barely touched hers. It was the slightest whisper of movement and yet, his world rocked on its heels. She reached up and her arms came around his neck. Her fingers tangled in his hair.

He turned her until she was flush against him. Her breasts were crushed against his chest. He kissed her again with increasing pressure, this time taking the time to learn the shape and feel of her mouth. She tasted faintly of coffee and of some kind of peppermint gum.

Over the years, he'd gained a little experience in kissing. Though he'd vowed to save himself for marriage, he hadn't lived a life totally devoid of passion. He'd dated girls on and off, nice girls one and all, and he'd enjoyed their company and their kisses, but none of them had ignited a need so great inside him he it threatened to consume him.

Dani angled her head, giving him more freedom to explore. Jett growled his satisfaction and kissed his way across her cheek and then nibbled on her ear. She gasped and shivered and tightened her hold around his neck. His tongue stole out to trace the delicate whorls and he heard her breath catch again.

Beyond thought and reason, he reached down and cupped her rounded ass and pressed her tightly against his erection. For a moment, she molded herself against him and he nearly died from the feel of it.

But then, she pulled away and her arms fell to her sides. He blinked at her abrupt departure and tried to get his bearings.

"Are... Are you all right?" he asked, his mind still full of their kiss.

A frown marred the smooth skin of her forehead and she stepped a little further away. "Yes, of course. I... It's just that... We're at the oval. Anybody could come by."

He looked around him, still dazed with passion and noticed a couple of students coming toward them, backpacks slung over their shoulders. It didn't appear they'd noticed them, but still... He understood Dani's reluctance.

Heat stole up his neck and spread across his cheeks. His embarrassment had nothing to do with the kiss they'd so recently shared. She was a pathologist at the nearby hospital. He was a detective. They had been making out like teenagers in the park.

"I'm sorry, Dani. I didn't mean to kiss you. It just sort of...happened."

Her face relaxed into a soft smile. "It's okay. I didn't mind. In fact, I liked it. I liked it a lot. It helped to...take my mind off things."

Once again, her green eyes deepened with emotion and his heart skipped a beat. He was falling for this woman and falling fast. The thought was both exhilarating and terrifying.

Dani perched on the edge of her couch, tense. She stared at her television screen in horror and watched the scene play out in front of her. Franklin being led down the front steps of his law firm in handcuffs, snarling at the gaggle of cameramen, to get the hell out of his way. *He must have returned to work...*

On one side, he was flanked by Jett and on the other, by another grim-faced detective. Dani was certain it was the same one who had attended the funeral.

She watched her brother-in-law being pushed into the back of a squad car and renewed waves of shock and disbelief shuddered through her. The cameras kept rolling as the car pulled away from the curb and sped away.

A reporter with a microphone in his hand turned back toward the camera, his eyes alight with the scent of the hunt.

"In breaking news, we've just witnessed the arrest of Franklin Cook for the murders of his wife and young daughter. Mr Cook is a high profile lawyer currently representing—"

Dani switched the television off, cutting short the man's sensationalized version of events. This was her family he was talking about. The thought of what would come over the next weeks and months filled her with dread.

She still couldn't bring herself to believe Sabrina had cheated on her husband. If Jett's theory was correct, the discovery of her perfidy led directly to her death. No, it couldn't have happened that way. Though Jett was a trained professional, she knew her sister better than she knew herself. There was no way Sabrina had gotten pregnant by her ex-boyfriend and then passed off the baby as Franklin's. Dani didn't care what the lab results showed.

Results could be falsified. Sometimes, the pathologist simply got it wrong, without any malice or premeditation involved. Just simple human error. It didn't happen often, but it happened enough that it was a possibility and one she now clung to with a vengeance. She needed to repeat the testing and ascertain for herself. Then, and only then, would she believe the results.

The idea took hold and grew wings. She jumped up off the couch. A surge of adrenalin poured through her veins. It was after five. Her lab would be closed, but that wouldn't deter her. Franklin had just been arrested. He'd be caught up at the police station for hours. She had plenty of time to get over to his place and source items that contained his and Marnie's DNA.

Fortunately, she still had a key, as well as after-hours' access to her place of work. She set her jaw with determination. She refused to see another day go by without knowing the absolute truth.

With her mind made up, she collected her handbag and car keys and locked the front door behind her. She thought briefly of Jett and wondered if she should call him, but then dismissed the thought. He'd be busy booking Franklin. Besides, she was the one who refused to believe her sister was a cheat. She needed to do this on her own. For her sake, and for Sabrina.

CHAPTER 16

Dear Diary,

Everywhere I turn, I see you. In your choice of cushions, the bed linens, the cheerful flowers in their pots. I can still hear the sound of your laughter. I know that if I just turn around, you'll be there with sweet baby Marnie chattering in your arms.

And then my dreams turn into a nightmare and all I can hear are your screams. There is blood everywhere. It stains everything I see, everything I feel, everything I touch...

I wake up cold...and remember. You are gone. Buried in the dark, damp ground. Far away from the home you decorated with such pride, the home you loved.

The police have arrested your husband. They are certain they have their man. It breaks my heart to think it might be true. Franklin loved you almost as much as I did.

How could it have come to this? How could he have felt such rage? To take your life and the life of your beautiful baby? Why? Why? Why?

Even if—God forbid—you were unfaithful, you didn't deserve to die. My perfect, beautiful angel.
Now you're gone forever... All I can do is cry...

Dani rode the elevator up to the penthouse, grateful that she was alone. No doubt the security cameras recorded her entrance, but she didn't care about that. Sabrina had given her a key to the condominium. Franklin was well aware. She wasn't exactly trespassing. After all, he hadn't asked for it back.

The *ding* of the elevator as she reached her destination made her jump. With a quick breath, she stepped out into the corridor and darted a glance right and left. *Nobody.* Her shoulders relaxed a little. *Good. It was time to get to work.*

She let herself in. The house was a mess. The police must have been looking for evidence. They hadn't taken the time to clean up after themselves. Papers and cushions were strewn over the floor. Drawers were left half open. With her lips compressed, she moved through the quiet rooms, her heart beating double time.

It wasn't that she was fearful of being discovered, more that without the presence of Sabrina—or even Franklin—it just didn't feel right to be there. But she needed DNA samples and there was only one way to get them. Ignoring the disorder and with renewed determination, she drew in a breath, squared her shoulders and entered Marnie's bedroom.

The cot stood where it always had, but the mattress was now stripped bare. Dani guessed the bedclothes had been taken by the police as evidence, soaked with her niece's blood. She shuddered and wondered how Franklin could bear to stay there. He'd be reminded every time he turned around of what had happened in these rooms...

Moving further inside, she walked over to an antique dresser that Sabrina had found in a little shop in Paddington. Dani had been with her the day she'd bought it. On the dresser, she spied a baby's silver-backed hairbrush and next to it, a matching comb. Her heart clenched. She'd given the set to Marnie as a christening gift.

Dani's fingers closed around the brush and she lifted it and turned it over. Fine strands of silken hair, golden like her mother's, were caught in the soft bristles. Dani's hand shook as she dropped the brush into her handbag and then hurried from the room.

Keeping her head down, she strode down the carpeted corridor to the bedroom her sister had shared with Franklin. The bed was neatly made and no discarded clothing lay on the floor. A book lay on the nightstand on Sabrina's side of the bed and Dani found herself drawn to it.

She looked down at the cover and her heart clenched. It was an historical romance by Jude Devereaux. Dani recognized the cover, depicting a beautiful buxom woman being embraced by a handsome Duke. Sabrina had always dreamed of her knight in shining armor and even after she was married, she still loved to get lost in the pages of a romance novel.

Dani had only ever admitted to her sister that she liked to indulge in romance novels, too. Despite her troubled and misguided youth, like her younger sister, she still dreamed of true love and happily ever afters. And then she couldn't help but think how Sabrina had found her prince and yet, her life had ended in a tragedy too sad to bear. *Where had true love gotten her sister?*

No, Franklin's actions weren't about love, if indeed, Franklin had committed the monstrous acts. They weren't called crimes of passion for nothing. What happened in this condominium had nothing to do with love. It was all about anger and resentment and jealousy and control. There had been no love present when Sabrina was stabbed thirty-seven times and then suffered the final indignity of having her throat slashed and there'd been no love when the killer stood over baby Marnie and took her life.

The sad thoughts weighed Dani down and as she made her way across the generous room with the gorgeous views of the harbour, her feet felt like they were dragging concrete pylons. She went into the bathroom that was situated off Sabrina and Franklin's room. A couple of toothbrushes stood in a glass near the sink. She didn't know which one was Franklin's but it didn't matter. If necessary, she'd test them both.

Working quickly now, she collected the

toothbrushes and placed them inside a Ziploc bag in an effort to preserve any genetic material. She spied a man's hairbrush on the vanity and for good measure, it followed the way of the toothbrushes, into her handbag.

She glanced at her watch and noted the time. She'd been in the condominium for less than fifteen minutes. Plenty of time to escape before Franklin was released. No doubt a prominent citizen like him, and a successful lawyer to boot, would make bail. That was why she'd come over right away, while there was still time.

Striding back the way she'd come, she peeked through the security hole in the front door and checked to see if there was anyone around. Satisfied no one was there, she quietly let herself out and headed straight for the elevator.

———

Hours later, she rolled her shoulders in an effort to relax the tension and stared at her computer screen in disbelief. With fingers that trembled and a mind still in shock, she dialed Jett's number, relieved when he answered.

"We have to talk," she croaked. That was all she could manage.

———

"The lab results were wrong."

Jett frowned in confusion and stared at Dani where she stood across from him on the other side of the room. He leaned against the opening that led into a tiny kitchen. Despite the late hour and the trying day, he'd hurried over to her bedsit the moment she called. She'd sounded stricken on the phone, but had refused to tell him why. His heart had been beating like he'd run a marathon ever since he'd taken her call.

"Honey, I thought we'd already been over this," he said quietly, keeping his tone mild. It had been a long day and he was ready for bed, but he saw that Dani needed him. Swallowing a sigh, he tried again.

"I understand how difficult it must be for you to accept Sabrina wasn't a saint. She was fallible, just like the rest of us." He shrugged. "She had an affair and got pregnant. It happens. It doesn't make her a bad person. We all make decisions we might live to regret. You know that better than most. It's life. It's just the way it is."

Dani's expression turned mutinous and she marched toward him with anger in her eyes.

"No, Jett. You don't understand. This was *Sabrina*. She didn't do that kind of thing. She'd never hurt someone that way. And now I have proof."

He frowned again. "What are you talking about?"

"I repeated the paternity tests. I got a profile of Franklin's and Marnie's DNA. He's her father, Jett. There's no doubt about it. The other lab made a mistake."

Her words registered in his brain and he gasped aloud at the implications. "They made a *mistake?* Are you *sure?*"

She moved even closer and crossed her arms over her chest. She glared at him. "Yes, of course I'm sure. I know how to run a DNA test. Marnie was Franklin's daughter. Only... Only, he didn't know it. The other lab sent him the wrong results."

All of a sudden, the anger went out of her and she seemed to crumple before his eyes. His head was still in a spin at her announcement, but without hesitation he stepped forward and took her in his arms. With tears glinting in her eyes, she looked up at him. Her voice broke on a sob.

"He-he killed them and it was all a *mistake!* Sabrina hadn't been unfaithful to him at all. He killed them for no reason. No good reason at all."

Her sobs turned into howls of anguish and he drew her up against him, holding her through her pain. Her hair had come loose and fell around her shoulders. He stroked it with a gentle hand. She opened her eyes and stared up at him and then stood on her tiptoes and kissed him.

A lightning bolt of electricity went through him at the feel of her soft lips on his. His heartbeat leaped into overdrive, but he wasn't sure she was in the right state of mind for this. He loosened his arms about her and tried to set her away, but she would have none of it.

"I want you, Jett. Please, kiss me, love me. For just a little while, I need to forget."

She reached for him again and he groaned in

an agony of indecision. He wanted nothing more but to give her the solace she craved. His body was hard with desire and need. *But what about his decision to remain a virgin until he married? Did that mean nothing when faced with making love to the woman in his arms?*

He was already well on the way to falling in love with her, but he didn't know how she felt. She wanted him, that much was clear, but she'd wanted plenty of guys. Was it different for her when she was with him, like it was when he was with her? Or was that just wishful thinking?

She didn't know about his vow of celibacy, of wanting to save himself for marriage. If he rejected her now, she might think he didn't want her at all and that couldn't be further from the truth. She was hurting so badly. She needed the escape he could give her, if only he was willing. The thoughts spun around inside his head until he didn't know which way to turn.

Gradually, her kisses became less frantic until finally, she pulled away. She stared up at him, her expression filled with confusion.

"What's the matter, Jett? Don't you want me anymore?"

She spoke the words in a tiny voice and wouldn't look him in the eye. His heart broke.

"Of course I want you," he said softly and tried to take her back in his arms. But she moved away.

"No, there's something wrong. I can feel it. One moment, you were there with me, consumed by the same fire, and the next, you were gone, withdrawing..." She shook her head. "I don't know where. Something happened to change your mind and I want to know what it was. Is it me? Are you remembering all the other men who've gone before? Is that the problem? Am I not good enough for you?"

"*No!*" he cried, tortured. "It has nothing to do with you. You're good and kind and beautiful. You're everything I could ever want."

She stared at him, bewildered. "Then what? What just happened, Jett? And don't you dare tell me it was nothing."

He stared back at her for a long moment and at last, breathed out on a heavy sigh. His shoulders slumped. He had to tell her. It wasn't fair to keep her in the dark. Taking her hand, he tugged her in the direction of the sofa. With reluctance dogging her every step, she followed.

Dani perched on one end of her faux leather couch, as far away from Jett as possible. As if she hadn't already suffered enough blows today. Now the man she was falling for didn't feel the same way. She thought she'd read the signs correctly. She thought he was as into her as she was into him; that amidst the turmoil and tragedy of the double murder investigation, somehow, they'd found each other.

But he'd withdrawn from her right when things were hotting up and his attitude had most certainly cooled. What else was she to think? She'd as good as begged him to make love to her and he'd all but turned her down.

He threw her a look of helplessness, like he didn't know what to say. She braced herself for his rejection and then decided to spare him the trouble.

"Don't worry about it, Jett. Save your awkward explanation. I get it. You like me a little, but not enough. Now that the investigation's winding down, let's just shake hands and agree to be friends. We need never run into each other again." She risked a glance in his direction. "What do you think? Does that sound all right to you?"

The helpless expression on his face was quickly replaced by a scowl. "No, it isn't all right with me," he retorted. "I'm not sure where you got the idea I don't like you enough, but you're way off base. The problem is, I like you too much."

She stared at him and her pulse picked up its pace. *Could she have been mistaken?* But then what the hell were the last few moments about? Earlier, at the oval, he'd matched her kiss for kiss. Now, he couldn't have appeared less interested. And yet, he said he liked her—too much, in fact.

Anger stirred in her belly. She was too old for stupid games. She'd worked hard to get where she was and she was damned if she'd let a man interfere with the reasonably stable mental status she'd managed to achieve.

"What the hell's that supposed to mean?" she

demanded, her tone probably a little harsher than she intended.

His gaze remained steady on hers. "I'm sorry, Dani. I'm not explaining myself very well," he said quietly. "I... I don't know how to say this. I—"

"Don't you *dare* tell me you're gay," she interrupted, glaring at him. "Because I flat out won't believe it. I felt every hard inch of you back at the oval. I *know* you were turned on as much as me. I—"

"I'm not gay. I like women fine enough. It's just that...I was raised in a loving Catholic family with parents who practiced their faith. I grew up believing it was a sin to have sex before I was married. Then, later, as I grew older, I realized what a special, beautiful gift it was and I wanted to save myself for marriage."

She stared at him without speaking, her mouth gaping open. If he'd told her he'd been born a woman, she couldn't have been more shocked. "You're... You're a *virgin?*"

"You don't have to sound so surprised," he replied, his voice dry.

She blushed, a little embarrassed, but how the hell was she to know? He looked close enough to her age. He must be nearly thirty. As far as she knew, thirty-year-old virgins were only the stuff of corny Hollywood comedies. She had no idea there were still men out there who felt the way he did. It was...sweet and refreshing and...oh so sexy.

A rush of feeling surged through her and her heart filled with tenderness and love. *Love?* Did she love him? She was suddenly sure that if she didn't already, it wasn't far away.

He was the kind of man she'd dreamed of, like the heroes that had filled her romance novels. The duke, or prince or knight who always managed to win the fair maiden's heart. But if he were a prince, where did that leave her? She was far from the innocent girl. He was aware of her past and he said that didn't matter to him, but what if later, it did? He was a virgin and she'd slept with more men than she could count. How would it ever work between them? Was there any point in even trying?

"Say something, Dani," he said quietly. "I'm dying over here. Does my virginity matter to you? Do you think I'm weird?"

Despite her misgivings, she scooted along the couch to reassure him. Her bare leg brushed against his. She reached for his hand and pressed it between both of hers.

"Of course it matters! But in a good way. I've never known a man who was a virgin. I'm intrigued and...incredibly turned on. Which doesn't help either of us, seeing as you're saving yourself for marriage. But you're into kissing, right? We were kissing earlier today."

His eyes flared with emotion and he stared at her with desire flooding his face. "Oh, yes, we were kissing all right and it felt...amazing."

Her hand stole up his thigh and then moved across to the bulge that filled his suit pants. She squeezed the firm flesh and was rewarded with a sharp intake of breath.

"So, kissing's okay," she murmured, hitching up her skirt so that she could straddle his lap. "What else are we allowed to do?"

Bending her head, her lips glanced off his and then returned to taste him over and over again. He groaned and encircled her hips with his hands, pressing her against his erection.

She sucked on the soft skin of his earlobe and then flicked her tongue inside his ear. His hold on her tightened and she smiled.

"Do you like that?" she murmured and laved him again with her tongue.

"Yes," he growled. "Do it again."

She complied with his order, rocking back and forth in his lap, loving the feel of the hard evidence of his desire against her butt. Emboldened, she loosened his tie and tossed it to the floor. Releasing the buttons on his shirt, she slipped her hands inside, gratified when she came in contact with his bare skin.

Chest hair tickled her fingers. She splayed her hands wide and caressed the flat planes of his pectorals. Firm and well-muscled, she yearned to see them finally bared to her gaze.

As if reading her thoughts, Jett tugged off his shirt and it went the same way as his tie. She stared at his broad chest and need burned deep inside. He was bronzed and perfectly proportioned, with dark chest hair shadowing his pecs. She buried her fingers in it and was surprised to find it was as soft as goose down. Her hands moved further apart. Her fingers grazed his nipples.

She smiled at the sound of his indrawn breath, pleased that he was enjoying her attention. He might be determined to remain a virgin, but she was going to do all she could to drive him wild and let him know just what he was missing.

CHAPTER 17

With her gaze locked on his, Dani slid off Jett's lap and knelt on the carpet between his legs. She reached for his belt. His eyes flared with heat and excitement and blood raced to her core. Her nipples tightened in response and her clit ached. She needed to be touched. But this wasn't about her. No, tonight would be all about him.

Tugging the belt out of his pants, she undid the button and slid down his zipper. Stealing inside his cotton boxers, her fingers closed around his warm, silky erection. She squeezed the firm flesh and his breath hissed. She stared up at him.

The desire that glinted in his heavy-lidded gaze sent another wave of need surging through her. Never had she touched a man so intimately without being fondled in return. Having the focus so squarely on him only highlighted the exquisite sensations that coursed through her and filled her with wanton need. She thrust the torturous thoughts away and took him in her mouth.

Her lips stretched wide around his erection. She sucked him in as deep as he could go. He made a low sound in the back of his throat and she glanced up. He lay back against the couch, his eyes closed, his face tense.

She wondered if this was the first time he'd had oral sex and all of a sudden, she wanted to know.

"Has anyone done this to you before?" she murmured.

He opened his eyes and she was stunned at the level of heat that burned from his gaze. "No," he rasped. "I've never been with anyone I wanted to do this with before."

A sense of power and exhilaration rose within her at the knowledge she was his first. It was a heady feeling and she vowed to make the experience something he'd never forget. Bending over his engorged cock, she renewed her efforts with her lips. Her tongue also joined in, swiping around the rim of his head and pausing to dip into his shallow slit. He groaned and thrust his hips toward her and she sucked him as hard as she could. With one hand, she reached down to cup his balls and fondle their taut weight. Her other hand stroked the length of his erection, keeping up the rhythm of her mouth.

"Dani, you're killing me!" he groaned. She merely smiled in satisfaction and increased her efforts.

His breath came faster, harsh in the stillness. He reached down and clasped her head between his hands, holding her in place. His hips bucked off the couch, his efforts becoming more frantic. His cock thrust hard. She kept her lips tightened around him.

"Oh, Jesus, Dani. I'm gonna come." He loosened his hold and tried to pull away, but she didn't release him.

"No, I want to suck you to the end," she told him and then followed through.

He groaned again and his hips moved faster. Her hand tightened around his cock. A moment later, he gave a triumphant yelp and rocked and shuddered against her.

Warm jets of fluid filled her mouth and she sucked and swallowed until it was over. Panting hard, he collapsed against the sofa. A moment later, he opened his eyes and stared at her in wonder.

"That was..." He shook his head. "Amazing? Unbelievable? The most incredible thing I've ever experienced. I can't find the words to describe it."

She smiled and was filled with warm satisfaction. Never before had she cared how her partners felt about her performance. It was all about finding a few moments of mutual, mindless pleasure and an escape from her troubles.

But with Jett, it was different. She was falling in love with him and that made all the difference. He wasn't just a nameless stranger she'd picked up in a bar. He wasn't someone she had no desire or inclination to ever see again. She wanted to get to know him better. She wanted more than just a few moments of physical pleasure. The truth was, she wanted to be part of his life.

But what if he didn't feel the same way? He liked her well enough and he'd certainly enjoyed their lovemaking, but was that as far as things went? Could he see her as something more? She didn't have any answers and the not knowing how he felt and where she stood was killing her.

Jett stared at her and his forehead creased into a frown. A hank of hair had fallen into his eyes and he brushed it away. "What's the matter, Dani? Did I say something wrong?"

She pressed her lips into a thin line, guessing that he'd seen something of her turmoil in her face. She wanted to reassure him, but she didn't know what to say. It was their first time together— way too soon to be talking about a future and yet the very thought of sharing a future with him, all but consumed her now.

And then, he sat forward and with his hands around her waist, lifted her to her feet and settled her in his lap. His eyes were a dark cobalt, deep and fathomless. His head lowered and her heart skipped a beat.

With a gentle hand, he cupped her cheek and kissed her softly, tenderly, taking his time to discover the shape and feel of her mouth. He kissed her like she mattered and the knowledge brought tears to her eyes.

Without pause, he kissed her closed eyelids and then kissed his way down her face. Her nose, her cheeks, her earlobe and then he nuzzled the side of her neck. Fire trailed in a sizzling path behind his heated mouth. Her hands clutched at his shoulders, at the soft warmth of his bare skin. Her heart pounded a rapid staccato in her chest and a pulse beat frantically in her neck. And still he kissed her.

Releasing his hold on her head, he reached out with fingers that trembled and released the buttons of her blouse. One by one, they opened to reveal another patch of creamy flesh until at last, he spread her top open and exposed her to his gaze.

She wore a white lacy bra beneath her pale blouse and her E cup was overflowing. His eyes flared. He stared like he couldn't look away.

She made a move to cover herself, becoming embarrassed under his prolonged steady and silent gaze, but he made a sound in the back of his throat and reached out and stayed her hands.

"Please," he whispered, his voice hoarse. "Please, let me look at you. I've never seen anything more beautiful."

She blushed under his praise and her tension eased. She was happy to let him look his fill. Men had always been fascinated by her breasts, but she'd never before cared much what they thought. They were her breasts, larger than most, but nothing very special. It had never mattered that men thought differently.

But with Jett, she cared a great deal what he thought, just like she cared how she made him feel. Being half in love with the man she was being intimate with, put everything in a completely different dimension. The feelings were new and confusing. She wasn't sure what to do. All she knew was that she wanted more of it.

Intimacy had never felt so good.

Jett reached out an unsteady hand and traced a hesitant path across Dani's breasts. He could feel the beat of her heart beneath his fingers, even through the lace of her bra. Though he'd been to second base before with other girls, those occasions hadn't been often and he'd never been there with someone he cared about as much as he cared about Dani.

Every inch of her was gorgeous, from her beautiful green eyes and wide, lush mouth, to her long, lithe body and bountiful breasts. His fingers continued their gentle exploration, down her breastbone, across her rib cage and then lower to skim over her concave belly. She drew in a quick breath, her stomach muscles tensing. He was filled with wonder that this exquisite creature was there with him, on his lap, responding to his touch.

"You're so beautiful," he said again and her eyes flared bright with desire.

He reached up and filled his hand with one of her breasts, scraping her nipple with his fingers. Her mouth parted on an indrawn breath and a surge of excitement went through him. He was far from the first man to touch her, but somehow, right here and now, she made him feel like he was.

He filled his palm to overflowing with her other

breast and at the same time, leaned forward and buried his face against the softness of her neck. He breathed in her exotic scent. She smelled of spice and vanilla, sweet and heady. It filled his senses and he breathed in deeply again. He wanted more.

He cupped the back of her head and tilted her mouth to his. He kissed her, softly at first, but within seconds, the kiss turned passionate. With increasing haste and pressure, he continued kissing her, moving his mouth more frantically over hers. His tongue pressed against her lips, seeking entrance and he groaned when she welcomed him inside.

Her arms came around him and drew his head close. They kissed until he felt like he was going to explode. He'd just enjoyed a mind-blowing orgasm, but his cock was once again rock hard.

He moved her against his erection, pressing her into his lap. She wiggled her butt and he bit back another groan, drawing on all his strength to detach his frenzied thoughts and concentrate on the woman in his arms.

He wanted to love her as she'd loved him, selfless and complete. He wanted to bring her to the edge of reason and watch her topple over the other side. He'd never given oral sex and was making up the moves as he went, but he knew with every fiber of his being that he wanted to share this incredible first moment of his with her.

Reaching behind her, he undid the clasp of her bra. Her breasts sprang free, so large and perfectly round. Her nipples were colored a soft, dusky pink and were as beautiful as the rest of her. Unable to help himself, he lowered his head and took one of the puckered buds into his mouth.

Dani gasped. She cradled his head, pressing him to her. He obliged by sucking her nipple deeper into his mouth and swiping across the pebbled surface with his tongue.

She moaned with desire and tightened her hold. Need burned through him and once again centered in his cock. He moved his attention to the other breast and gave it the same attention. By the time he was finished, she moved restlessly in his lap.

Taking his hand, she brought it up to her lips and kissed his fingers, staring at him all the while. Then she brought his hand between her legs and pressed it against her mound. He could feel the heat of her through her panties and almost climaxed again.

She removed her hand and he continued to fondle her through the silky fabric. Staring at him with eyes that were dark with desire, she ground herself against his fingers. It was the most erotic moment of his life.

He yearned to see her naked and with a sudden surge of impatience, he moved her off his lap and lowered her to the couch. Sliding to his knees on the floor, he undid the button and zipper of her short skirt and slid it down over her hips. He reached for the brief scrap of fabric that passed as her panties and sent it the way of her skirt. At last, she was naked.

His gaze started at the riot of curls that framed

her beautiful face. Her eyes were wide and shadowed, desire and anticipation in their dark green depths. He moved lower and paused on her breasts, heavy and round and perfect. Still lower, he skimmed over her flat belly and at last, rested his gaze on her mound. He couldn't wait to taste her.

Grasping hold of her thighs, he pulled her closer to his waiting mouth. His tongue swiped from top to bottom and then back up again. Increasing the pressure, he continued to stroke her with his tongue. She tasted like warm, sweet honey. She tasted like heaven.

She moved against him, her fingers tangled in his hair. Holding his head in place, he took her cue and increased his efforts. He opened her up with his fingers and delved into her moist warmth with his tongue. She groaned and her hold on his head tightened. His fingers replaced his mouth and stroked her in and out. His tongue caressed her lips in time with the rhythm of his fingers. She groaned and rocked her hips against his hand.

"Oh, Jett, that feels so good," she gasped and he kept up the rhythmic pressure.

Her cries of pleasure grew louder and were interspersed with breathy gasps. And then she was pulling on his hair until it hurt, begging for him not to stop. His fingers pumped faster and his tongue kept up the frantic pace until at last she cried out and shuddered. Her muscles clenched around his fingers.

His cock throbbed almost painfully and his balls were once again heavy and full. Now that she'd reached her orgasm, he was desperate to relieve the pressure. His cock stood hard and erect. It poked out of the elastic of his boxers. Dani half sat up and stared down at him. Her eyes widened at the sight of his erection. Seemingly oblivious to her nakedness, she tucked her legs beneath her and moved across on the couch, beckoning to him.

Needing no further encouragement, Jett stood and shucked off his pants and underwear before joining her on the sofa. If ever he was tempted to break his self-imposed ban on making love, it was now. He wanted nothing more than to bury himself in her moistness and lose himself in her heat.

She lay back down on the couch and he positioned himself between her open legs. With the taste of her still on his lips, he burned with the need to have her. His cock pressed against her entrance. Any moment, he'd be inside her, surrounded by her wetness, encompassed by her warmth.

But she moved slightly and dislodged him and pulled him up until he was lying prone on top of her. His cock pressed against her stomach, still hard and throbbing with need.

"I think we should wait," she whispered and the tension went out of him.

He slumped against her and blew the air out of his lungs on a sigh. "Really?" he panted against the soft sweetness of her hair, his heart still beating fast.

"Yes. You've waited so long. There's no need to

rush things." She offered him a lopsided smile. "I don't want you to regret it in the morning."

He lifted his head and opened his mouth to protest. He loved her. He wanted her to be his first. But she reached up and pressed her fingers against his lips.

"*Shh,*" she whispered. "Trust me. I know about these things. What you have is special. It's worth waiting for."

With another sigh, he slumped back against her and then lifted his weight off her and rolled onto his side. He took her with him and they lay there, skin to skin, heart to heart. She felt so good beside him, in his arms, pressed against him. He never wanted to leave her side.

CHAPTER 18

For a long time afterward, Dani lay in the stillness with Jett. The night folded in around them. His breathing was slow and deep. Light from a streetlight outside the front room window seeped through the open curtains, breaking through the dimness.

She thought of Sabrina and Marnie and Franklin and was filled with a wave of sadness. Jett had shared his suspicions about Franklin with her and she'd watched the arrest on the news, but she hadn't heard any details. All of a sudden, she needed to know what had happened.

"Are you still awake?" she whispered into the dark.

A second passed. Two. And then he answered. "Yes."

"Did Franklin kill my sister and niece?"

There was another moment of silence and then he replied. "We talked about this already, Dani. Franklin was arrested this afternoon."

"Yes, but did he kill my sister?" she insisted.

Jett sighed heavily and turned around to face her. "Do you really want to know?"

A block of cold concrete weighed down her stomach. Her limbs felt too heavy to move, but she held his gaze in the dimness and nodded.

"Yes, Dani. I think Franklin murdered your niece and sister."

Though she'd come to the same conclusion, his stark words broke her heart in two. "Do you think it had something to do with the lab test?" she asked in a small voice.

Jett sighed again and pulled her into his arms. She rested her head on his chest, loving the feeling of safety and security she found there.

"There's no way of knowing for sure," he replied heavily, "but your brother-in-law said he hadn't opened the results, and yet it's clear from the crime scene photos he had. The fact that he lied not only about it, but also the lab that had done the testing, makes me think those results certainly factored in."

Tears burned Dani's eyes. Her chest felt tight. "I still can't believe it!" she choked out. "His reasons for killing her were based on an error. Sabrina *wasn't* unfaithful. She loved him far more than he deserved. She was good and kind and wonderful. She was an angel. Why would God punish her like this?"

The tears slid down her cheeks. "Why not *me?*" she cried on a sob. "*I'm* the one who lived the life of a sinner. If anyone deserved to be punished, it was *me*."

"No, Dani! No!" Jett replied, tightening his arms around her. "Please don't talk like that."

"It's true," she sobbed. "I grew up in a household where my parents were drunken bullies. I couldn't wait to leave. But I sought out the wrong kind of attention and I enjoyed it! I enjoyed it because all of a sudden, the attention was on *me*! I craved the feeling of being wanted, even for just a little while. For those few minutes in the dark, I was the center of someone's universe."

She gulped and sobbed harder. Jett stroked her back and murmured words of comfort, but Dani needed to get it out.

"My behavior was wrong on so many levels. I knew it then and I know it now. You're a Catholic. You know it, too. It was completely amoral, against every principle you were raised with. I'm not making any excuses, but that's why it's so hard to accept Sabrina was the one who was taken!"

"Don't be so hard on yourself, Dani. We're all sinners. Not one of us can claim to be any different."

Dani sighed heavily. With an effort, she got herself back under control. "Let's just agree my family's a stuff-up. Why don't you tell me about yours?"

Jett turned his head and looked at her. He cocked an eyebrow. "There's nothing special about my family."

"Of course there is," she replied with a mock frown. "Your mom and dad are still together, right?"

"Yes," Jett replied.

"And you have brothers and sisters who love each other?"

"Three brothers and two sisters. And I guess we get on most of the time."

"And I'm betting none of you are drunks or drug addicts or murderers. Am I right?"

"Yes," he conceded with a brief smile. "I guess you're right."

"See! I told you your family was special! How many families these days can answer all of those questions in the affirmative?"

He looked thoughtful and eventually nodded. "I see what you mean. I guess I've never thought of my family as anything unusual. We're just the Craigdons. Mom, Dad and six kids. We were a bit of an anomaly growing up in the beachside suburb of Maroubra, because there were so many of us, but other than that, we got on with life like everyone else."

She stared at him, her heart filling with yearning. "No, Jett. Not everyone else got on with life. Some of us came home to parents too drunk to get out of their own way. I never saw either of my parents go out to work. I bet yours went out every day, or at least, your dad."

Jett's expression turned serious. "Yes, you're right. Dad was an accountant for a local firm. He eventually made partner. Mom was a secretary. In fact, they met at the accounting firm when they were both in their twenties. Dad was fresh out of college. Mom was answering the phones. She eventually worked herself into the position of office manager. They both retired a couple years ago."

Dani stared at him and was filled with sadness

for the parents she'd never had. Oh, they'd provided for their children in a physical sense, with a patched-up roof over their heads and food mostly on the table, but their efforts at parenthood had hauled up short. No effort had been made to see to their daughters' emotional needs. Dani marveled how Sabrina had been able to rise above the poverty and disregard and become the person she'd become. Dani hadn't been so strong. At least, not back then.

"Tell me more," she murmured, squeezing his arm.

Jett raised an eyebrow. "It's not exactly thrilling storytelling. Are you sure you want to hear this?"

Dani held his gaze and simply said, "Yes. I am."

Jett heaved an exaggerated sigh. "Okay, you asked for it. I'm the oldest. Then comes my brother, Callum. He started out in the police force, but somewhere along the line, he felt called in another direction. He's now training to become a priest."

Dani was flooded with surprise. Jett had already told her he'd been raised in the Catholic faith, but she had no idea the devotion went as far as that. She didn't know of anyone who entered the priesthood these days.

Jett noticed her response and grinned. "Yes, it was a surprise to all of us. Callum's probably the best looking of us all. He was always surrounded by girls in high school. Anyway, a few years ago, he decided he'd been called to a life of Christ."

"Is he ordained?" Dani asked.

"No, he hasn't gotten that far through yet. It

usually takes seven years to become a priest. He has a degree in theology from the Australian Catholic University and entered the seminary twelve months ago."

"What if he changes his mind before he finishes?"

Jett shrugged. "Then I guess he changes his mind. It's one of the reasons the training is so rigorous. It's a tough life and I'm sure it can be very lonely. There are a lot of dreams and other things they're giving up: a wife, children; a normal life. The Church wants to make sure they're ready and that they have a clear appreciation for what life as a priest will be like."

"Your parents must be proud," she commented.

"Yes, of course, but then, they're proud of all of us. After Callum, there's Joel. He's twenty-five and is a lawyer. He works in the city. Isabella comes next. She's twenty-three. She went into nursing."

"Does she work at the Sydney Harbour Hospital?" Dani asked.

"No. At the moment, she lives in the country, in Armidale. It's—"

"I know where it is," Dani interrupted dryly.

"Really? Where is it, smarty pants?" Jett challenged, a teasing glint in his eyes.

"It's in the New England area of north west New South Wales."

Jett nodded. "I'm impressed."

"I went to college there," she admitted with a cheeky grin.

"Not in Sydney?" he asked in surprise.

"No," Dani replied as memories of her troubled youth rushed to the fore. She'd needed to get out of her hometown in the outer western suburbs of Sydney, away from the past that could only drag her down.

"I wanted a fresh start. The country sounded like the perfect choice. And it was. I loved my time in Armidale. The warm summers, the crisp winters, the snow that lies on the ground. It's so different from western Sydney."

"Is that where you grew up?" Jett asked quietly.

"Yes. Mount Druitt. A long way from the beaches and chic city feel of Maroubra."

Jett pressed a kiss against her hair. "It doesn't matter where we were born or where we lived as kids. After all, none of us had a choice in that. It's what we choose to do when we're adults that counts and you've done everything you could to turn your life around. That's what matters, Dani. The *only* thing that matters."

With her heart flooding with tenderness and love, she cupped his cheek in her hand and kissed him softly on the lips. "Thank you," she whispered.

His eyes darkened with emotion. "Anytime," he whispered back.

Something indefinable passed between them. It was so charged with emotion, Dani got frightened. Things between them were moving so quickly. She wasn't sure she was ready. She'd been single for so long and entering a relationship with a guy who wanted to remain celibate until he was a married man—the irony wasn't lost on her.

She lowered her gaze and cleared her throat

and the moment between them was gone. She swallowed a surreptitious sigh of relief.

"So, tell me about your other siblings. Another sister and brother, right?"

Jett stared at her a moment longer, his expression inscrutable and then looked away and nodded. "Yes, Nicholas is twenty-two and Sophia's nineteen. The two of them are still at college."

"What are they studying?" she asked, genuinely interested.

"Nick's studying business, although Dad swears he hasn't got a business bone in his body and Soph's doing a Bachelor of Education."

"Where are they?"

"University of New England," Jett replied with a smile.

Dani smiled back at him. "In Armidale. I guess that explains why your other sister lives there."

"Yes, she wanted to get out of Sydney and experience the country life. From all accounts, she loves it. I'm not sure if anything will drag her back."

Silence fell between them. Dani picked up Jett's hand and idly traced swirls across his palm. "You have such a wonderful family," she said quietly.

Jett looked at her, his gaze steady on hers. "Yes, I do."

"You're lucky," she whispered.

"I know that, too," he replied and then added, "I'm sorry about your childhood. No kid should have to grow up like that."

A rush of sadness welled up inside her at the

compassion in his eyes. She blinked back tears. "You're right."

He leaned closer, intent on kissing her, but she turned her face away. A ball of concrete had lodged in her belly. She was overcome with feelings of inadequacy. They came from such different backgrounds and he deserved the very best. His parents were pillars of society. Hers were the scum of the earth. She was unworthy of this kind and wonderful man. He might not see it yet, but over time, he would—and so would his family.

Pushing him away, she struggled to her feet. Bending down to collect her clothes scattered on the floor, she held them to her in an effort to shield her nakedness from his gaze.

"I think you should go," she said quietly, staring at the carpet.

Jett sat up on the couch, a frown marring the smooth skin of his forehead. His face filled with confusion. "What is it, Dani? What did I say?"

She shook her head with increasing vehemence, suddenly determined to make him understand.

"Don't you see? You have the perfect family. A mom and dad, brothers and sisters who love each other and are doing something with their lives. I come from poor white trash. I haven't spoken to my parents in years. I don't even know where they are and I don't want to know! My sister was murdered by her husband. He killed their baby girl!"

She shook her head again, her breath coming fast. "The very thought of the two of us... I don't know what I was thinking! Please, just leave. This thing between us, whatever it is... It's never going to work."

Dani stared at the bottle of scotch that sat on her coffee table, only a few feet away. It beckoned to her in the dark, promising sweet oblivion. Desolation crept into her bones.

The imitation Christmas tree she'd bought on sale weeks earlier remained unopened in the box. The very thought of Christmas made her shudder. Christmas was a time for celebration, a time of sharing with the people you loved. The people dearest to her were gone forever. She had no one. Right now, it felt like she'd never celebrate again.

Jett had left hours ago, concerned about her abrupt change of heart. He'd tried to argue against her, to protest that she had it wrong. It didn't matter to him where she'd come from, or what she'd done. That was the past and it would stay in the past. He wanted to be part of her future. As much as she wanted to believe his words, she knew better.

He was a virgin. He held love and marriage and the special union between husband and wife very dear. She was the antithesis of all that he believed in, and all that his family prized. They'd discover her past and that would be the end of it. They'd shun her. Jett would be forced to choose sides.

She refused to drive a wedge between him and his family.

No, as much as it felt like her heart was breaking, she had to let him go. It was the right and honorable thing to do; the *only* thing to do. The thought sent another surge of tears flooding into her eyes. She sniffled and swiped at them, but they kept coming. Once again, her gaze was drawn to the bottle of scotch.

As soon as Jett had departed, closing the door quietly behind him, she'd thrown on her clothes and picked up her keys. She'd left the house and headed straight for the nearest liquor store. She walked with purpose to the row of whisky bottles glittering in the light and picked up a bottle of Johnnie Walker. She had yet to taste its bite.

It had been so many years since she'd had a drink, but the yearning never quite went away. She still remembered the burn of the alcohol like it was yesterday, the glow of the aftermath, the sleepy, sweet oblivion.

She'd stumbled through her teenage years in a fog of alcohol-induced pleasure. It had been the only way she could survive the neglect she'd suffered at home. Then she finally started listening to her sister and went to an AA meeting. She met Ben—gorgeous Ben—and worked hard to get her life back under control.

She picked up the tumbler she'd collected on her way through the house and stared through the crystal glass. The bottle of whisky looked weird and distorted. With a muffled oath, she set the glass back down and pushed away from the couch and temptation. She looked around for her phone.

Finding it in her handbag, she tugged it out and dialed a number she knew by heart. Despite the late hour, he answered on the second ring.

"Dani? Are you all right?"

"I need you," she choked. "Can you come over?"

Chapter 19

Dear Diary,

I worked so hard to put that life of degradation behind me and now my efforts have been for nought. My world is crashing down around me. My beautiful sister—gone. She was the only person who believed in me, who loved me, faults and all. How can I cope without her? Who will help me bear my shame?

Ben, dear Ben. He's always been there for me, to help me fight the fight. But is it fair to burden him with my troubles? After all, he battles his own demons through the long and lonely nights.

I pray for strength and courage to stand tall, to hold my head high. I have done much to be proud of—and I am. But every now and then, I am reminded of my shortcomings, of the girl I used to be and despite everything—my efforts, my determination to remain clean—I am back there again, amidst the filth and sordidness; I am that no-good poor white trash girl again.

How can I expect anyone to love me, when I cannot love myself?

Dani heard the knock on the door and rushed over to open it. Ben stood on the other side, his face filled with concern. At the sight of him, her courage failed and she threw herself in his arms.

"Ben! Oh, Ben! Thank you for coming."

His arms came around her and he held her close, murmuring words of comfort against her hair. Closing the door behind them, he took off his coat and led her to the couch. Spying the bottle of whisky, he came to a sudden halt.

The heat of shame burned a path across her cheeks. "I-I'm sorry," she stammered. "I… I didn't open it. I swear."

The look he threw her was filled with compassion and understanding and not an ounce of judgement. It brought a fresh bout of tears to her eyes.

"It's all right, Dani," he said gently. "I believe you. I'm so glad you called me when you did."

"I… I didn't know what else to do. It's been so long since I was in this position… Desperate and terrified."

Ben took her hand and squeezed it. "Come on," he said. "Talk to me." Together, they lowered themselves to the couch.

Brushing the tears away, Dani leaned back against the faux leather with a heavy sigh.

"What's going on, Dani?" Ben asked gently. "What brought this on?"

She bit her lip against a surge of pain and sat up straighter, determined to talk it out. She'd phoned Ben so that he could help her. She had to let him do what he did best.

"It's Jett Craigdon," she whispered.

Ben frowned. "The detective?"

"Yes. He was here. We...talked. I... I really like him."

Ben stared at her in surprise. "You mean like, in a romantic way?"

Dani nodded.

"Wow," Ben exclaimed. "How did that happen?"

Dani shrugged and stared at her hands where they were clasped together in her lap. "I don't know. He's physically attractive, of course, but that's not what drew him to me. He's so good and kind and...wonderful. He understands me."

"I thought he was investigating the murder of your sister and niece? I didn't realize the two of you had connected on a deeper level."

"It just kind of...happened," Dani admitted. "It wasn't exactly planned. We met to talk over the case. Things just went from there."

"I saw Franklin's arrest on the news," Ben murmured. "The police think he did it."

A surge of resignation went through her and she bowed her head under the weight of it. "Yes."

In quiet tones, she recounted Jett's theory and what the police had found. And then she told him about the lab test and how she'd repeated it and discovered the truth.

Ben shook his head in shock. His tone reflected his sadness. "What a waste! To think he killed her in a jealous rage and the test result wasn't even true." He looked at Dani. "Have you told him yet?"

She shook her head. "No."

"He was released on bail about fifteen minutes ago. I heard it on the radio on my way over."

Dani absorbed the news without reaction. It didn't come as a surprise. She wondered if he'd gone back to his condominium and guessed that he probably had. *After all, where else would he go?*

"You've had a tough time of things, lately, Dani," Ben said quietly. "Is that the reason for the scotch?"

She looked at the bottle. "Yes. No. What I mean is, I guess it had something to do with the scotch, but tonight was all about Jett. And my past. And the knowledge that I'm falling in love with him. It terrifies me. I don't know what to do."

It was a relief to say it out loud, to share her burden with someone else. Ben regarded her solemnly.

"What is it about falling in love that terrifies you?"

Impatience surged through her and she cast around for the right words, trying to make him understand.

"It isn't the falling in love bit, so much; it's the fact I'm falling in love with *Jett*. He comes from a fine upstanding family. He was raised in the Catholic faith. He's still a virgin, for goodness sake! How can I hope to measure up to that? You know about my family. You know about my past. You helped me drag myself out of it, remember?"

"Of course I remember," Ben replied, his voice annoyingly calm. "Just like I remember how hard you fought to put it all behind you." He turned to her, his eyes bright. "And you have, Dani. You *have*. Nobody could argue with that. If this detective's worth even a fraction of you, he'll see that."

"You don't understand," she argued. "It isn't him I'm concerned about. It's his family. When they find out who I was, what I was, where I came from... They won't want to have anything to do with me, least of all with me dating their son." She lifted her gaze to his and swiped angrily at her tears. "I don't know what to do."

"Have you talked to Jett about it?"

Dani nodded. "He said it didn't matter. That my past was my past. But he's not right. It *will* matter! It will matter to his family and then it will mean something to him. It's only a matter of time. And then it will become this *thing* between us."

"How does he feel about you, Dani? Does he love you?"

She shrugged, uncomfortable. "I'm not sure. Maybe."

"So he hasn't said the words?"

"No, but neither have I."

"Well, whether he loves you or not, he cares for you. Of that I have no doubt."

"What makes you say that?" she asked, curious.

"You said he told you your past doesn't matter. Do you think he was sincere?"

Dani thought about it. "Yes, only he doesn't know what will happen when his family finds out. They don't know me. I'm sure they won't be so quick to discount what I've done, how I lived."

"You're right," Ben agreed, "and a lot of

boyfriends wouldn't be able to discount it. The fact your detective has been able to do it so easily tells me a lot more than words about what kind of a man he is and how much he cares."

Silence fell between them. Dani was lost in her thoughts. *Was she brave enough to take the chance and find out if she and Jett had what it takes to make the distance?*

Ben squeezed her hand and stood. He picked up the bottle of Johnnie Walker and strode across to the small kitchen. He opened the bottle and poured it into the sink until every last drop of whisky had gurgled down the drain. He looked over at Dani.

"You don't need alcohol, Dani. You're so much stronger than that. What you need is to believe in yourself, in the good person you've become. This detective sees your specialness and wants to be part of it. You owe it to yourself to take the risk and see where all this might lead. If his family reject you, then that's their loss. You need to look past that. If Jett Craigdon really loves you, his family's opinion won't matter."

"How can you *say* that?" Dani cried, coming up off the couch. "You don't know him, or how much he adores his family. He has five siblings, for goodness sake! He could tell me the age of every one of them and what they were doing with their lives. He spoke about them with genuine love and respect. His family means *everything* to him."

"And yet, he cares for you and has openly put himself out there. He's a smart man. He must know your past isn't what his parents would necessarily want in a daughter-in-law, but guess what? They're *his* parents. He knows them better than you. It's my guess they'll open their hearts to you, just like he has."

Ben came around the kitchen counter and didn't pull up until they were almost nose to nose. "Are you going to walk away from an opportunity of a lifetime?" he asked. "This man cares for you. He knows about your past. You've told me how good and kind and wonderful he is. Are you prepared to let your fear get in the way of what could be the best thing that ever happened to you?"

Dani stared at him in silence, still struggling with the notion that what Ben said was true. With a muffled oath, Ben ran a hand through his hair and turned away, his frustration evident.

"Do you know what I'd give to find someone who cared for me like that?" he asked, spinning back around to face her. "Someone who knew all my dirty secrets and yet wanted to be with me? You don't know what kind of rare gift you've been given, Dani. Please, don't screw it up."

Dani's jaw dropped open in surprise. She didn't know much about Ben's past. In the early days, when they were getting to know each other, he'd hinted at a family as dysfunctional as hers, but he never seemed inclined to talk about himself and she respected him enough not to pry.

Now, she couldn't help but wonder what had brought him to the point where he found himself on the doorstep of an AA meeting. From the closed look on his face, now wasn't the time to ask if he was ready to share.

Moving toward him, she came to a stop in front of him. In silence, she put her arms around him and hugged him. For an instant, he resisted her efforts to pull him close, but then he relaxed against her. They stood together, each taking comfort from the other, grateful for the support.

A long while later, Ben pulled away. He surreptitiously swiped at his eyes with the back of his hand and then hunted around for his coat.

"It's way past late, Dani. I have to get going. I have court in the morning. I'm the duty lawyer with a list as long as my arm and Judge Bridges waits for no one." He gave her a small smile.

"Thank you for coming, Ben. You don't know how much it means to have your support. Here," she said, collecting his coat from the back of the couch and handing it to him. "Let me walk you out."

Jett tapped the steering wheel of his Jeep with impatience as he waited for the light to change. He'd almost made it back to his apartment, when he decided to turn around. He wasn't prepared to walk out on Dani without talking things through. His parents had raised him not to let the sun go down on an argument and their wisdom now rang true.

It was obvious he and Dani had a connection and he knew she felt it as strongly as he. The way she'd made love to him with her lips and tongue... It was the most magical night of his life. He'd bared his soul to her—his Catholic faith, his set of beliefs that many would have found comical and old fashioned—and yet, she'd accepted them without a qualm; had even encouraged him to uphold them when he'd been sorely tempted to set them aside.

And then the beautiful woman before him, the woman who had captured his heart, turned him away on the grounds she wasn't good enough for him. It was bullshit and he intended to make that clear. He didn't care if she refused to listen. He'd stand outside the door of her bedsit and tell her at the top of his voice. He'd wake the neighbors; he'd upset the dogs; he'd do whatever it took because he was in love with Danielle Porter and she was in love with him. At least, he hoped so.

The traffic light finally turned green and he stepped hard on the gas. The Jeep leaped forward, as if sensing his eagerness. It was now going on eleven, but what did time matter in situations such as these? If he went home and let things be, no doubt she'd be even harder to convince in the morning.

He understood her concerns. They were two people who came from miles apart. Literally and figuratively. He'd been raised in comfort and security near the beach in Sydney's sought-after eastern suburbs. She'd come from the west, with barely a penny to her name and not only poor, but poor in spirit, with parents who didn't deserve the name.

But none of that mattered to him and he knew it wouldn't matter to his family. They were Christians in name and in nature. There was always forgiveness in their hearts. They'd meet Dani and they'd love her as surely as he did and it wouldn't matter about her past. He need only convince her and all would be well.

He turned into her street and his heart leaped in anticipation. Lights still shone in her front windows. Pulling up to the curb outside her house, he switched off the ignition and went to climb out.

Movement snagged his attention. He squinted into the darkness. The silhouettes of a man and a woman were outlined against the porch light of her house. He heard the murmur of voices, of soft laughter and then finally, the couple kissed. Slowly, lovingly, like they were reluctant to part. He stared harder. Something about them was familiar...

And then, with a savage curse, he realized who it was.

Chapter 20

Jett stared with narrow-eyed concentration at his computer screen. The office was filling up with his work colleagues as they arrived for another day. Though many of them swapped casual chit chat and tossed greetings in his direction, he barely mumbled a response.

He'd spent the night fuming over Dani's betrayal and his own gullibility. *How could he have been so stupid? How could he have been so blind?*

She and Ben Fitzgerald. They'd been an item in the past and despite what they said, it was clear they still were. He'd seen them on her front porch, kissing like lovers, doing their best to delay the moment when they had to say good-bye. He was a fool to believe she felt something for him. To think he even thought they were both falling in love. What a joke! They were falling in love all right, just not with each other.

He made a sound of disgust in the back of his throat and pounded harder than necessary on his keyboard. Franklin Cook had made bail. No surprises there. Until the murders, he'd been a fine, upstanding citizen, much admired among his peers and members of Sydney society. He and Sabrina had made a striking couple. It just went to show how much appearances could deceive.

And now he'd been deceived by none other than her sister. It was enough to turn his stomach.

Forcing the thoughts aside, he focused on the computer screen. During the long hours before dawn and in between bouts of anger and self-pity, he'd recalled the threatening letter Cook had received. It seemed so long ago and given what he now believed had happened, it was almost certain the letter was a hoax.

It had to have been written by Cook. With the man now headed for arraignment, Jett wanted to shore up the evidence against him. Another search warrant on the man's condo was the first place to start and securing the warrant had engaged Jett's attention since he'd arrived at work.

Adding the final details, he hit "print" and pushed away from his desk. Collecting the warrant off the printer, he strode to his superior's office and knocked briefly on the door. Detective Superintendent Michael Collins looked up at Jett's approach.

"Jett, good work on that Cook arrest. How are we looking?"

"Thanks, boss. We haven't found the murder weapon yet or the original set of clothes, but we have quite a bit of other circumstantial evidence. I have a few more leads to follow up. There's a threatening letter Cook allegedly received from an anti-Islamic group and a call he says he made to his mistress to conveniently explain a gap in his timeline. I think the letter is a hoax written by Cook to put us off the scent and I'd be surprised if the mistress exists. Don't worry, I'm confident we'll get the murder charges to stick."

"Good. So, what can I do for you?" Collins asked.

"I've prepared another search warrant for Cook's condominium. I need you to authorize it."

Collins gave a brief nod of assent and Jett handed the document over. Collins scrawled his signature where it was needed and handed the warrant back. "What do you think was missed the first time, Detective?"

"A computer or laptop, for starters. One wasn't found the first time we searched, but I'm convinced Cook must own one. If we don't find it this time, the next warrant will be for his office."

"That will be sure to raise the hackles of the fine and mighty lawyers of Harris & Birmingham. Keep me posted, Detective. This case has all the hallmarks of being a media circus. We want to make sure our actions are aboveboard. We don't need any bad press."

"Of course, boss. No problem. Lane and I have it under control."

"Good." Collins returned his attention to the

paperwork spread over his desk and Jett took his leave.

Franklin poured two fingers of scotch into a cut crystal glass and threw the liquor back neat. The alcohol burned his throat and stole his breath, but within moments, the warmth of it steadied his nerves. It was strange, being back in the condo after being released on bail. He'd been arrested on suspicion of a double murder. The media camped outside his building were baying for his blood. How quickly things changed.

He wouldn't have come back if he'd had a choice, but he had nowhere else to go. Though he owned a couple of investment properties in the eastern suburbs, both of them were tenanted. He could have gone to a hotel in the city, but with his face plastered all over the television, it was only a matter of time before he would be recognized. Someone would be sure to tip off the media and his hideout would be discovered. At least, at home he was surrounded by his things and he could spend his time hunkered down in comfort.

Of course, he had a lot more downtime now than he'd anticipated. Edward Birmingham had phoned him that morning. The other partners of his law firm had met. They'd taken a vote. By unanimous decision, they'd agreed it might be best for Franklin to take a leave of absence—at least until the pesky matter of his trial had been resolved. Of course, no one believed he was guilty and of course, the firm would help with the legal fees, but surely he understood? They were a firm with an enviable reputation, a reputation they simply couldn't put at risk...

The bullshit had gone on a little longer and Birmingham had offered commiserations and words of support that sounded completely insincere. Franklin had thanked him politely before ending the call.

He poured another two fingers of scotch and threw himself down on his couch. The harbor sparkled in the morning sunlight. Usually the view lifted his spirits, but today, nothing could lighten his mood.

He still couldn't believe his family was gone. His beautiful Sabrina and sweet baby Marnie—dead. Every time he thought about it, he was stunned all over again. He'd never meant for it to happen. None of it had been planned. After it was over, he'd stared at the carnage in shock.

His wife lay dead in the bath, the water stained bright crimson. More blood than he'd ever seen in his life was sprayed up the walls, the tiles; the door. It was like someone had come in with a garden hose filled with red paint and had turned it on full pelt. His clothes were soaked with it.

And it hadn't stopped there... He'd been bleeding from a cut to his hand where the knife had slipped on one of the downward strokes. He'd applied pressure to it and stopped the flow and then had calmly stood and proceeded down the hall...

Now, memories of his little daughter made his stomach twist and heave. He raced down the corridor and only made it as far as the main bathroom, before bending over the toilet and losing his breakfast in the porcelain bowl.

When the retching was finally over, he sat back on his haunches and looked around. It was the first time he'd stepped inside the bathroom since it happened. Though it had been weeks since the murders and the room was once again sparkling clean, all he could see was the blood. He'd see it until the day he died.

Like the suit he'd been wearing. In fact, all of his clothes from that day had been stained beyond repair. After the stabbings, he'd gazed down at himself in disbelief. He realized he was in trouble and raced to his bedroom to shower and change. Later that night, he'd disposed of the stained clothes in the wood behind the complex. He'd stood over the pile for as long as he dared, careful to watch every last piece of them burn.

When the detective had requested the clothes he'd worn on the day of the murders, it had been a simple matter to retrieve the second set. He'd relied on the fact that the police wouldn't know the difference. After all, he had plenty of suits and one looked much the same as the rest. But now, the clothing gave him pause. He hadn't yet seen any of the evidence against him, but he was concerned he'd made a mistake.

The suit he'd been wearing the day of the murders was a navy-blue. He'd changed into a charcoal-gray number before he'd made the emergency call. He couldn't believe such a little thing as the color of his suit might be the one thing that brought him down. And then, he dismissed the idea as nonsensical. It would take more than one piece of circumstantial evidence to prove his guilt.

The sound of a sharp knock on his door snagged his attention and he frowned. He'd stuck a sign on the front of his door requesting privacy and assuring the media he would call a press conference in the next few days.

But when did the media ever respect anyone's privacy? He'd been kidding himself. Still, he could always sit on his couch and enjoy the view and wait for the unwelcome visitor to give up and go away. They couldn't stay out there forever.

The knock came again and it was followed by the sound of a woman's voice. "Franklin? Are you in there? It's me. Danielle."

Franklin's frown deepened. *Danielle?* Why would she be here? She couldn't possibly have missed the news of his arrest. *Could* she? A sudden surge of optimism rushed through his veins and his heart leaped in hope. Perhaps Dani was still ignorant of yesterday's happenings. Perhaps she was still on his side.

All of a sudden, he wanted to spend whatever time he had left, with her, before she discovered the truth. He'd pretend nothing terrible had ever happened, that his wife and baby were still alive. He'd act like the Franklin of a few weeks ago, before he'd gone crazy with jealousy and hurt. He'd act like they were still part of a family who loved each other.

Pushing away from the couch, he set his glass on the coffee table and then walked a little unsteadily toward the door. He lurched and made a grab for the kitchen counter and took a moment to regain his balance. He wasn't usually much of a drinker. The scotch had gone to his head. He blinked and tried hard to clear his vision and then continued to the door. Fumbling with the security lock, he eventually pulled it open and greeted his sister-in-law with a lop-sided smile.

"Dani! It's good to see you! Come in." Standing back to allow her to enter, he closed the door after her.

"Cut the bullshit, Franklin. This isn't a social call."

The iciness of her tone pulled him up short. His heart skipped a beat. *Perhaps she'd heard about his arrest, after all?* He hurried to assure her of his innocence.

"I'm not sure what you've heard, Dani, but I can tell you, it wasn't me. I loved your sister and my daughter with everything that I was. I would never have harmed them and I won't rest until I find the bastard who did. The police are pinning this on me because it's easy. It's always the husband, right? They can put this case to bed and claim another victory. It's always about their statistics, making their conviction rates look good. They—"

"Shut up, Franklin. Just shut up!"

The sharp command startled him, almost as much as the cold fury in Dani's eyes. "B-but—" he stammered.

She strode back toward him, her eyes

narrowed dangerously. She got up close and personal, crowding his space. He could see the dark flecks in her eyes. He'd never noticed them before...

"For Christ's sake, are you deaf?" she shouted. "I said, shut the fuck up!"

The blasphemy and cursing shocked him to the core. He'd never heard Dani speak like that before. Of course, he knew her history, about the slut she used to be and he assumed she'd picked up some bad habits while she was fraternizing with the bottom dwellers of her town, but in the past he'd never seen any hint of the poor white trash she'd been.

She waved something in front of his face and for the first time, he noticed the piece of paper. He frowned in confusion, at a loss as to what it could be.

"Do you know what this is?" she growled.

He shook his head and attempted a smile. "Of course not. How could I?"

"Do you remember the paternity test?"

Once again, he wondered where this conversation was going. "Yes, of course."

"You received the results the day of the murders, remember? You told the detective and I that they'd arrived at your work and you'd brought them home, unopened. Right?"

Her tone remained icy and her eyes were hard.

"Yes, I remember," he replied more cautiously.

"But you lied, didn't you Franklin?"

He feigned confusion. "Excuse me? I don't understand."

Her smile was feral. "Oh, you understand, all right. Let me tell you what really happened."

She spun on her heel and stalked away, coming to a halt halfway across the room. Behind her, was the plate glass window, framing the perfect view.

"You received those results at work, like you said, only you *did* open them and you read their contents. You discovered you weren't Marnie's biological father and immediately thought of Sabrina's ex-boyfriend and the love letters you'd found."

Surprise shot through him and disquiet stirred in his gut. He had no idea Sabrina had told her sister about their argument over Scott. He forced his expression to remain neutral, unwilling to let her know how much she'd rattled him. There was something about the unnatural look in her eyes that unnerved him.

He laughed in an effort to disarm her, but the sound of it was strained. He didn't want to listen to any more. It was time to see her out.

"Look, Dani," he said, "this is all very fascinating, but I think it's time you left. I have a few things to attend to and I'd rather do it alone."

"Like the way you murdered Sabrina and innocent baby Marnie?" she threw at him, her lip curled up in disgust.

He chuckled again and shook his head. "My, my, my, Dani. You have such an imagination. I see you've been watching too much television."

Instead of pacifying her, his words only raised her fury. She came at him like a banshee, screaming at him about murdering her sister and how it was all for nothing.

"The lab made a mistake!" she shouted. "Sabrina was never unfaithful to you! I redid the test, you worthless bastard! You were Marnie's father, after all!"

Her words stunned him. He stared at her in shock, gaping, speechless, his mind whirring out of control. *What was she saying? The lab results were wrong? He was Marnie's father?* That meant Sabrina hadn't...

"*Nooo!*" The howl of pain was torn from the very bottom of his soul. Horror filled his every nerve and blood cell. He'd stabbed his wife and baby to death...for nothing. She hadn't been unfaithful at all. She'd loved him and only him, like she'd said. And now it was too late...

A rush of helpless anger, so hot and vivid, momentarily blinded him. He'd murdered his wife and daughter based on information that was wrong. The lab had made a mistake so huge, so momentous, it was incomprehensible. The consequences of their error consumed him, the pain of it so great he gasped and wheezed and tears burned a path down his cheeks.

He glared at Sabrina's sister. Her mouth was still moving, her face was contorted with anger, but he could no longer hear what she said. He stumbled toward the kitchen. The only thought in his mind was to inflict pain like it had just been inflicted on him. He spied the knife block where it stood in its usual place. One slot remained empty. Of course it did. He'd taken the missing knife with his bloodstained clothing and burned them in the woods until there was nothing left.

Without conscious thought, his fingers closed around yet another black handle and he tugged the vicious-looking blade free. With a yelp of triumph that almost deafened him, he spun on his heel and brandished the knife in Dani's direction. He couldn't stand to hear another word she said or think for another moment about his despair. The lab test had been wrong. Wrong, wrong, *wrong!*

With a bloodcurdling howl, he lifted the knife high above his head and charged at the woman in front of him.

CHAPTER 21

Jett glanced across at his colleague and then stepped forward and pressed the call button for the elevator that would take them to the Cook family penthouse.

"What are we looking for?" Lane asked.

Jett shrugged. "I'm looking for the murder weapon, which is probably removed already, and a computer. A desktop or laptop—maybe both. The first team that searched didn't find one. I want to make certain. It's either here or at his workplace. It'll be much easier to prove he was behind the threatening letter if it was written from a home computer."

"You think Cook wrote it?"

Jett nodded grimly. "It's the only thing that makes sense."

"Yeah. When you mentioned the letter to Barber, he didn't have a clue what you were talking about and if it had originated from someone in his faction, you would have thought he'd know."

"Coupled with what we already have against

Cook, my money's on finding something on his computer that links him to it."

"How did things go with the mistress?" Lane asked. "Any luck tracking her down?"

"Oh, yeah, I tracked her down all right," Jett said. "I traced the phone number back to a prepaid Telstra account."

Lane's eyebrows rose in surprise. "So, she did exist after all. I must admit, I had my doubts."

Jett laughed without humor. "Oh, yes, she existed. The only thing was, her name wasn't Angel Lockhart."

"Really? Why would Cook lie about something like that?"

"The phone account was held in the name of Sabrina Cook. That's why the bastard lied. He gave us his wife's phone number."

"For Christ's sake!" Lane cursed, incredulous. "What kind of sick fuck does something like that?"

Jett glanced at his partner. "I think he panicked. He knew we'd found a discrepancy in his story. The timeline didn't fit. He gave us the first number that came to mind. Besides, he knew darn well Sabrina wouldn't be answering it. It was a pretty smart move, when you think about it."

Lane was still shaking his head back and forth when the elevator arrived. Both men stepped in and Jett reached over to press the button for the top floor. The search warrant was in his top pocket. He wasn't sure if Franklin was home, but judging by the number of reporters and cameramen camped out on the doorstep of the building, the likelihood was fairly high.

The elevator came to a stop and the steel doors slid silently open on well-oiled hydraulics. The corridor was bare. Jett strode over to the door that led to the only residence on the top floor. Lane followed closely behind him.

Jett lifted his hand to knock on the door in order to announce their presence. Cook wasn't legally entitled to refuse them entry, but it was a courtesy extended just the same. The sound of shouting from behind the door stayed his hand. He motioned to Lane to come closer and to keep quiet.

The two of them put their ears to the door and this time, there was no doubt. A woman and a man were arguing. They couldn't catch the words, but the conflict was clear. Anger reverberated behind the closed panel.

Jett glanced at Lane and together, they silently debated whether to interrupt or to stay quiet and see what they could find out, but a moment later, a blood curdling howl ripped from deep inside the man's throat was followed by the woman's ear-piercing scream.

Without hesitation, Jett turned the doorknob, expecting it to be locked. To his surprise, it turned easily beneath his hand and he and Lane shoulder-barged their way in. It only took seconds for Jett to take in the scene: Franklin hurtled toward Dani with a wicked-looking knife; Dani, her eyes wide with shock, screamed in terror. Jett's heart leaped into his throat.

"Freeze! Police!" Jett screamed, drawing his gun. Out of the corner of his eye, he was relieved to see Lane had done the same.

The two of them kept their guns trained on Franklin. Jett hardly dared to breathe. Dani's brother-in-law was breathing heavily and a feral glint sparked wildly in his eyes. His gaze skittered from one to the other, the knife still held high in his hand.

"Drop the knife, Franklin," Jett ordered. "You're in enough trouble. Don't go adding to it with another murder charge."

Franklin continued to stare at them, as if debating his chances of getting away. He glanced at the open door behind them and then at Dani who stood not very far away. Jett's heart pounded. Any moment, Franklin could make a move and it might not be the one Jett hoped for. He stared at Dani, willing her to move further away, out of the danger zone, but it was almost as if she was transfixed by terror, her feet refusing to move.

And then with a guttural growl, followed by a savage curse, Franklin spun on his heel and flung the knife away. It landed with a clatter on the polished marble tiles near the kitchen, well out of harm's way. Jett's shoulders slumped on a sigh of relief. He went to holster his gun.

"Franklin! No!"

Dani's terrified scream made Jett's blood run cold. He looked up in time to see Franklin hoist up one of the heavy dining chairs and run toward the plate glass windows. A moment later, there was a crack like a bullet.

Broken glass sprayed out all over the place. With a triumphant yell, Franklin followed the chair through the jagged opening. Jett didn't have to see his landing or hear the thud as he hit the ground to know that Franklin Cook had just jumped to his death, ten storeys below.

Dani's heart beat so hard she thought it might jump right out of her chest. Her breath still came fast and it was all she could do to ward off a panic attack. In the space of a few minutes, she'd been threatened with a knife, rescued just in time, and then watched her brother-in-law jump to his death. Coupled with the sure knowledge he'd murdered her niece and sister, she didn't know how much more she could take.

She risked a glance in Jett's direction and noticed he was still talking on the phone. She figured he'd be busy for some time. A suicide in the course of an arrest would do that.

He'd come over to her briefly, immediately after Franklin's jump and had asked about her welfare. *Was she all right? Did she need an ambulance?* She'd assured him she was fine and he'd thrown her a long, inscrutable look, but had then nodded, taking her answer at face value. He'd been on the phone ever since.

She didn't know what she expected. After all, the night before, they'd departed on rather abrupt terms. She'd asked him to leave and he had, but he'd been far from happy about it. She hadn't seen or heard from him since.

The room filled with more police officers, including two with the word "Forensics" printed in bright yellow across the back of their dark-blue overalls. Jett gave orders and officers moved to do his bidding. Dani stood where she was, halfway across the room. She hadn't moved since Franklin dived out the window, despite Jett's gentle urging that she might want to find somewhere to sit.

What she wanted was to leave this place and everything in it and never, ever come back, but she was required for further questioning and had been asked to stay put. An older man with graying hair and a weary expression on his face came over and introduced himself.

"I'm Detective Superintendent Michael Collins. I'm from the State Crime Command. I understand you're Danielle Porter. Is that correct?"

"Yes," Dani replied softly, bracing herself for what was to come. This would only be the first of many times she'd be forced to recount in vivid detail what had happened and every time she'd remember Franklin and the shock and horror on his face and then she'd remember the feeling of satisfaction that it was right he feel like that. He'd murdered her sister and baby niece in error, out of misplaced jealousy and rage and he wouldn't be forgiven for that. She hoped he rotted in hell.

The superintendent pulled out a notepad and with a little prompting, in a monotone, she recounted exactly what had occurred. It seemed to take forever, but finally, he tucked the notepad away in his shirt pocket, and throwing her a grave look of understanding, thanked her for her time and moved away.

Unsure what to do with herself, Dani wandered out of the living area and walked down the carpeted hall. She found herself in the spare bedroom—the room Sabrina had laughingly referred to as "Dani's room."

Like the rest of the house, it was tastefully furnished with expensive pieces. The heavy damask curtains alone must have cost a bomb. The pale blue-and-white color scheme was so pretty and Dani had always felt comfortable here—wanted, loved.

Moving further into the room, Dani perched gingerly on the edge of the bed. Once upon a time, she would have thrown herself across the expensive fine cotton bedspread and let her troubles melt away. But those days were long gone and would never be again.

Moisture burned behind her eyes. There was nowhere she could go, to talk things out, nowhere she could go to unwind. She had Ben, of course, and a truer friend didn't exist, but Ben had his own issues and it wasn't fair to expect him to deal with hers.

"What are you doing in here?"

She looked up at the sound of Jett's voice and hurriedly swiped at her tears. "I... I'm sorry. I gave a statement to the superintendent, but I wasn't sure if I was free to leave. I... I didn't know what to do. So, I came in here."

Jett nodded. He eased further into the room, his expression grim. He looked around at the feminine furnishings and then glanced back at her. "Was this where you slept when you stayed over?"

"Yes." Her breath caught on a sob. She couldn't believe she'd never see her sister again. Never hear her laughter, tell stories; share secrets in this very room. *It wasn't fair. It darn well wasn't fair.*

"We've had another witness come forward," he said quietly. "A guy who lives in the apartment two floors below. He says he saw a fire in the woods behind the building on the night Sabrina and Marnie were killed. I despatched a couple of officers to investigate. They found the remains of some clothing and the blade of a knife. It matches the set in the kitchen."

"One of the same knives Franklin was going to use on me. I… I just c-can't believe they're gone!" She hiccupped. "Sabrina, my beautiful sister and sweet baby Marnie. And Franklin…"

Jett moved to sit beside her. In silence, he put his arm around her and drew her against his side. She tensed momentarily, but it felt so good to be held. She dropped her head on his shoulder and allowed herself to cry.

Her gasps of distress were noisy in the silence. Jett murmured words of comfort against her hair and stroked her back and shoulders. She took comfort from his quiet strength and knowledge that he was there. If he'd arrived a few moments later… She shuddered to think it could have easily been her with the forensics officers standing over her body, photographing her remains.

"I'm sorry, Dani," Jett whispered and tightened

his hold around her shoulders. "I wish I could have done something, stopped him."

She looked up at him through her tears. "You did more than enough. You got here just in time." She shuddered. "I don't even want to think about what might have happened if you hadn't. Franklin... He just went berserk when I told him about the lab results, how he'd made a terrible mistake. I think he was shocked beyond belief. He went crazy. The next moment, I realized he was coming at me with a knife. I screamed..."

She couldn't go any further and Jett seemed to understand. He shushed her quietly and once again, drew her close against his side. Grateful for his presence, she slipped her arms around his waist and clung to him.

A long moment later, he lifted his head and gently loosened his hold. "I'm sorry, honey. I'm going to have to leave you. I have to get back to work."

She stared up at him. His use of the endearment filled her with surprise and warmth. Perhaps there was a chance for them, after all. A tiny spark of hope ignited deep inside. She nodded slowly in response to his statement. "It's all right, Jett. I understand."

He got to his feet and pulled her upright and enveloped her in a strong hug. "You're free to go home now. I'm going to be stuck here for quite a while, but... Do you mind if I come by later? We need to talk."

He spoke the words quietly and without inflection, his expression somber. Butterflies of dread filled her stomach, but she held his gaze bravely and nodded. "Okay."

He blew his breath out on a heavy sigh, but offered her the slightest smile. "Okay. I'm not sure what time it will be. I'll get away as soon as I can."

"It's all right," she assured him softly. "I won't be going anywhere. Come by whenever you're free."

"Thank you." He moved toward the door. With his lips compressed, he threw a final look over his shoulder and left the room.

The late afternoon sun was poking its face through the low cloud cover when Dani answered Jett's knock on her door. She'd spent the rest of the day staring into space in her living room and talking to a few close friends on the phone.

She'd called Ben, but her call had gone through to his voicemail and she remembered him telling her he'd be in court. When he finally received her message and called her back, he'd been shocked at what had happened. He wanted to come over right away.

He'd offered to explain to his remaining clients that an emergency had cropped up and get instructions to seek an immediate adjournments from the judge, but Dani assured him she was doing okay and that he was needed more where he was.

And now, Jett stood in her doorway, looking tired and disheveled, but there was an air of tension around him that sent her nerves into overdrive.

"Come in," she said and stepped back to allow him to enter. "Can I get you something to drink?"

"A beer, if you have it," he said and then grimaced. "I'm sorry, Dani. I forgot. Water's fine."

She nodded and walked across the modest living room to the fridge that stood at the end of the kitchen. Opening the door, she retrieved a bottle of water and handed it to him.

"Thanks," he said and unscrewed the cap and swallowed half the contents in one gulp.

"Wow, I guess you must be thirsty," she murmured and allowed herself the tiniest smile.

"It's been a hot day," he replied.

An awkward silence fell between them and Dani averted her gaze. It was like neither of them knew where to start or what to say.

"I'm sorry about last night—" he started.

"I've been thinking about what I said—"

They spoke simultaneously and then stopped. Nervous laughter fell from their lips. Dani looked at Jett and then glanced away. Jett stared down at his feet.

"Do you mind if we sit down?" he asked quietly.

"No, of course not."

Dani moved to the couch and then froze, remembering the last time they'd been there. Heat spread from her neck and across her cheeks. She snuck a peek at Jett and saw his embarrassment.

She guessed he was also recalling their last time alone at her place, but there was nothing for it. She only had one couch. Unless they departed for her bedroom, there was nowhere else to sit. The tiny bedsit wasn't big enough for a dining room table or chairs. The sofa and her bed were it.

CHAPTER 22

Jett watched Dani move past him, head toward the couch with a no-nonsense approach, and sit at one end. Pushing away his memories of the last time they'd been there, he took her lead. He wasn't sure where to begin and earlier that morning, he hadn't wanted to begin at all, but the events of the day had made him realize he cared for her deeply and wanted to try again.

"Last night, I was so angry at you," he began in a matter of fact voice, "but I was even angrier at myself."

She blinked and her eyes widened in surprise.

He understood her reaction. He'd left her home unhappy and upset that she refused to discuss her ridiculous claim that she wasn't good enough for him, but he hadn't been angry. No, it wasn't until after he'd seen her with her ex that the anger had set in.

"Why were you angry?" she asked.

"I was frustrated and hurt about what you'd said—that we couldn't make things work. I argued back and forth about your ridiculous attitude all the way home, but before I climbed out of my car, I made up my mind to go back and talk to you. I wanted to do what I could to make you see sense."

Her eyes grew wary. "Okay. I still don't know what got you so angry."

"I pulled up at the curb outside your house. It was late. You were standing nearby, with your ex. Only, he didn't look like an ex. The two of you were enjoying a very intimate embrace."

She frowned in confusion. "Me? And...Ben? Are you *sure*?"

"Yes, of course I'm sure. It was dark, but I'm not blind. You and Ben Fitzgerald had your arms around each other and were kissing. I didn't hang around."

She was silent for a moment and a frown still marred her forehead. A few seconds later, it cleared and she chuckled. "Oh, yes, you're right! I remember now! It *was* Ben and I on the front porch and we *did* kiss."

A fresh wave of hurt and anger surged through him. He went to get up off the couch. Dani's arm came out and restrained him.

"Please," she said. "Let me explain."

With a sigh of resignation, he let her draw him back beside her. When he tried to retrieve his arm, she tightened her hold.

"I was upset when you left here," she started, her tone quiet. "Last night was magical, something out of this world. I'd been with a lot of men, but no one as special as you. I started thinking about how wonderful you were—how kind and loving and good—and not only you, but your family. I realized how inadequate I was and how my family and I could never measure up. It wouldn't be fair to you or to your family to ask that they ignore the many shortcomings of my past and focus only on my present."

She heaved a heavy sigh before continuing. "So, I pushed you away. I thought it was the best and fairest thing I could do. I was falling in love with you and it wasn't right. I wanted to break things off while I could."

Jett stared at her and hope trickled into his heart. "You're falling in love with me?" he asked, almost scared to repeat the question.

Dani looked at him, her eyes full of sadness. "Yes. But, like I said, it was all wrong. I'm not good enough for you. At least—"

"Dani, that's nonsense!" he interrupted, his anger stirring. He ran a hand through his hair and made a sound of frustration deep in his throat. *How could he make her see? What could he say to convince her?* With an effort, he tried again.

"Like I told you last night, I don't care about your past and my family won't either. They—"

"If you'd let me finish," she broke in, "I would have told you that I felt that way last night. It was awful after you left. I felt like my heart was breaking. After all that I'd been through with Sabrina and Marnie and Franklin... I went out and bought a bottle of scotch."

Jett's breath caught in his throat. She'd told him weeks ago that she'd been sober for more than ten years. He stared at her and dread formed an icy lump deep in his gut.

"I came home with a bottle of Johnnie Walker and I stared at it for quite a while. Finally, I got the courage to call my sponsor."

Jett's eyes widened in sudden comprehension. "Ben."

"Yes, Ben," Dani sighed. "Dear, dear Ben."

"He came over," Jett stated.

"To help me, yes."

"And somehow, you both picked up where you'd left off a few years ago." It took everything Jett had, to say it, but they needed to be honest. If they were ever going to have a chance at a relationship, there could be no misunderstandings.

"No."

He frowned. "What do you mean, no?"

"I mean, Ben came around and helped me by talking me through so much of what had happened. He convinced me alcohol wasn't the answer. When I told him about you, he also persuaded me to trust myself and you and have faith in what we felt together. He convinced me to give things with you another shot."

Jett sat forward, his body angled toward hers. His heart picked up its pace. "You mean, he encouraged you to see me again, to...start a relationship?"

Dani stared at him, her eyes huge in her face. She looked scared and excited and happy, all at the same time. "Yes. That's exactly what he did."

The trickle of hope in Jett's gut morphed into a

river, but he had to make sure. "So, what I saw outside your house—the two of you...?"

"What you saw were two very close friends being grateful they had each other. Nothing more."

Jett let out a holler of excitement. Unable to contain himself, he stood and scooped Dani up into his arms. He swung her around amidst laughter and tears and plastered her with kisses. She'd been through such a horrific time, but right there and then, he couldn't be happier.

Finally, he slid her down his body and set her on her feet. He stared at her in wonder and disbelief. "I love you, Danielle Porter. Now and forever."

She blinked and smiled through her tears. "I love you, too."

Chapter 23

Five months later

Dear Diary,

The crisp May air filters through my gauzy curtains, but the sun is shining bright. I'm glad. No bride wants it to rain on her wedding day. Once, I would never have dreamed I could be so happy. I thought my world came to an end the day my beautiful sister died... And Marnie, sweet baby Marnie...

But it's strange how things work out. Without their deaths, I would never have met my future husband, never have known love as deep as this. They say all clouds have a silver lining and I can't help but feel it is true.

I know you're up there watching, little sister and I'm sure there's a wave for me from my niece. I miss you now; I'll miss you forever, but finally, I am at peace...

Dani took the hand of her new husband and pressed a soft kiss against his palm. She never got tired of touching him. The wedding had gone well and though the bride's guest list was a little on the light side, the crowds of Craigdons more than made up for it. They'd welcomed her in as if she were a precious jewel, unique and highly prized. His parents had called her their daughter and shyly asked her if she'd like to call them Mom and Dad. She'd brushed back tears when she'd nodded. They couldn't have made her feel more included.

"A penny for your thoughts, Mrs Craigdon?" her handsome husband asked.

She looked up at him, so resplendent in his formal wedding attire, and offered him a smile.

"I'm so happy," she whispered. "I never imagined I'd feel this way again."

His steady gaze held hers and he nodded. "You've made me the happiest of men."

Coming to a halt outside their hotel room, she waited for Jett to swipe the key. The door opened with a soft *beep*. A moment later, she was taken by surprise when he bent and swept her up in his arms. Carrying her over the threshold, he kicked the door closed behind them and deposited her gently on the carpet.

His hands went to her bare shoulders, and pushed down the thin spaghetti straps that held her sequinned bodice in place. Moments later, he captured her mouth in a kiss. As if finally being given permission, desire swept like wildfire through her veins. Out of respect for Jett's beliefs, they'd done little more than heavy petting since the time they'd become engaged. It had been a long five months and Dani could hardly wait to feel him on top of her, inside her, surrounding her, loving her.

She reached up and undid his bow tie. The black satin slid through her fingers and she nonchalantly tossed it away and went to work on the tiny black buttons that decorated his white pleated dress shirt. It was the first time she'd seen him in such formal attire and the sight of him waiting for her at the end of the aisle had stolen her breath.

His longish dark hair had been tamed with a brush, but still looked roguishly sexy. His blue eyes shone with happiness and love. He looked like a man who couldn't wait to be married—and knowing she was on the receiving end of that look had warmed her all the way through.

Spreading open his shirt, she splayed her fingers across his warm skin, sliding through the light covering of chest hair to caress his firm muscles. Her fingers grazed over his nipples and knowing how much he loved it, she paused to tweak them into hard nubs.

His breath hissed between his teeth, but he remained still and submitted to her attentions. In her five-inch satin heels, they were almost the same height. She bent her head and flicked her tongue over his nipples.

"Dani, you're killing me," he groaned and his hands tightened on her hips. He pulled her in close and his hard cock pressed into her belly.

She pressed back against him, loving the feel of his hardness. With her arms around his neck, she buried her face against his skin and breathed in deeply of his scent. Warm, masculine, spicy. Every part of him smelled divine. Though they'd served alcohol to their guests at the wedding, Jett had chosen water over wine.

Curious, Dani had questioned him about it. His eyes were bright with love and desire when he told her he wanted a clear head for his wedding night. He intended to remember every single second of it.

The heat in his gaze had sent her pulse racing and it was the same heat that coursed through her now. His expression was filled with deep yearning and she was in awe at the thought that his desire was all for her.

Desire from men was nothing new, but with Jett, everything was different. When she'd suggested they refrain from making love in the fullest sense until after they were married, she had no idea how difficult it would be.

She'd always been a passionate woman in touch with her sexuality. Though she'd done a lot of things in her youth she wasn't proud of, that didn't change who she was. The months of enforced abstinence had sharpened her needs to the point she was about to explode—but this wasn't so much about her. Not only had Jett given her the gift of his heart, he'd given her an even greater gift: his purity.

All of a sudden, she was beset with nerves. It was his first time. He'd waited for this his entire adult life. *What if she disappointed him? What if the experience didn't measure up?*

"Dani? Is everything all right?"

Jett's quiet query cut through her increasingly panicked thoughts. She blinked rapidly and drew in a quick breath.

"Yes, of course." She offered him a smile, but it came out shaky. The concern in his eyes increased.

"Dani? What's wrong? Please, talk to me."

His somber plea cut through the noise that had been building in her head. Her shoulders slumped on a sigh. Though the thought of sharing her fears with him had her burning with embarrassment, he was her husband. There was nothing she couldn't tell him.

"I... I don't want to disappoint you," she mumbled and fire exploded across her cheeks. Her confession was met with silence. She snuck a peek at him and found him gaping at her, a stunned expression on his face.

"*Disappoint* me? How the hell could you do that?" he finally managed, his tone incredulous.

Dani averted her gaze, still embarrassed. With her eyes fixed on the carpet, she offered him a shrug.

"Dani, look at me." His voice was soft, but commanding.

With reluctance, she lifted her gaze. Jett reached out and grasped her chin between his fingers, removing any means of escape.

"I love you, Dani. I'm proud to call you my wife. I promised to honor you with my heart, my soul and my body. I promised you all of my worldly goods. Everything I have, everything I am, is yours."

"And I promised you the same," she whispered.

"I've been waiting for this moment all my life, Dani. To make love to the woman who is my wife. The woman I chose above all others. The woman I will love until I die. There's nothing you could do to disappoint me. At least, not in a sexual way. I love you and the physical act we share will be the epitome of that, but I don't just love you for your body. I love *you*. Danielle Veronica Craigdon. My wife." He sighed quietly. "I don't know what else I can say."

Dani swallowed the lump in her throat and stared at him through her tears. The love she felt for him overwhelmed her. Sabrina had been the only person in her life who had shown her such unconditional love and her sister was gone forever. While it still hurt to think about what had happened, having Jett beside her helped ease the pain.

She reached up and pressed her lips to his and kissed him with all the love she held in her heart. Within seconds, the kiss caught fire and their lips moved with a frantic haste. She tore off his shirt, he tugged at the zipper of her dress and then cursed when it got stuck.

She giggled. He tried again, but the zipper was still firmly caught. He cursed a second time and she giggled harder. A grin tugged at his lips. On the third attempt, the zipper gave way. Jett pushed her dress off her shoulders and Dani shimmied it over her hips, revealing lacy white underwear beneath.

She heard Jett's breath catch at the sight of her and was filled with a shy kind of warmth. With her gaze locked on his, she stepped out of the white satin and lace concoction and reached for his hand. She walked backwards until she came up against the side of the bed and sank down onto it, bringing him with her.

"Let's take it slowly," she whispered. "I want this night to last forever."

"Me, too. But I can't make any promises." His gaze drifted down her near-naked body and then back up again. "I feel like I'm going to explode."

His words sent a fresh wave of desire coursing through her. Need burned even hotter in her core. His naked chest gleamed golden in the soft lamplight.

Pushing him back against the mountain of pillows, she straddled him, deliberately pressing her butt against the hardness in his pants.

"Dani," he cried out hoarsely.

She smiled, loving the power she had over him. She bent over and kissed him once again. Next, she moved across his stubble-roughed cheeks and his chin, before burying her face in his neck. She breathed in deeply of his scent and nuzzled him. Nipping at his skin, her hands wandered across his chest. She found his nipples, pebble hard and teased them with her fingertips.

His breath came faster in her ear. She pressed back against his crotch. She moved slightly lower and captured his nipples in her mouth, licking and sucking the hard nubs. He groaned and his hands came around to tighten on her hips. He ground her against his erection and she tingled all the way through to her cleft.

"I want you," he growled, his eyes glittering in the light.

"And you shall have me," she quipped, her voice a little tremulous from the desire that held her in its grip.

Releasing his belt, she slid it out of the loops and then went to work on his pants. First the button, then the zipper. Her hand stole deftly inside. He wore black satin boxers and the shiny fabric slid over her seeking fingers. The sensation of the silky soft fabric across the hardness of his erection was exhilarating.

She encircled his erection and gave it a firm squeeze. His hips lifted and his breath hissed. He looked flushed, like he was in the throes of a fever. She worked his pants down, along with the satin boxers. He lifted his hips to assist her and then kicked away his clothes.

Naked and magnificent, he lay sprawled on the bed before her. His cock stood at attention, thick and long and proud. She ached to feel it inside her, but she wasn't anywhere near ready yet. This was his first time and she wanted to make it a night he'd never forget.

Reaching behind her, she undid the clasp of her bra and tossed it to the floor. Free from their restraints, her breasts bounced and jiggled. She leaned over and brushed them across his chest and her nipples hardened from the contact. Jett reached out to fondle them and she couldn't hold back a groan.

Rolling her nipples between his fingers, he lifted his head and began to suckle. First one, and then the other. Fire burned between her thighs. She pulled away gently and moved lower, kissing her way down his chest. Pausing at his belly button, she flicked the slight indentation with her tongue.

Jett stirred restlessly beneath her, but she wasn't done yet. She lifted his erection and swiped his head across her lips. He gasped and dug his fingers in her hair, holding her head in place. Her tongue swirled around his tip then she opened her mouth and sucked him all the way in. She tasted his desire.

Jett's grip on her hair tightened almost painfully, but Dani wasn't through yet. Without releasing his cock, she reached down and cupped his heavy balls. Fondling them in rhythm with her mouth, she continued to work his shaft, driving him to the edge of reason. She pulled up just before he toppled over the other side.

"Dani," he gasped. "You need to stop."

She stared up at him. His face was flushed, his eyes glittered; there was tension around his mouth. She nodded. With a swift movement, Jett rolled her over and positioned himself between the legs.

With hands that were far from steady, he undid the clasps on her stockings and peeled them down her legs. Her garter belt and lace panties quickly followed. She lay before him, naked and let him look his fill, loving him and the wonder and awe that lit up his face.

"You're so beautiful," he breathed. "I can't believe you're mine."

She smiled and reached out for him and he immediately complied. Drawing him down on top of her, the feel of his weight and hardness pressing against her drew forth a sigh. There was nothing about this man she didn't love. She would love him until she died.

Jet's cock throbbed with so much pressure, he didn't know how much longer he could last. He hadn't been exaggerating when he'd told Dani if she didn't quit her teasing, he'd explode.

The day had been perfect and now he was there, in the bridal suite, making love to his beautiful wife. It was everything he'd ever dreamed of and he couldn't believe this was only the first night of the rest of his life.

She'd walked down the aisle toward him on the arm of her best friend. Ben had handed her over to him with a low word about keeping her safe and never breaking her heart.

He didn't need to be told. She was a treasure beyond value. He couldn't ever imagine not loving her or yearning to hold her close. Now, she lay beneath him, naked and resplendent and even though she'd blown his mind with the sexy underwear, the feel of her warm, soft skin against his was beyond wonderful.

She moved beneath him and lifted her hips, as

if encouraging him to take the final step needed for them to become one. He wanted so much to keep loving her with his mouth, his hands, his tongue, but his cock was throbbing with a need so great, he couldn't ignore it any longer.

Pushing her legs wider, he hesitated. *Should he just do it? Thrust into her in a single stroke? Is that how it was done? Would it hurt her? Maybe he should just ease his way in, provided he could hold onto his self-control.* He didn't want to come the moment he got inside her. That would be beyond embarrassing.

He cursed silently under his breath. He should have taken the pressure off the night before, like he'd thought about doing in the shower. Then he wouldn't feel such a desperate need to explode. It was too late now. He'd have to deal with it the best he could. *Perhaps he could think of his present police investigation?* A distraction like that would be sure to take the edge off his need.

Once again, Dani moved restlessly beneath him, silently encouraging him to proceed. With a deep breath, he probed her entrance. She was already slick with need.

His cock slid into her moist warmth, only an inch and then two. He clung to his control with his fingernails. She felt better than anything his fantasies had revealed. He eased in a little further and her hands tightened around his shoulders. She made small murmurs of encouragement and all at once, he couldn't hold back.

With a guttural groan, he plunged into her, all the way to the hilt. It was like nothing he'd ever felt before, wild beyond his dreams. She surrounded him with her warmth and wetness, her cries of pleasure were music to his ears. He thrust his hips and stroked her, his rhythm picking up speed.

He didn't know how much longer he could last. He didn't want to come before her, but he wasn't sure how far away she was from her climax and his was banging on the door.

"Yes, Jett, yes!" she said breathlessly as her fingernails dug into his skin.

He plunged into her again and again and all of a sudden, she gasped and panted and then cried out her relief. The feel of her inner muscles contracting against him pushed him over the edge. He thrust harder, faster and then he was flying through heaven, past the stars, past the planets, until long moments later, he finally came back down to earth.

Breathing hard, he stirred and realized he was lying full against her, crushing her with his weight. He immediately propped himself up on an elbow and looked down at her, unable to keep the smile off his face.

"That was..." he started.

"Amazing," she finished and reached up to push back the hair that had fallen across his face.

"And so much more," he added, still feeling the remnants of his orgasm.

She stared at him with an expression that was filled with so much love it made his heart ache.

"I love you, Jett Craigdon," she whispered.

He kissed her softly on the lips with all the love and joy he felt inside. "I love you, too, Dani. I'll love you until I die."

Epilogue

Dear Diary,

It's the day after the most magical night of my life. My husband and I made love for the first time and I don't have the words to describe it. For so many years, sex was nothing more than a commodity, a way to escape and feel wanted. While the attention from strangers wasn't pleasurable, it helped fill the loneliness for a little while.

But now I know what it feels like to make love to the man of my dreams. A man I love beyond reason, beyond anything I ever imagined I could feel. I now know why they call it making love. There's no comparison to the frantic, emotionless couplings I sought out in the past. I think back on those days and shudder with revulsion, self-hatred and disgust.

But I guess my past and everything in it, as sordid as it was, has helped shape me into the woman I am today: strong, resilient and a woman who knows what it's like to love and be loved.

I think about my sister. The memory of her is never far away. I'm grateful for the time we had, though it wasn't nearly enough. I think of her husband and I am devastated that love drove him to the point of madness. He had a perfect life, a perfect family. He loved his wife and daughter like crazy, but he destroyed it because of his insecurity and blind jealousy and the innocent mistake of lab technician. The knowledge saddens me deeply.

I hope and pray that time and the deep and abiding love of my husband will help me forgive Franklin for what he did. Right now, I can't see it happening, but then again, I never believed in miracles before and yet I woke up this morning and turned to the love of my life. Even better, he feels exactly the same way.

So yes, miracles do happen. I am proof of that. All you have to do is believe...

Note to Readers

I do hope you have enjoyed reading Danielle and Jett's story. If you've enjoyed this book, please feel free to leave a review for The Lab Test at Goodreads and your favorite digital retailer. Every review is very much appreciated.

If you would like to receive news on upcoming stories, release dates, book launches and other snippets, please feel free to sign up for my newsletter. You can do this by visiting my website at www.christaylorauthor.com.au and clicking on the "Subscribe to my Newsletter" link on the right.

The Stolen Identity is the next book in the Sydney Harbour Hospital Series.

Here's a sneak peek:

Morgan O'Brien is in love with her job.

As a midwife at the Sydney Harbour Hospital, there's nothing more exciting than being present at the birth of a baby. But being around newborns night and day only emphasizes the fact she doesn't have a family of her own. At thirty, her biological clock is ticking and she can't help but remember the baby she chose to abort all those years ago...

But then her father disappears in mysterious circumstances and babies are the last thing on her mind. Where has he gone and why has he left without telling her? She's his only child. They keep in regular contact. He would have told her he was going away...

Concerned, Morgan arrives back in her hometown and immediately runs into sinfully good-looking, Detective Sergeant Colt Barrington. She hasn't seen him since college and there's a good reason for that... He's the father of the baby she never had...

But her father has disappeared and Morgan wants to know why. Will she turn to her ex-lover in the hopes he can find her father, or will they both end up regretting the fact Morgan O'Brien is back in town...?

The Stolen Identity will be released on 30 October, 2016 and is available now for pre-order from your favorite digital retailer.

About the Author

Chris Taylor grew up on a farm in north-west New South Wales, Australia. She always had a thirst for stories and recalls writing her first book at the ripe old age of eight. Always a lover of romance and happily-ever-afters, a career in criminal law sparked her interest in intrigue and suspense. For Chris to be able to combine romance with suspense in her books is a dream come true.

Chris is married to Linden and is the mother of five children. If not behind her computer, you can find her doing the school run, taxiing children to swimming lessons, football, ballet and cricket. In her spare time, Chris loves to read her favorite authors who include Richard North Patterson, Sandra Brown, Kathleen E Woodiwiss and Jude Devereaux.

You can find out more about Chris and sign up for her newsletter at her website:

http://www.christaylorauthor.com.au